THE CHINGLES
FROM THE
EAST

Also by Patricia Murphy

The Chingles Go West

THE
CHINGLES
FROM THE
EAST

PATRICIA MURPHY

POOLBEG

This book is entirely a work of fiction. The names, characters and incidents portrayed in it are the work of the author's imagination. Any resemblance to actual persons, living or dead, events or localities is entirely coincidental.

957, 809/JF1

Published 2004
by Poolbeg Press Ltd.
123 Grange Hill, Baldoyle
Dublin 13, Ireland
Email: poolbeg@poolbeg.com

3 5 7 9 10 8 6 4 2

A catalogue record for this book is available from the British Library.

ISBN 978 18422 32163 (from January 2007)
ISBN 1 84223 216 9

Typeset by Patricia Hope in Goudy 16/21
Printed by Litografia Rosés, Spain

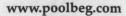

www.poolbeg.com

About the Author

Patricia Murphy grew up in Ballygall, Dublin, the eldest of six children, and turned to storytelling to amuse her brothers and sisters and sixty cousins. After reading English and History at Trinity College Dublin, she worked in television as a reporter and documentary maker and got to travel the world from the Arctic Circle to the Amazon Jungle. She is now a producer/director and has made a number of acclaimed documentaries for BBC and Channel 4, including several on children's lives. She is married and lives in Oxford.

The Chingles from the East is the first book in a trilogy and the winner of the Poolbeg 'Write a Bestseller' Competition 2004.

This book is dedicated with love to my parents
Betty and Charlie, my brothers and sisters
Stephen, Audrey, Neil, Kenneth and Karen,
my goddaughter Aoife, godsons James and Jack
and nephews Patrick, Cian and Senan.

Pronunciation Guide for
"The Chingles from the East"

This list (using the English spelling system) is to help you pronounce the Irish words in the book. Remember it is a rough guide only!

Áine – Awn-yah
Amandán – Om-a-dawn
Balor – Bal-ur
Beith – Beh
Cailleach – Kyle-uch
Cernunnos – Ker-nuh-nohs
Clíona – Clee-on-ah
Cluain Meala – Cluu-in mal-ah
Cnoc Áine –Kuh-nuk awn-yah
Coll – Cul
Conán – Con-awn
Connle – Con-leh
Dair – Dahr
Dúlachán – Duul-uch-awn
Eadha – Ah–dah
Fearn – Fyarn
Ferdia – Ferd-ee-yah
Finbhearra – Fin-varra

Geas – gyas

Gruagach- Gruuh-uh-guch

Inish Álainn – In-ish awl-ing

Leath sí – lah-shee

Lugh – Luu

Manannán Mac Lir – Mon-an-awn mac lir

Muiris – Mwir-ish

Ogham – Oe-am

Róisín – Roe-sheen

Rua O'Rogan – Ruu-ah o-roe-gan

Saille – Sahl-yah

Scáthach – Skaw/huch

Sean Gaels – Shan Gwales

Segais – Seg-ish

Sí – Shee

Síonna –Shun-ah

Tadgh – Tie/ig

Tír na nÓg – Tir-nuh-nogue

Tuatha dé Danann – Tuu-ah day dan-an

Úna – Uuh-nah

Uath – Uuh-ah

Uath Mac Immomuin – Uuh-ah mac imm-ov-in

INISH ÁLAINN

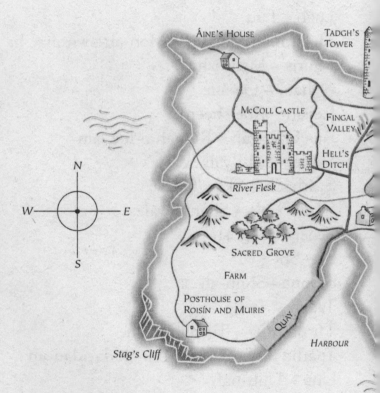

INISH ÁLAINN — 3km LONG — 6km WIDE

〰️ Boreen
━━━ Main Road

FAIRY FORT
& FIELD

FAIRY FORT
HOUSE

Marsh

POOLBEG ROCKS
& COVE

·BO MEN BOG

FLOWER
MEADOW

GLIMMERING LAKE

River Flesk

BOOGAN BEACH

ULALLY'S
UB

JARLATH'S WORKSHOP

TEASHOP

FERRY

TO MAINLAND
ONE HOUR

CHAPTER 1

Cassie caught her first glimpse of the island from the ferry, in between trying to poke her brother's eyes out. Thomas was really, really winding her up that day, singing that she looked like a monkey and lived in a zoo to the tune of 'Happy Birthday'. Of course, it wasn't even her birthday. Then he started an argument about the colour of the sea. She said it was the colour of green Wellington boots. He said it was the colour of mushy peas. She had just caught him by the throat when the island popped up suddenly out of the sea, like a sponge that had been pushed down in the bath.

Instead of throttling him, Cassie let go and

1

shouted out: "I saw Inish Álainn first, *na, na, na, naanaa!*" But almost as suddenly as it had appeared, the island disappeared behind a curtain of mist. Instead Cassie's attention turned to the fat little birds with multicoloured beaks that were skimming along the water near the boat.

"Look, look, Pouting, over there! They are puffins!" she called to her brother, forgetting in her excitement that they had been deadly enemies only seconds before. 'Pouting' was her evil nickname for her brother. After 'Doubting Thomas' in the Bible, except her mummy said their Thomas pouted more than doubted. It was true. He did have a way of sticking out his lower lip that made him look sulky. She commanded him to come and stand beside her.

"How can I look if you are going to poke my eyes out?" he asked in an annoying voice that he knew wound her up.

An old lady, who had been enjoying the sun on the deck and was going back into the cabin, gave them both a hard stare. Cassie smiled innocently. As soon as the old lady was gone, she stuck her tongue out. Thomas joined her at the rail. He pointed up to the sky. Cassie looked up. There was nothing there.

Thomas chanted,

"I made you look, I made you stare,
I made a barber cut your hair,
He cut it long, he cut it short,
He cut it with a knife and fork!"

But suddenly there was something there and their mouths hung open in amazement.

Flying over the boat was a strange ugly bird. On closer inspection, they saw that it had no feathers. It had an enormous wingspan and its skin was pimpled like a plucked turkey except it was sooty black. Its big red beak looked ready to gobble them up. The bird was so large that for a moment it blotted out the sun. It looked almost prehistoric and it iced their hearts with fear.

"Ugh, horrible bird!" Cassie shuddered and held on to Thomas.

"Puffins aren't horrible," a voice rang out.

It was their Uncle Jarlath and they were glad to see him. He came up on deck carrying Nancy, their toddler sister, as if she was a sack of potatoes. She wouldn't be three until Hallowe'en but already she had Jarlath wrapped around her little finger. That was an expression of her mother's. Cassie wasn't entirely sure what it meant but had something to do with Nancy's ability to turn everyone into her personal slave.

"Not those birds," explained Cassie. "You missed it. It was an ugly black bird with no feathers."

"It disappeared into thin air," Thomas added.

Jarlath looked puzzled. "We'll have to ask Tadgh when we arrive. He's the librarian and knows everything. Now, puffins," he continued, "they are interesting. They spend most of their lives on the open waves and their young are called pufflings." He spoke facing out to sea with his back to the children.

They forgot their fear of a moment ago and Jarlath now became the butt of their jokes. Cassie mimed blah, blah, blah! Thomas turned his eyes until only the whites showed. Suddenly, Thomas leaned forward and tickled Cassie. They both exploded with laughter.

"My gosh, children, what is so funny?" asked Jarlath, turning round.

"You are," said Nancy.

Jarlath laughed good-naturedly. Little did he realise that Nancy was telling the truth. Nancy always told the truth.

Cassie, Thomas and Nancy were on their way to spend the summer with their Uncle Jarlath on Inish Álainn, a remote island off the West Coast of Ireland. They were to stay in the summerhouse where their mother and her brother and three sisters always spent their holidays when they were children. It was their first holiday without their mum and dad and they felt sick with excitement.

Cassie was desperately hoping to have a holiday adventure although she was secretly worried that she was just too ordinary. Her friend Maya had nearly been trampled to death by an elephant in India, and Quentin, a horrid boy in her class, had spent a month in quarantine after he caught a deadly virus in the jungle. The worst thing that had ever happened to Cassie on holiday was sunburn. But she had high hopes for Inish Álainn despite her mother describing it as 'peaceful', that being the adult word for dull.

Uncle Jarlath was their mother's youngest brother, the 'baby' of the McColl family, although he looked pretty old to the children. He had lots of dark brown curly hair and freckles and was still at university – a 'big person's school', their mother had explained to Nancy. Thomas joked that this was really because he was the most stupid boy in Ireland. But their Aunty Angel, who was an actress, said it was quite the opposite. He was very, very clever and was doing this big long sum that took years to add up and take away and multiply.

Cassie who knew her one hundred times table wasn't impressed. She thought Jarlath certainly looked like a baby who was just learning how to get dressed all by himself. Today, he had on one green sock and one red sock. His jumper was on inside out and, even though it was a sunny day, he was wearing a woollen cap. Thomas thought he looked cool and turned his jumper inside out as well.

Nancy was trying to count his freckles. She pointed and said, "One, two, four, twelfty, seven!"

The island was one hour away from the mainland by ferry and was often cut off by storms but today the sea was as smooth as a mirror. As they got closer to the island the mist cleared and they could make out a few buildings set among lush green fields. Some of the houses had roofs made of straw and Jarlath said they were called thatched cottages. Cassie knew that already. She was just about to tell him this and recite her one hundred times table when a massive black yacht with blood-red sails loomed into view and headed towards them at a frightening speed.

The children screamed. Thomas dropped to the deck and Cassie jumped on top of him to protect him. Jarlath huddled by the side of the cabin, trying to shield Nancy in his arms. The yacht sliced through the water like a killer whale ready to gobble them up.

"Look out!" shouted Cassie, trying to warn the other passengers.

Podge, the captain of the ferry, sounded the

warning bell. The yacht loomed nearer and nearer. Then *WHOOSH!* At the very last moment, it changed course. Everyone on deck got drenched in the backwash of the wave. Cassie looked across at the black yacht speeding away and caught a glimpse of a big fat ugly man with an eye-patch, chomping on a cigar. She could have sworn that she saw fire coming out of his mouth and that big black ugly bird hovering overhead again! Her blood ran cold and her heart pounded with fear. She didn't understand it but she had a funny feeling that this man spelt big trouble for herself and her brother and sister.

"You horrible rude so-and-so!" shouted Jarlath. "If it wasn't for the children, I'd call you every name under the sun!"

The old lady who had scowled at Cassie and Thomas earlier, appeared on deck with towels to help them dry themselves. Luckily it was a warm day and soon there was steam rising off their clothing. Jarlath introduced the old lady as Róisín McGonigal, who ran the island's post office with her husband Muiris. They were bringing back a special delivery from the mainland.

"That blackguard, whoever he is," Róisín said, "if I ever get my hands on him, I'll wring his neck!"

"She doesn't really mean that," said a merry voice. Her husband Muiris appeared on deck. He was smoking a pipe.

"I'll give him a piece of my mind!" she said.

"Is that wise," said her husband, "when you haven't got much to spare?"

"You know what I mean." Róisín glared at her husband. She then smiled and poked him playfully in the ribs.

"Don't mind us fighting," explained Muiris. "It's our hobby. But I'd like to know who it was gave you a free shower."

Cassie told them about the fat man on the deck wearing an eye-patch and smoking a cigar. She didn't tell them that he filled her with dread. Róisín's eyes narrowed shrewdly. "I wonder if that is to do with the special delivery we had to pick up on the mainland?" she said, rummaging in a damp postbag. "I'd ask you to give me a hand," she said to her husband, "except you are a boss-eyed gombeen, who is half blind!"

"No need to mock the afflicted," he laughed, " you bad tempered oul' biddy!"

Róisín took out a notice that was a bit soggy around the edges from the drenching. "These have to be delivered to every home on the island," she said. "By hand, if you please." She held up the dripping notice. It bore a picture of a fat man wearing an eye-patch and smoking a cigar.

"That's him!" exclaimed Cassie.

"Well, more fool him for getting his own blasted notices wet!" pronounced Róisín.

She read it out:

"Dear Islander,

"You are invited to a very important meeting tomorrow at Mulally's pub at 3 pm. Everyone must attend. We have a proposition that will make you all very rich.

From Sir Dignum Drax

The DUM CORPORATION (Drax Universal Media)

Thomas and Cassie were very excited by this. Jarlath looked doubtful and said there was bound to be a catch in it with a wealthy magnate like Drax. Thomas wondered if it was tough being a magnet with iron things sticking to you all the time. But Jarlath explained he wasn't that sort of magnet but someone who owned television stations and newspapers and lots of everything.

"He can stick it where the monkey stuck his nuts," Róisín said with scorn. "Wild horses wouldn't drag me to that meeting even if he was handing out gold bars. I don't care how rich he is," she sniffed.

"Don't mind yer one," Muiris winked at the children. "We'll keep a seat for ye in the front row."

Róisín merely stuck her nose in the air because her attention had turned to the children. "So you must be Theresa McColl's little ones," she said, smiling at them and her face was so crinkly that her eyes disappeared. "Where's your mammy and daddy?"

"They've gone to Sweden. Dad has to search for something – a comet, I think," Cassie replied.

"She means 'research'," Jarlath cut in.

"So you must be Cassie," Róisín said. "I haven't seen you since you were a baby. How old are you now?"

"I'm ten and a half going on forty, my mum says."

Róisín and Muiris laughed.

"He's Thomas and he's nine but we call him Pouting Thomas because he's sulky."

Thomas stuck out his bottom lip and interrupted, "I'm not sulky. I'm changeable."

"You're close in age," Róisín said. "Almost like twins."

Cassie ignored her because she hated when people said that. In Cassie's opinion they didn't even look like brother and sister. For a start she had long nut-brown hair and Thomas's spiky blond hair was like a toilet brush. So she continued, "Nancy is three on Hallowe'en."

"I'm a wish," Nancy pronounced.

"She thinks she's a witch because she was born on Hallowe'en," Cassie explained.

"We are the Chingles from the East," Nancy sang out.

"She means we are children from East Croydon," Thomas piped up. "She can't say 'children' properly."

"I *can* so say ch– them!" Nancy insisted.

"Now where have I heard that word before?" said Muiris, talking to himself. "It's to do with some prophecy about the island but I don't know what it is."

"Pay no attention to yer man muttering away to himself," said Róisín.

"It's only a problem when I answer myself as well," Muiris grinned.

Róisín shushed him. "Go on, tell us more about yourselves," she urged Cassie who needed no encouragement.

"Do you know what?" Cassie rattled on. "Our mother says she's a Roman Catholic, which means she's a Catholic who came roamin' over from Ireland."

"Oh, I've met your daddy before," Róisín said. "He's English, isn't he? He must feel swamped by all the McColls."

13

"Yes, his name's Ivor Nelson and he's an only child and half an orphan because his father is dead," Thomas volunteered, which was most unusual for him. He wasn't normally chatty with strangers.

"My dad has funny names for all the McColls," Cassie whispered in a confidential tone. "Do you want to hear them?"

Róisín's eyes glistened as she prided herself on being the nosiest woman in Ireland and that was really saying something!

So Cassie rattled off all the family information. How their dad called their Aunty Angel 'Radio 4' because she was always droning on and on and on. And their Aunty Holly 'Aunty-biotic' because she was always ill and her twin Ivy 'Aunty-dote' because she was a doctor and was always trying to make her sister better. Then she whispered very quietly in Róisín's ear that their dad thought Jarlath was bonkers.

"And how are your grandparents?" Róisín asked. "Are they still living on the houseboat on the Grand Canal in Dublin?"

"Yes," said Cassie. "Dad says that it's amazing that two nearly normal people could produce such mad children."

"I'm hungry in my tummy," Nancy said.

Muiris rummaged in his pockets and took out three chocolate bars wrapped in gold paper. "I don't have any gold bars like Sir Dignum Drax," he said. "Will chocolate ones do?"

The children's eyes lit up.

"That's much nicer than gold bars," Thomas said.

"How would you know if you've never tasted a gold one?" Cassie said. She was just about to ask Róisín and Muiris if they'd seen the ugly featherless bird but there was no time because the boat was coming in to land.

CHAPTER 2

The quayside was packed with people waiting for the arrival of the ferry. Complete strangers waved at the children as if they were their long-lost relatives and Thomas and Cassie felt like royalty as they waved back from the boat.

As the ferry drew up alongside the quay and the gangway was positioned, an extraordinary thing happened. Three rainbows formed over the harbour. They shimmered above in the shape of an arch – red, orange, yellow and green, blue, indigo and violet.

"Wow!" said Cassie and Thomas in unison. Even Jarlath was impressed.

"Now you know why Inish Álainn got its name. It means 'beautiful island'," said Muiris proudly.

"It's a good omen," pronounced Róisín. "Your visit here will be magical!"

"I'm glad to hear it," muttered Cassie, "as the bird and the yacht have scared us out of our wits twice already!" But nobody heard her with the hurly-burly and hubbub rising from the quayside. She was relieved, as she helped carry the luggage down the gangway, that it wasn't in the least bit peaceful.

When they reached dry land, everyone made a huge fuss of them, saying how Cassie was the image of her mother and that Nancy was the spit of the twins. This unfortunately encouraged Nancy to start spitting until Jarlath told her to stop. Thomas, they said, must look like his father. He replied by making his devil's face at them. Mr Mulally, who owned the only pub and hotel on the island, told the children to drop in any time for lemonade. He introduced them to his twin teenage sons, Macdara and Conán, who helped Cassie and Thomas get their bikes off the ferry.

The twins were big strapping lads and friends of Jarlath's. They asked to see Thomas's muscles and laughed when Cassie said hers were bigger. They promised to teach them all a game called hurling. When the barrels of beer they were waiting for rolled off the ferry, they walked on them to the pub like circus performers.

Also waiting for a delivery off the boat was a tall thin man – Tadgh, the island's librarian. The ferryboat captain, Podge, handed him a pile of books tied up with twine. Jarlath just about managed to introduce the children to Tadgh, among all the commotion of people shouting and talking, and boxes and packages being passed back and forth.

"This fella might know about your weird bird," Jarlath said.

Cassie and Thomas described the bird that they'd seen from the ferry. Tadgh scratched his head. "A big ugly black bird with no feathers? It sounds a bit like the Corra. That's the old Irish name for the flying state of the water monster. A ferocious beastie that likes to gobble little children."

The children shuddered.

"Oh, it's only a legend – an old, old story," he laughed.

957, 809 / JF1

Róisín joined them and handed him the Drax notice from her postbag. "Well, this monster isn't a legend," she said. "The bully nearly drownded us."

Róisín and Muiris handed out all the notices from Sir Dignum Drax and soon everyone was talking about the mysterious stranger.

But Jarlath looked at his watch and began to fret. "I wonder if Connle is having trouble with the donkey again?" he said.

Connle was the caretaker of the summerhouse and was supposed to have met them off the ferry.

Right on cue, a donkey shot out from behind the hill and reared up on his hind legs. On his back was a small man with flaming red hair.

"Oh, there he is!" said Jarlath.

"Down boy, down boy!" shouted Connle, who was barely hanging on.

The donkey stopped abruptly and Connle flew over his ears into a ditch. Everyone laughed, especially Thomas and Cassie who enjoyed a good accident more than most. Only Nancy shouted, "Stop laughing!"

A strong-looking young woman with plaited golden hair was first on the scene. She pulled Connle out of the ditch as if he was as light as Nancy.

She spoke in a strange language to the donkey who nuzzled Connle as if to say sorry. Then Connle said something to the young woman the children couldn't understand. Jarlath explained that they were speaking Irish. The young woman, Áine, had told the donkey to be quiet and Connle had thanked her.

"So will Connle be able to understand us?" asked Cassie. "Does he speak English?"

Jarlath laughed. "Oh, Irish, English – it's all the same to him! He switches from one to the other all the time!"

The children noticed that Áine had a tattoo in a swirly design on her upper left arm. And she had impressive-looking muscles too.

"That Áine has a witchy way with her,"

Róisín whispered, none too quietly, "She's always appearing out of nowhere."

Jarlath shot Róisín a look, then stammered: "Sh-she was only trying to help."

Róisín smiled knowingly at Muiris. "Oh, somebody has a soft spot for Áine!"

This made Jarlath blush to the roots of his hair. Connle was tiny, not much bigger than Cassie. He had a mop of red hair that he had tried to comb into a quiff, except it kept collapsing into his eyes. The children couldn't figure out if he was an old-looking young person or a young-looking old person. He wore a green shirt with orange trousers and an extraordinary patchwork waistcoat that had loads of pockets. On his feet were cowboy boots with spurs and clicky heels. He winked at Cassie and Thomas.

"I know what you are thinking," he said. "I look like a leprechaun. Well, I'm Ireland's tallest leprechaun." He clicked his heels and did a little dance.

"I'm Cassie – and don't mind Thomas, he's sulky and nicknamed 'Pouting'."

"And she's ten going on forty, Mum says," Thomas piped up.

"Ten and a half," Cassie shot back.

Connle laughed.

Nancy shook his hand. "My name is Nancy and I am a wish."

"Oh, just like your great-great-great-great-great-great-great-great-great-great-great-great-etcetera-grandmother," said Connle, impressed.

At this, Thomas and Cassie both rolled their eyes up to heaven and pointed to their heads, agreeing he was a bit mad.

Without turning round Connle said, "Oh, I don't mind if you think I'm mad – once *I* don't think I'm mad is all that matters."

They were both too shocked to react. They could have sworn he had his back to them.

Nancy then said: "We are the Chingles from the East."

A funny look came over Connle's face. "What was that?" he asked her.

"She means we are children from East Croydon," Cassie explained. "She can't say the words properly."

But Connle had nipped off to talk to Áine, muttering about "the Chingles". She in turn looked at them with special interest.

Soon all the bags were loaded on the unfortunate donkey, who was called Derry.

As they were leaving, Muiris handed them the notice from Drax. He grinned when Nancy spat at it.

"Come and visit us at the Post House before the meeting," he said. "Róisín bakes the best fairy cakes on the island but don't tell her I told you that."

They thanked him but before they could begin their climb up the hill, a dark shadow appeared over the little harbour. It was the black yacht of Sir Dignum Drax with its blood-red sails. Up close they saw it was named *The Ocean Beast*. It was ginormous and had a helicopter on the deck, a swimming-pool, and tennis court. There was also a huge telescope on a moving platform. It had a curious sign on its flag: an upside-down cross with a snake curled round.

Tadgh, the librarian, gazed at the standard. Áine asked him if he recognised it but he said he didn't.

"I'll have to consult my manuscripts," he said.

The islanders watched closely for any signs of life aboard.

Two men dressed in black blazers with gold tassels came out on to the deck. Neither of them looked like the picture of Sir Dignum Drax. Róisín hissed and booed as soon as she laid eyes on them. One of the men held a megaphone. He didn't really need it because he shouted loudly anyway, nearly deafening everybody.

"*Attention, all islanders! My name is Stinchcombe! On behalf of the DUM Corporation, Sir Dignum Drax invites you to his public meeting tomorrow at 3 pm. You are advised to attend so don't be late.*"

Stinchcombe touched a button and a recorded fanfare blared out. Next thing, he and the other member of the crew disappeared below deck. There was no sign of Sir Dignum on board.

Everyone stood well back as the boat sailed off again to the mouth of the harbour.

"I've heard a rumour that he's bought the castle," said Stephen Guilfoyle the farmer, who was rounding up the sheep that had come off the ferry. "I wonder if he'll let me use the west field for grazing the sheep."

The castle was a derelict ruin in the centre of the island, heading west.

"It would be great if he rebuilt the old place, all the same," said Mrs Prendergast the teashop owner. "It is a bit of an eyesore."

"Don't say that in front of Jarlath and Connle," Muiris whispered to them. "It used to be the ancient house of the McColls."

"I suppose we'll find out tomorrow," said Mr Mulally. "Doesn't look like Sir Very Important Drax will be over to try my beer."

"All the more for us," laughed Eamonn the fiddler.

With that, a few islanders slipped into the bar for a quick drink and the other folk began their separate journeys home. From the top of the hill,

Cassie looked back to see Róisín hauling Muiris out of the pub by his ears.

Cassie and Thomas rode their bicycles ahead of the others. Jarlath had told them to stay close so they didn't get lost down any of the boreens (which he explained was the Irish word for little roads). From the crest of the hill they saw what he meant. They could see a few 'main' tarred roads running through the island like major arteries in the human body with a maze of connecting 'boreens' like blood vessels. But they couldn't stop themselves from freewheeling down the hill.

"I hope Jarlath doesn't think we've disappeared down a 'boreen'," Thomas joked when they reached the bottom.

They dawdled along, waiting for the others to catch up.

"I think Áine is Jarlath's girlfriend," Cassie said.

"Ugh!" said Thomas. "I think Sir Big Bum Drax is your boyfriend!"

"No, he isn't!"

"Is!"

"Isn't!"

"Is!"

They kept this up until the others came in sight and then they set off up the next hill. As they reached the top, Jarlath called out to them to wait.

The donkey was making slow progress up the hill. Nancy was now perched on his back among the bags and Jarlath held the reins, with Connle bringing up the rear. Nancy played with the donkey's ears.

"I think you have some special powers over the donkey," Connle said to her. "That's the first time he's ever let a soul touch his ears."

Cassie and Thomas chased each other up the road, but they soon cycled back to the others who sounded as if they were having more fun.

Nancy was singing a song. Out of tune.

"I'm sitting on a donkey,

And looking at a tree!

And soon I'll be having my tea.

And wetting my knickers!"

Cassie and Thomas burst out laughing but Jarlath looked worried.

"She is toilet-trained?" he asked Cassie.

"Nearly," Thomas answered. "Sometimes she forgets."

"But then she only pees," Cassie added. "She tells you when she wants to poo."

Connle snorted with laughter. "Hah, you were nearly Thomas's age and you still had to wear a nappy at night," he said to Jarlath. "Do you not remember Theresa and Angel and the terrible twosome calling you piss-in-the-bed and making you wear dandelion –"

Jarlath went bright red and interrupted Connle. "Children, you can just see the house around the next corner."

The white summerhouse was on the crest of a hill, on the highest point of the island. Below it there was a field that was lumpy and bumpy and covered in luxuriant green grass. In the centre of the field was a ring of hawthorn trees growing around a raised grass-covered circle of earth.

Beyond that was a bog. A sign at the gate said: *Fairy Fort House.*

"Now that field there is called the Fairy Field. And the circle with the hawthorn trees is a fairy fort – home to the Little People," explained Connle.

"Oh, our mother has told us all about them," Cassie said importantly. "They're the Irish fairies but they're only stories."

"Well, who knows," said Connle. "There's many a story that has a grain of truth in it. What do you think, Jarlath?"

"The significance is in the number 9," he blurted out, miles away.

Nancy meanwhile was babbling to the donkey and getting on famously, judging by the donkey's brays. It was almost as if she was talking fluent donkey.

"Have you noticed anything special about the island?" Jarlath asked them.

"Everyone's mad," Cassie said.

"No," said Jarlath. "Stop and listen."

They dismounted from their bicycles and stood still for a moment. All they could hear was birdsong, the wind rustling in the trees and beyond that the gentle roar of the sea.

"I can't hear anything," said Thomas.

"That's just it," said Jarlath. "There are no cars here. The farmer has use of a tractor and there is a car for emergencies, an old fiat 127, but it has engine trouble. This is a car-free paradise."

"Call that paradise!" said Thomas, disgusted. "I love cars."

"There's probably nowhere to visit anyway." Cassie sounded grumpy.

"Can we watch telly when we get home?" Thomas asked.

"Didn't your mammy warn you? We can't get a signal on the island. And mobile phones don't work either. And I try to limit our use of electricity to a couple of hours a day."

"So that's why Mum didn't pack our DVD's. I thought she was just being forgetful," said Cassie, in her none-too-pleased voice. "And let me guess, you don't have a computer so I won't be able to play my helicopter game."

Jarlath shook his head.

"I suppose we'll only be getting bread and water to eat," said Thomas, panting with the exertion as they pushed their bikes up the last stretch of the hill.

"That's if you have water," Cassie said, her breath coming hard.

Suddenly Thomas said, "I want to go home. This is horrible!"

He went red in the face and started sniffling and next thing Nancy joined in: "WAAAAH!" Jarlath didn't know what to do. Cassie would have helped but she was feeling sorry for herself too and then she got a bit tearful.

Jarlath tried to cheer them up by calculating the square root of their great-great-great-great-great-great-great-great-great-great-great-great-great-granny. But this only made them all the more irritable. Connle scratched his head and led Derry the donkey and the three children up the path. And it was in this unhappy fashion that they all trooped up to the house.

The house was painted white with a door in the middle and two windows on the downstairs and two upstairs. There was also a dormer window in the attic, tucked into the roof. It looked such a friendly house, with a red door and smoke coming out of the chimney. The sight of it cheered them all up a bit and they were pleased that the door opened in two halves like their fridge freezer at home. So if a knock came to the door you could lean out the top half without having to bother opening the bottom.

Inside, the children stopped crying long enough to tell Jarlath what they wanted for their tea.

"We only ever eat cake," Thomas said, wiping his snotty nose on his sleeve, "and sweets and jelly and chocolate and Starlight Stoppers."

"I want bread," said Nancy, "with jam and ham."

Cassie said she had a pain in her tummy.

Connle scratched his head, knocking his quiff

over his eyes. "I'll see what I can do. I could manage cow-tongue sandwiches, sheep's-eye trifle and some fried chewy pig-tails."

All three children shouted "*Yeuch!*" and Thomas said he'd rather starve. But Connle ignored their protests. He settled Cassie down in the rocking chair in the kitchen with a patchwork quilt over her knees. Then he put on an apron and got busy. He soon rustled up a tea of brown soda bread, cheese, homemade Rice-Krispie buns and fruitcake. Relieved to be eating normal food, they soon polished it all off.

After their tea, Jarlath showed them to their rooms. They were delighted that their bedrooms were in the attic, right under the eaves of the roof: a single room for Thomas with an adjoining door to the girls' double bedroom.

"This was always our summerhouse," said Jarlath. "I thought you'd like our old toys." They were a motley collection of old-fashioned dollies and cuddly toys, all battered and patched up as if they had survived several wars. Thomas and Cassie turned their noses up at them but Nancy immediately grabbed an old teddy, which for reasons of her own she named 'Dog'.

Jarlath was delighted. It used to be his old teddy but he called him Number 2, he explained, because it was his second teddy. This made Thomas and Cassie laugh.

"Imagine calling your teddy Number 2! When you wanted to do a Number 2, did you say you wanted to do a teddy?" Cassie asked.

Jarlath looked totally puzzled but he was so relieved that they were laughing he didn't mind that it was at him.

"Now I think you should all get washed and changed for bed – you've had a busy day," he said.

Cassie looked at her watch. It was only seven o'clock in the evening.

"But it's way too early!" she protested through a yawn.

"I have a special treat for you," Jarlath said. "But get ready for bed first."

Cassie helped Nancy have her bath and dressed her in her red pyjamas and night nappy. Cassie wore her purple-striped pyjamas and dressing-gown. And Thomas donned his Superman pyjamas. They trooped down to the kitchen.

"I wonder what's Jarlath's idea of a special treat?" wondered Cassie to Thomas.

"He's probably going to give us some maths homework," said Thomas in a worried voice.

They soon found out. Áine was in the kitchen and she had brought her harp. They had already taken a liking to Áine. She had golden hair like Auntie Angel except Áine's wasn't black at the roots. They also liked the tattoo on her upper arm, which she explained was a Celtic design from a long, long time ago. She was kind to them but they could tell that she would be fierce to anyone who got on her wrong side.

Connle had his tin whistle out.

"We'll start by playing you a medley of Elvis Presley tunes," he announced.

The children knew all about Elvis because their granddad liked him. He was a dead singer who died of eating too many burgers. But they didn't recognise any of the songs because the combination of the tin whistle and the harp made it sound as if someone had tried to strangle Elvis Presley's songs and had succeeded.

Then they played nicer music and Áine sang in Irish. It sounded like whispers and wind rustling and birds chirping in the field and sometimes as if Áine had a cold and was trying to clear her throat.

Soon Nancy dropped off to sleep.

Cassie and Thomas tried to hold open their eyelids to stay awake.

"You are very lucky to have each other," Áine said to them. "That was a song about my sister whom I lost long ago."

But they didn't really hear her because they were now falling asleep themselves. And Jarlath was gently snoring in the corner.

Cassie drifted in and out of sleep, lulled by the sound of Connle and Áine talking, as if she were listening to a radio.

But then there was an urgency in their voices that snagged her attention.

"Can this really be them?" Áine was saying quietly to Connle. "I did not expect them to be so young."

They must be talking about her and Thomas and Nancy! But what did they mean? Who were they supposed to be? Cassie kept her eyes closed and tried to catch the next bit of the conversation but their voices were low. She thought she heard Connle mutter something about Drax and his arrival in the yacht.

"I don't know, Connle," Áine replied, "but the Corra –"

Nancy murmured in her sleep and Áine stopped talking abruptly. Cassie lay as still as a statue with her eyes shut tight. She thought she heard Connle whisper something about a lake. Or was it a cake?

Then there was a rustle of cloth. Cassie risked half opening her eyes and watched as Áine put her cloak on.

"It's getting late. I must be gone before nightfall," Áine whispered, pulling her cloak tightly round her and picking up her harp carefully so as not to make any noise. She began to tiptoe out of the room. Connle let out a deep sigh and Áine said something to him that was muffled. Every fibre in Cassie's body strained to hear what they were saying but all she caught was Connle mentioning something about 'the Chingles'. That word again! But she distinctly heard Áine's reply.

"It is our task to prepare them," she said. "Sometimes the dark force can be overcome by the power of the weak."

Cassie lay deathly still.

Áine paused at the door and whispered. "Keep an eye on them, Connle. They may have special powers hidden to us. We will look for a sign."

A sign? What on earth was going on? Their voices drifted away from her and Cassie risked turning towards the door, pretending she was moving in her sleep. But she overdid it. Áine and Connle froze.

"And you, listening one, will remember nothing after you sleep," said Áine as she walked out the door.

CHAPTER 3

That night, Cassie had a strange dream. She, Thomas and Nancy were sailing in a boat, the shape of a walnut shell, on a green lake. All was calm but then the Corra, the black featherless bird that they'd seen from the ferry, swooped down upon them. Just as they were about to be gobbled up, the wind blew them out of the bird's path. But there was something lurking in the water, and they were afraid. Below the surface, they saw a monstrous, ugly worm with one great eye. They heard voices coming from above and, when they looked up, they saw a giant Áine and Connle looking at them and muttering about 'the Chingles

39

from the East'. Áine asked, "Have they caught the Pike? Is this the sign?" Then they heard Jarlath saying, "Oh, we mustn't lose them – whatever will I tell their mother and father?"

Cassie woke up shaking in the bed.

She recounted her dream to Thomas and Nancy at the breakfast table.

"I saw the fish," said Nancy.

"Yes, I had a dream too," said Thomas. "And there was a fish."

"He was called a bike!" said Nancy.

"He was called a *pike* not a bike," said Cassie.

They looked at each other in wonder.

"Do you think we were all in the same dream?" Thomas asked.

"I think so," said Cassie.

"Cool," said Thomas.

"I heard Áine and Connle talking about us last night," Cassie said.

"Oh yeah, what did they say?" asked Thomas, idly picking his nose.

"That you're the most revolting boy who ever lived!" Cassie exclaimed.

"Liar!" said Thomas defiantly. "What did they really say?"

Cassie scratched her head. "I can't remember . . . but they were worried about us or something."

"Grown-ups are always worried," said Thomas

Cassie shrugged her shoulders. "Maybe I was dreaming."

They only realised Connle was in the kitchen and had been listening to their conversation when he placed bowls of steaming porridge before them.

"Ugh!" Thomas made a face of pure disgust. "There's no way I'm eating that sh–"

"Mind your manners, you little brat," Cassie interrupted him. Then she said to Connle, "But I'm not eating that porridge either. It looks like sick."

"Now, children," Connle said mysteriously, "this is magic porridge. It will taste of whatever you want."

They looked doubtfully at him. Connle sighed and took the bowls away.

"You are right," he agreed. "It's probably too special for you."

Suddenly they really wanted to try it.

"Ah, please?" Cassie begged.

"Pretty please," lisped Thomas with his hands raised in prayer.

"All right," Connle said in a weary tone, placing the bowls back on the table. "What's your favourite food, Thomas?"

"Starlight Stoppers," he said.

Connle held up a spoon to Thomas's lips.

Thomas ate the tiniest mouthful. He licked his lips. "Strawberry flavour! Wow!"

"Well, I don't like Starlight Stoppers," Cassie insisted in a hoity-toity way. "My favourite food is Death by Chocolate, a cake that Nan Nelson makes. That's our English Nan. And I bet –" but she soon shut up when Connle shoved a spoonful of porridge in her mouth. Cassie was amazed. The porridge tasted not just like Nan Nelson's famous cake, but it was almost as if she'd been transported to her nan's kitchen and the cake had just come out of the oven, all moist and warm. She closed her eyes with pleasure and when she opened them she was surprised to be in the summerhouse in Inish Álainn.

"And what about Nancy?" Connle asked.

"I want broccoli and bloody orange juice," she said. But soon she was rolling her eyes with relish and lapping up her porridge.

By the time Cassie thought it would be interesting for them to try each other's porridge, no one had any left.

Jarlath had already departed for his workshop in another part of the island. The plan was that Connle would take them on a tour and they would join Jarlath for lunch. He slung some saddlebags over Derry's back, plonked Nancy on top, and they set out.

The island was no more than three kilometres long and about six wide and from their hill they had a great view of the sea.

Connle pointed out a school of dolphins out at sea.

"Have you heard tell of Funghi who lives in Dingle?" he asked them. "Well, that's his brother Mossy and he has his own school."

"Is he the teacher?" Thomas asked. "But what do they have to learn? Dolphins can't learn to read and write, can they?"

Cassie tutted. "Honestly, Pouting, sometimes you are sooooo stupid! School is the name for a group of dolphins."

Thomas stuck his tongue out at her. "It takes one to know one!" he shouted.

"Children, children," Connle intervened, "you'll get yourselves into real trouble bickering so. Now shake hands and promise to be better friends." Thomas held out his hand but as Cassie went to shake it, he thumbed his nose at her.

"See what I'm up against?" Cassie said to Connle as she tried to trip Thomas up. "There's no way I'm ever saying sorry to him, ever."

Connle looked at them with resignation. "What am I going to do with the pair of you?" he sighed. "What do you think, Nancy?"

"Throw them in the bin," she said.

Connle winked. "I'll make them walk backwards instead."

So Thomas and Cassie had to walk backwards down the narrow boreens. It was torture because they both nearly fell over several times and Nancy kept exclaiming, "Oh, look, look!" and they weren't allowed to turn round. Actually, they couldn't turn round, even though they tried to cheat. There seemed to be some magnetic force stopping them. Soon they were straggling far behind and feeling very sorry for themselves.

"I thought Connle was going to be a pushover," Cassie complained.

"It's your fault," Thomas sulked.

"It's yours, fathead!"

They carried on like this for a few steps but their legs felt like lead. They soon realised that every time they insulted each other, it got harder to move. They finally agreed that they'd better say sorry, and called Connle. He made them shake hands, not just with each other but with Nancy as well.

"You have to learn that bickering just holds you back," Connle said.

"It doesn't stop Róisín and Muiris," Cassie said, quick as a flash but one look from Connle made her regret it. Already she could feel her legs getting heavy at the thought of having to walk backwards again.

"That's different," Connle said sternly.

"But why?" asked Thomas all innocence. "Just because they are grown up! It's one law for children and another for adults."

"Exactly so," said Connle. "For a start, they don't hit each other and they are funny, whereas you two are just boring."

That shut them up.

They were about to turn down the boreen to the lake when they heard a loud clatter and soon a dark shadow was swooping towards them across the adjoining field. It was Sir Dignum Drax's helicopter flying overhead and it was striped black and yellow like a big angry wasp. The whoosh of the propellers blew all their clothes and the children crouched down low and put their hands over their ears. Connle watched the helicopter with narrowed eyes. "It's heading over to the east of the island where Jarlath has his workshop. I wonder if Drax is looking for Jarlath?"

"Well, whatever he wants, he won't get a straight answer from Jarlath," Cassie said wisely.

Connle laughed. "Cassie, girl, you've got a

right tongue in your head! Well, we'll just have to wait until lunch-time to find out."

They headed through the green fields to Glimmering Lake in Fingal Valley. At the side of the water were standing stones with unusual swirling signs on them.

"That there is Ogham script," Connle explained, "that the druids used to do in ancient times."

"What are druids?" Cassie asked, trying to sound polite

"Oh, here we go again. School lessons," Thomas groaned.

"Stooopid boy!" Cassie sniffed. "I'd like to know what it says."

"I'd like to know what it says too," Connle said. "I knew once and I've forgotten. But druids were people who knew a lot of things."

"Unlike you," Cassie murmured under her breath, forgetting her manners.

"I've forgotten more things than you'll ever know," said Connle.

"Sorry," said a contrite Cassie. "I didn't mean to be cheeky. It just came out. Sometimes people laugh and other times I get into trouble, so I get confused."

"Sometimes it depends on how you say it. The McColl women all have sharp tongues," said Connle, "but you're so sharp you'll cut yourself."

"That'll teach you," Thomas gloated.

But Cassie didn't respond because her attention was distracted by the sight of a little upturned boat shaped just like a walnut shell at the water's edge. She eyed it suspiciously. It was just like the boat in her dream! Cassie ran towards it but Thomas hung back.

"I'm not going near that," he said.

"Ah sure, that's a brave little boat, Thomas," Connle said. "We call it a currach in these parts."

"Currant," Nancy repeated.

Connle turned the boat over. "All aboard," he said.

They rowed out to the centre of the lake. It was a still day and the sun crept gently up in the sky towards noon.

"I wish we could fish," said Thomas, forgetting his earlier fear.

"Just what I was thinking," said Connle. And as if out of nowhere, he produced from his pockets three pens that turned into fishing-rods.

"Magic!" exclaimed Thomas.

Connle attached some bread to the hooks as bait.

"You certainly have a lot of stuff in those pockets!" Cassie said, amazed.

Connle squinted, rummaged around some more and pulled out a net.

After about ten minutes with no sign of anyone catching a fish, Thomas sighed.

"How deep is this lake?" he asked. "Are there any fish down there at all?"

"I've heard tell it's bottomless," Connle said, "but folk don't like to explore on account of the . . ."

The children's eyes opened wide.

"I'll tell you when we are back on dry land," he said. Instead, he sang them a song with a country and western twang that was so mournful even the fish would have felt sorry for him.

"*Swim around, swim around, little fish!*
Deep in the water, you go swish,

49

Back and forth with your mouth open wide.
You surge through the lake from side to side.
But if the powers would grant me one little wish,
You'd bite on my line and become my dish!
Little fish, little fish, little fish!"

He'd only just finished singing when Cassie felt a tug.

"It's a monster!" she screamed.

Cassie thought her arms were going to be wrenched out of their sockets by the strength of the fish. The pull on the line was so strong that at one point it seemed that they were the fish and the fish was reeling in the boat. They were dragged along hook, line and sinker.

"By the Cape of Ferdia," Connle exclaimed at the fish, "I'll have yeh, yeh brute!" He took hold of Cassie around the waist. Thomas held on to her leg and Nancy clung on to the back of her jumper. There was much squealing and screaming.

"It's a shark!" Thomas shouted.

One minute they whirred around in a circle, the next they were pulled back and forth like water-skiers.

The sky grew dark and a great wind blew up. There was a thwack and the fish flew out of the water, circling above their heads. For a moment, they were all lifted clean out of the boat, clinging onto Cassie and drifting in the air like a human, multicoloured kite. Then the wind died just as suddenly as it had risen and they landed back in the boat with a thump. They looked up. For a split second the fish hung in the air and then landed straight in Connle's lap. Cassie and Thomas were ready with the net and, as the fish thrashed about, Connle rowed for the shore.

The fish was nearly as big as Connle who looked it straight in the eye.

"Well, if it isn't the old legendary Pike of Glimmering Lake or my name isn't Connle O'Flaherty Finnegan Kennedy O'Leary Killykelly Murnaghan Downey Deery O'Donovan!"

Back on dry land, the Pike flailed on the grass.

"Will you grant us our wish if we put you back?" asked Connle.

Thomas and Cassie hung back in fear. But

curiosity got the better of Nancy, who tiptoed over for a better look.

"I show Dog the fish," she said, running back to the currach for the teddy. But her teddy wasn't there. "I want my Dog!" she cried. "Where's my Dog?" In all the commotion, the ancient teddy had fallen into the water. Nancy stamped her foot.

A straggly wet bundle flew out of the lake.

Thomas ran to retrieve it. It was Nancy's teddy. Thomas handed it to her with distaste, as if it was a nappy full of poo.

"Well, I never," Connle said, shaking his head in disbelief. "To think we caught the legendary Pike of Glimmering Lake and all we got was a wet teddy bear!"

Nancy hugged her teddy and ran back to the fish to thank him.

"There's no way I'm going near that thing!" Thomas made a face and hid behind a rock.

"Me neither," said Cassie in exaggerated horror.

Both of them were rather afraid of the pike

and were trying to cover up that fact by their play-acting.

"Look!" Nancy pointed at the fish's mouth.

At that, Connle, who was rolling up the net, thought he caught sight of something glistening out of the corner of his eye. But at that moment he was distracted by Cassie and Thomas who popped up from behind the rock, ready to cast their fishing-rods in the direction of the Pike.

"Quit messing about or you'll take each other's eyes out!" Connle shouted at them.

"It was Thomas's idea," said Cassie.

"No, it wasn't!" protested Thomas.

Connle glared at them as they made a big fuss about reeling in their lines, arguing all the time.

Only Nancy paid attention to the large stone like a crystal in the fish's mouth, its many surfaces catching the sun's rays.

"Look!" she exclaimed, squatting down close to the Pike's mouth and peering in.

As Connle turned back to her he was caught on Cassie and Thomas's fishing-lines, the hooks sinking into his jacket.

"Drop those lines immediately!" he shouted at them, swinging round again.

"We didn't mean it," pleaded Thomas. "We were only trying to straighten the lines."

Cassie and Thomas slunk out from behind the rock. They went to help Connle untangle himself but he shooed them away.

"You two have caused enough trouble!" he said impatiently. "Just keep an eye on Nancy!"

Shamefaced, Cassie and Thomas watched their little sister as she bent her head close to the Pike's mouth.

"I think she's going to kiss it," shrieked Cassie to Thomas in disgust. They both turned away and pretended to be sick.

With that, the Pike jumped in the air and disappeared back into the lake.

"Oh no!" Connle cried. "I wanted to get a closer look at that fish!"

He managed to get the hooks out of his jacket and ran back to the spot on the grass where the fish had just been. He dropped to his knees and started to rummage around in the grass.

"Did he give you a stone like a crystal, Nancy?" he asked Nancy urgently.

Nancy held out her empty hands. "Gone," she said.

"I could have sworn I saw something glinting." Connle scratched his head. "It's not lucky to accept gifts from any passing fish," he muttered to himself as he peered under stones and swept his hands through the grass. To make amends, Thomas and Cassie helped him comb the surrounding area.

"Don't tell me you swallowed it," Connle said to Nancy with a groan.

Nancy laughed and said, "I won't tell you I swallowed it." She giggled and flapped her mouth like a fish.

Thomas wanted to give her a Chinese burn as a torture but Connle wouldn't hear of it. Cassie caught hold of her and thumped the poor child on the back. Nancy let out a scream and a big belch. She wriggled away and ran into Connle's arms to stop the others bullying her.

"That fish has never been caught before except once by Ferdia," Connle said.

"With our wish we could have asked for all the gold in the world," said Thomas.

"Or all the money to buy all the gold," argued Cassie.

They glared at poor Nancy.

"Leave that poor child alone!" scolded Connle. "If you pair hadn't been acting up like a right pair of babies, I might have seen what happened."

Cassie and Thomas went into a sulk. Connle realised they were hungry and said no more about the missing stone.

They set off down another twisty turny boreen lined with stone walls to join Jarlath for lunch. Nancy whispered in Derry's ear and it was as if he knew exactly what she was talking about. The other two made a point of dawdling behind. Everyone was out of sorts.

Connle knew what to do to make them snap out of their bad moods: he told them the story of the Pike.

"Long ago," Connle began, " there was a war in the heavens between Balor of the Evil Eye and the Sun Goddess for control of the skies. Balor had captured a precious crystal called the Star Splinter, which had magical properties that could help him take control of the sun. But he had been badly injured in the battle so he came to Glimmering Lake to bathe in the magical waters, which could cure any ailment."

"So does Balor die?" Thomas interrupted.

"Listen to the story," said Connle. "Now, the Keeper of Glimmering Lake was known as Finnen and she could take the form of a swan."

"How?" interrupted Cassie. "Was she a witch?"

"No, not a witch," answered Connle, "but a goddess with magical powers. She could also sing sweeter than anyone in the whole country."

"And the Sun Woman, was she a goody or a baddie?" Thomas asked.

"She was a goody," sighed Connle. "In fact, Finnen was the sister of the Sun Goddess. So when she caught Balor trying to sneak into the lake, she hauled him out by his big hairy toe. She looked at him and recoiled in fright. He had seven toes on one foot and five on the other and twelve fingers like claws. He wore an eye-patch over his one huge eye in the middle of his forehead. He was bleeding so heavily it was like a stream and his blood was green."

"Yeuchy!" Nancy made a face.

"How was his blood green?" asked Thomas.

"Look, do you want me to tell this story or don't you?" Connle sounded a bit irritated.

They shut up.

"Finnen offered him a deal," continued Connle. "She would allow him to heal in the Sacred Lake if he surrendered the Star Splinter. Instead, he offered her an eyelash that he plucked from his eye, a toenail that he bit from his toe and a big lump of snot that he blew from his nose. She was disgusted and threw them all into the lake."

Thomas, who'd been idly picking his nose, quickly extracted his finger and flicked the contents away. "What happened next?" he asked to distract attention from his nose-picking.

Connle described how Balor attacked Finnen but she transformed into a swan and flew away. Balor thought he'd won but he had forgotten that the waters of the lake were magical. When he got to the centre of the Lake he felt something nibbling his toes. His eyelash had turned into a pike in the enchanted waters. He managed to kick it away with his many big toes but then he bashed his foot into a massive stone rising up out of the lake. This was his toenail transformed into a big boulder. Staggered by the blow, he sank to the bottom where he came eye to eye with a hideous huge white worm with a mouth and a head on either end of its body. "Guess what that was?" Connle looked at Thomas. "Yes, his dirty big lump of snot!"

"That's just too disgusting!" Thomas exclaimed.

"And that's why you shouldn't flick snot all over the place!" Connle gave Thomas a disapproving nod.

"What happened next?" asked Thomas, eager to change the subject from snot.

"The massive worm swallowed him at one end and spat him out at the other, one bit at a time. First his arm, then one leg, then his body, then his other arm, then his head. Balor managed to put himself back together again but this time he had only one leg. Then the worm spat the Star Splinter out but the pike jumped up and grabbed it before Balor could even see what was going on."

"That fish we caught is a smelly old beast's eyelash and Nancy kissed it," Thomas said with revulsion.

"That whole story is *yeuch!*" said Cassie.

"You two are very delicate altogether!" Connle shook his head.

"What happened to Finnen?" asked Cassie.

"She disappeared, nobody knows where. But the boulder rose out of the lake and had that druid's Ogham writing on it that we were talking about earlier. And some say it means that one day Balor will come back to look for the Star Splinter."

"So that jewel of the Pike might be the Star Splinter?" Cassie said. She glared at her little sister.

Connle looked sad. "It's back in the lake now anyway," he said.

Nancy just flapped her mouth like a fish.

"I'm going to keep an eye on Nancy's nappies just in case she did swallow it," Cassie whispered to Thomas.

They finally arrived at Jarlath's workshop. There was no sign of the helicopter. Perhaps it hadn't visited Jarlath after all. The workshop was a big wooden barn with a massive door at one end and windows high up by the tin roof. Jarlath was stuck in the open doors, struggling to pull out a strange machine. It looked like a giant vacuum cleaner with a long wriggly hose at one end and a massive balloon gadget attached to the rear. Jarlath wriggled out from under the balloon when he heard their greetings.

"Oh great," he said. "You'll all be able to help me tame this big yoke after lunch."

"We are only children," Thomas replied, showing off his new-found manners, "but we'll help you all we can."

Connle beamed at him with approval.

Jarlath took them down to a sweet, sunny spot in the meadow and Connle got the picnic ready.

He took a cloth no bigger than a postage stamp from his pocket and when he shook it out it became a fair-sized tartan blanket. Out of another pocket he pulled out plastic beakers and plates.

The picnic basket was in Derry's saddlebag and was no bigger than a child's lunchbox. Yet it contained boiled eggs, barbecued sausages, pizza slices, tasty pastries and Rice-Krispie cakes for afters.

In between stuffing their faces, they told Jarlath about their day, all about the magic porridge for breakfast and the Pike of Glimmering Lake that used to be a giant's eyelash. The thing that interested Jarlath the most was how they fared with the fishing-rods.

"Good, aren't they!" he said with pride. He told them how he decided to invent them one day when he was out walking and saw a plump trout in a stream. He would have caught it but he only had a pen with him and thought how useful it would be if it could turn into a fishing-rod.

"They're a bit flyaway," Connle said, "but they were just what we needed. One of your better ones, I think." Connle explained that Jarlath was always inventing things to take his mind off his big sum.

Jarlath promised to show them more inventions, like his 'Shoes-off', a device for taking shoes off after a long walk when people are too tired to bend down and do it for themselves. And his 'Cooler-hat', a bobble hat with a propeller on the top for cooling you down on a warm day. He'd also invented indelible pens where the ink couldn't be erased and that changed colour depending on the background.

"Oh, we forgot to tell you about the angry-wasp helicopter we saw," Cassie said.

Jarlath nearly blew all the crumbs in his mouth on top of the children.

"That was none other than Stinkbomb, the servant of Sir Dignum Drax," he fumed. "Interrupting my work just as I had nearly cracked the significance of the number 9!"

"You mean Big Bum Drax!" said Thomas.

"Language," scolded Connle.

Jarlath calmed down. "I'd got as far as pi

multiplied by a square root of the cardinal number, subtracted from the integer of a prime number, when he barged in wanting to sell me something, or buy me something." He hung his head in shame.

"Oh no," Connle shook his head. "You didn't lose your temper? Not the Jelly Belly?"

Jarlath looked sheepish. Connle explained that this was a machine that covered people in gooey jelly and then feathers, so they looked like moulting birds.

"You're a terrible boy – what am I going to do with you?" said Connle.

"But I was provoked," Jarlath pleaded. "Look at this horrid letter." He handed a torn, crumpled letter to Connle who read it aloud.

It said:

"Dear Sir,
The DUM Corporation wishes to buy Fairy Fort field and house. We can offer you a high price for a building that is, after all, falling apart. If you do not comply we will inform your university that you waste

all your grant money on stupid inventions instead of finding out the significance of the number 9.

Yours insincerely,

Sir Dignum Drax
The DUM CORPORATION.

Connle patted him on the shoulder. "I can see how you got annoyed," he said.

"I couldn't resist showing him just how useful my inventions are for dealing with pests like him," Jarlath said.

They all laughed and wished they could have seen it. Jarlath brightened up and they went to look at his latest contraption that was stuck in the barn doors. Cassie suggested using Derry the donkey to help pull it out, so they tethered ropes to the poor animal and, with much huffing and puffing, they finally managed to get the machine outside.

"Behold the fog-buster!" Jarlath said with a flourish.

He then explained that as his workshop was at the bottom of the valley, he was much troubled by mists and fog that rolled in off the sea every morning. He lived in constant fear of it erasing his sums written in chalk on the blackboard. But no more! He undid the nozzle of his machine and pressed a large button, which started a whirr-clonk-crack racket.

The children held their ears but Jarlath shouted, "This works on the principle of the centrifuge, two interlocking spirals. It is like a wall of death where the rider stays on his motor bike through the velocity of resistance to his motion." But he might as well have said, "I'm a giant banana and I wear gobstobbers in my green hair," for all they heard or understood.

The large twisty hose juddered into life like a mad snake. There was more whirring and whooshing and Jarlath got so excited that he nearly got sucked into the hose. Luckily Connle turned the machine off in time. Jarlath's hair was standing on end when they managed to get the hose off his head and his face was purple. But far from being annoyed, he smiled and hollered and hugged them all.

"This is a breakthrough!" he cried. "It works. Just a few wrinkles to sort out."

Cassie and Thomas exchanged glances. Uncle Jarlath was turning out to be as nuts as their father claimed he was.

"Well," Connle said, scratching his head, "perhaps you should wait until there really is a fog."

Jarlath thought this was a great idea and he made them all promise to get up at dawn the following morning so that they could witness a real-life experiment. He also asked Connle to make him his special treat to celebrate. While Connle was helping Nancy on to the donkey, Cassie asked Jarlath if he was ever made to walk backwards by Connle when he was little.

"I'm afraid so," he grinned. "It was the weirdest thing. Like he'd given you a dead leg without touching you. It's almost as if there's a magnetic field and you just can't disobey him."

Cassie and Thomas nodded their heads in recognition.

"Ah, you've been done. You'll learn to watch

your p's and q's," Jarlath continued. "You might think Connle's as soft as butter but I'd swear he has special powers – if I believed in all that sort of thing."

They said goodbye and thanked him for the advice.

They were off to meet Áine, before going to the Drax meeting at the pub. As they walked down the lane with Nancy on the donkey, Cassie made a special effort to be polite. She asked Connle what was Jarlath's special treat.

"Plain porridge," said Connle, "made with water, no sugar, lumpy and allowed to go cold."

They knew then that Jarlath definitely was bonkers.

"And why doesn't he use a computer or a copybook for his sums?" asked Thomas.

"He's says he can think better if he sees it on a blackboard," Connle replied.

"Sometimes clever people can be very stupid," said Cassie.

"You'll have to remember that for yourself," shot back Connle.

Cassie was going to say something but decided to be cleverly silent on this occasion.

"Good girl," said Connle. "Sometimes it's better to hold your tongue." Cassie looked at him with amazement. It was almost as if he could read her mind!

They were so absorbed in their discussions that nobody noticed a figure, dressed all in black but covered in jelly and feathers, slink away in the opposite direction.

CHAPTER 4

They walked through the rustling wood and came to the Field of Flowers, a meadow where herbs and flowers grew in a thick carpet. Áine was in the middle picking blossoms and putting them in a basket. They joined her and she handed them each a basket of their own.

They told her all about their action-packed morning, catching the legendary Pike of Glimmering Lake.

Áine looked significantly at Connle.

She questioned them closely about the stone that was in the Pike's mouth. Cassie and Thomas told her that Nancy was the last person who saw it. Áine asked Nancy about it but Nancy's only reply was to flap her mouth like a fish. The children also described the helicopter buzzing the landscape like an angry wasp and told her of the letter to Jarlath from Sir Big Bum about wanting to buy the house.

"I've also had a visit from Stinchcombe, his slimy servant," Áine said, a flash of annoyance in her voice. "He was horrible, covered in jelly and feathers."

When she heard that this was Jarlath's doing, she looked pleased.

"They want to buy my little cottage too," she went on, "and said I could make a range of herbal remedies for sale in Sir Drax's big shop in London."

"What are herbal remedies?" asked Thomas.

"Oh, ointments and soaps, candles and creams," replied Áine.

"Yeuch," Thomas said, "girl's stuff."

"Don't mind him, he's a moron," Cassie said. Thomas stuck his tongue out at her.

Connle frowned at them and they remembered their manners.

"I don't like any of this," said Connle to Áine. "We must talk."

"Now you've done it!" Cassie hissed at Thomas. They expected a right telling-off but Connle had other things on his mind. He took the picnic blanket out of his pocket and laid it out in the meadow. Áine handed them a beautiful red poppy and asked them to smell it.

All of a sudden, the children felt drowsy and yawned in turn. For the first time in her life, Nancy volunteered to have an afternoon nap. Cassie didn't have time to comment on this surprise because she herself felt all warm and toasty as she lay down beside her little sister. Thomas tried to resist the desire for sleep and stumbled around like a drunk, until he too finally fell in a snoring heap. Gently, they slept on the blanket while Áine and Connle talked.

All three children had a strange dream. They heard Áine say that Jarlath had his head in the clouds and they saw Jarlath at his workshop with his fog-buster surrounded by fluffy white clouds. Then he was on his own little planet. Stinchcombe arrived with another servant of Drax who was carrying a big ball of wool on a silver platter. Stinchcombe took the yarn and wrapped it around Jarlath's eyes until it completely covered them like a mask. A mist appeared and all three of them and Connle were piled on to unfortunate Derry the donkey. They were about to enter a lion's den but Connle pulled the reins. The air was filled with hundreds of flying pike. A giant wasp appeared and out of its belly crawled a huge, wriggly worm that told them there was more to Sir Drax than met the eye. Out of the giant worm popped the ugly face of a giant with a huge eye in the centre of his forehead.

"Give me the Star Splinter or I'll eat you up!" he roared.

"No, no, no!" they all screamed and tried to get away on the donkey.

Then the children realised, as they sat up on Connle's tartan blanket in the field of flowers, that they had screamed themselves awake and once again must have shared the same dream.

Áine and Connle comforted them.

"That was horrible," said Thomas. He explained to Connle and Áine about the dream.

"Remember the horrible worm!" Nancy shuddered.

"I didn't like the giant with one eye," Cassie said.

"So they do travel in dreams!" Áine looked at Connle.

"Just like I told you. They foretold the capture of the Pike." Connle beamed at them proudly. "Surely it's a sign that they are the Chingles from the Prophecy of Ferdia's Cape!"

"What do you mean about Chingles? What's the Prophecy of Ferdia's Cape? Is it something to do with the Pike? " asked a sharp-eared Cassie.

Connle stuttered. "Don't mind me. I'm a silly old fool. I was trying to say I'd like a pot of tea with fairy cakes. I'm always getting things duddled mup."

"You mean muddled up," Thomas laughed.

But Cassie decided that Connle and Áine were pulling that old adult trick, trying to cover up something they didn't want the children to know about. Cassie whispered to Thomas that they would just have to find out about this mysterious Prophecy of Ferdia's Cape all by themselves.

The mention of a pot of tea and fairy cakes reminded them that they had arranged to see Róisín and Muiris when they had met them on the ferry. Áine gave them a garland of herbs and flowers as a gift and said she'd see them later at the public meeting. They said goodbye and set off for the Post House.

The Post House was near the Harbour, nestled into Stag's Cliff. The children were enchanted to see that it had a thatched roof. But not just any old thatched roof. This one had straw animals popping out of it. There was a straw dog chasing a straw cat that was chasing a straw mouse across the top. Muiris stood in the half-door, smoking a pipe. He waved to the children.

"Now there's a sight for sore eyes," he said. "Come on in. The Missus is cooking up a storm."

Connle wished them well and said he had to nip home and would see them later at the pub.

Muiris and Róisín had a little dog, Scalpeen,

who was equally delighted to see them all. They spent a happy half-hour playing a game of catch with the lively dog. Nancy won every game even though she was the slowest because it seemed that the dog did whatever she said.

Róisín brought them out a glass of lemonade.

"Sure isn't it great to see young people all about the place," she said.

"Are there no children on the island?" Thomas wondered.

"Since the school closed down all the young families moved to the mainland, leaving all the old codgers behind. But the grandchildren come at holiday times," Muiris said.

A few moments later Róisín called them in to the kitchen.

"Tea's up," she called. "Come and get it. You must be all starving."

"Our Granny McColl says only people in Africa are starving. We are just hungry," said Thomas.

"It is a wise woman your old granny is," said Muiris, "unlike a certain other ould wan I could mention."

Róisín glared and then grinned at him. "Two nil to you today."

Muiris explained that every day they had a competition to see who could come up with the best insults.

"They're worse than children," Thomas muttered to his sister.

They all piled into the kitchen where a big cosy fire was burning in the hearth. The table was laid with a red-and-white-check tablecloth and it was heaving with food. The children's eyes were wide with astonishment. Róisín really did make the best fairy cakes. There was a sugar-plum fairy decorated with icing and whipped cream, another iced cake shaped like a leprechaun and yet others in the shapes of pixies and goblins decorated with icing, with currants for eyes and cherries for mouths. There was a row of gingerbread men marching across a plate and a plum pudding with chocolate flakes sticking out of it like a hedgehog, surrounded by sugar mice. Jelly babies made from real jelly wobbled on a dish. And in the centre was a cake decorated with three smiling children who looked just like Cassie, Thomas and Nancy. There was also a chocolate donkey surrounded by little piles of chocolate donkey droppings that made them all laugh.

"I told you she was the best," whispered Muiris, proudly.

They ate so much they thought they would burst and at last sat back with a sigh of contentment.

Róisín had loads of questions for them, in between trying to stuff more cakes into their mouths. Even Thomas couldn't fit any more in. And all the while Róisín was asking them who and what and why and where and which and when and how.

"That woman is worse than a quiz programme. I thought she'd already pumped you for information on the ferry," sighed Muiris.

But Cassie and Thomas didn't mind. Cassie always loved talking. And when Thomas got to know people, he really was a friendly boy.

They told her about all the things that had happened that day, the Pike and the lake and

Jarlath's fog-machine and the herbs and the flowers with Áine.

"Sure isn't a child's imagination great?" said Muiris.

"Connle should have more sense than to take you out on that lake," tutted Róisín. "Mind you, they say he's one of the Little People himself."

"He's Ireland's tallest leprechaun," said Thomas.

"Now whist, woman, don't be filling their heads with nonsense," scolded Muiris.

But Róisín was off.

"Legend has it," she said, "that when Saint Patrick banished the snakes out of Ireland, he also threw out all the ancient gods and goddesses and all the fairies known as the Little People. Now some went off to other places but a group of them settled here and hid themselves in our famous island mist. Now long ago, the God of the Sea, Manannán MacLir, put down a veil between their world and ours. But in some places that veil is quite thin. And it's thinnest of all here on Inish Álainn."

"No, it's thinnest of all in your head," scoffed Muiris.

Róisín started clearing away the plates with a noisy clatter. "But Muiris McGonigal, don't you ever tell me I didn't see the Dúlachán holding his own head in his hands as he rode on that fiery horse over Hell's Ditch out by Castle McColl!"

"Whisht, you, now, I'm more worried about that other demon by the name of Drax." Muiris went to the mantelpiece and fished out a letter from behind a clock. It was just like the ones sent to Jarlath and Áine.

"That horrible Drax says he wants to buy our house and we can rent it back from him for favourable terms," said Róisín. "I'll give him favourable terms!" She grabbed the letter from Muiris and threw it in the fire. It hissed as it burnt. "Somebody is going to have to put a stop to that Drax!"

"There's something about that fellow that gives me the creeps," said Muiris, shuddering. "The way he's just turned up out of nowhere!"

There was a pause in the conversation as they all brooded on Drax.

"Do you know anything about the Prophecy of Ferdia's Cape?" asked Cassie, all innocence.

Róisín shrugged her shoulders and Muiris scratched his head.

"I've heard tell of it," said Muiris. "It is something to do with the Pike of Glimmering Lake and maybe them Chingles whoever they are but more than that I couldn't say."

"Oh, you know about the Chingles?" Cassie asked.

"I only know the name," Muiris said. "You'll –"

"We know," Thomas interrupted him. "We'll have to ask Tadgh."

Róisín disappeared into her bedroom and came out with an enormous handbag and wearing her coat, even though it was a warm summer's day.

"Where are you going to?" said Muiris. "I thought wild horses wouldn't drag you to that meeting?"

"Do you think I'd let that article Drax sell the house from under me without giving him a piece of my mind?" she said, sweeping out the door and down the road.

Muiris winked at the children and they all followed her down Stag's Cliff to the pub in the harbour. They had no idea what went on at a public meeting but they felt this one wasn't going to be dull!

CHAPTER 5

From all over the island, people streamed into the harbour, making for Mulally's pub. Macdara and Conán, Mr Mulally's twin teenage sons, were delighted to see the children and brought them up to sit on the stools at the bar. They gave them three glasses of red lemonade complete with straws and umbrellas. The pub was heaving and looked like it would burst at the sides. Drinks seemed to move over people's heads without anybody holding them and there was a big clatter of voices. Mr Mulally pointed to a small, important-looking man trying to jostle his way through the crowd to the bar. A tired-looking woman clacking along on high heels followed him.

"See that fella there," said Mr Mulally. "From the television he is. Sir Dignum Drax has his own television station, would you believe."

"Big Bum!" said Thomas and everyone laughed.

The television man approached them with his mouth in the shape of a smile, revealing large white teeth like piano keys.

"I can't seem to find your electrical sockets," he said, sounding pained.

"That's because I don't have any," Mr Mulally said. "May I introduce you to these young children, Mr Finbar Flash?"

Mr Flash didn't even look at them but went off muttering to his assistant with the big dark circles under her eyes. "Typical of these gombeen places. We'll just have to use the generator." He pushed his way out through the crowd, using his sharp little elbows.

Mr Mulally winked at the children. "Of course, I do have a socket but I'd be damned if I'll help that insolent pup, swanning in here demanding this, that and the other. And another thing –" but he didn't get to finish his sentence because a large woman in a tracksuit, the island aerobics instructor, came to order five lemonades which she drank on the spot.

"That TV man has no manners," said Thomas to Cassie.

"He should come and stay with Connle for a while," she replied. "I bet you he'd never walk forward again."

From across the bar, Muiris and Róisín who were seated in the corner beckoned them over. The children were passed over everyone's heads and their drinks followed.

"There you are," said Muiris. "I told you yer one would bags the best seat." He pointed at Róisín who was looking very pleased with herself.

Everyone kept coming up to talk to Róisín and Muiris about the letters that Drax had sent. Tadgh the librarian had been offered a 'state of the art' library and a folklore centre if he signed all his precious manuscripts over to Drax. The farmer, Stephen Guilfoyle, had been told he could have a new milking parlour and the use of the helicopter to transport his cattle if he agreed to rent his land from Drax.

"I must admit it is tempting," he said.

"It's all a bit fishy," said Muiris. "There has to be a catch. Fish – catch," he repeated, laughing at his own joke.

Mrs Moriarty, the craft-shop owner, was offered an exclusive deal to sell her Aran sweaters in Mr Drax's top London shop, Posh Shop. But she was a bit disappointed that they were only interested in her sweaters. Mrs Moriarty liked to knit everything – apart from clothes, she had knitted curtains, knitted tablecloths, even knitted pyjamas and swimsuits. She herself was dressed head to toe in a distinctive swirly pattern known as Aran and measured up the children for sweaters as she talked. She asked them if they'd like to buy an Aran bra and knickers set for their mother or some Aran boxer shorts for their dad, as she was shortly branching into underwear.

"Are you thinking of doing nappies?" Cassie asked, trying not to laugh and not really succeeding. Thomas began to giggle hysterically and had to pretend the pompoms on Mrs Moriarty's Aran poncho were tickling him. Mrs Moriarty said she'd certainly consider the idea.

Emer Cassidy, the cheesemaker, was also interested in the deal promised in her letter. She stuffed their faces with little morsels of cheese as she chatted about Drax and about how he would collect the cheeses by helicopter and have them in London the same day. Donnacha who made the goatskin hand-drums known as bodhráns had also been promised loads of cash and couldn't make up his mind. They could hardly hear what Donnacha was saying because he banged away on his bodhrán as he spoke. But it was clear that Mr Drax was dividing the islanders with his offers.

Nancy was getting restless in the pub so Cassie took her to the play area outside, which was behind a hedge. They could overhear two people arguing and Cassie soon figured out it was Finbar Flash the television man and his worried-looking assistant, who apparently was called Katy.

"I don't want anything to go wrong," hissed Flash. "This is my big chance to impress Sir Dignum and get out of this god-forsaken hole."

"But we don't know which way the islanders will vote. They might decide they don't like Drax trying to muscle in on their island."

Finbar Flash laughed. It wasn't so much a laugh as a harsh shriek like a hyena being strangled.

"Do you really think Sir Dignum Drax would bother wasting his time turning up to this backwater if it wasn't already a done deal?" he sneered.

"But what if they vote against the offer and throw Drax off the island?" she argued.

"You just make sure to get a good clean shot of Sir Dignum. Did you bring the wide-angle lens?"

Cassie didn't hear any more because someone rang a bell to summon them all inside. She didn't have time to warn anybody that Drax was up to no good. The pub was stuffed to the gills and Finbar Flash was interviewing Mr Mulally who was pulling a pint at the bar.

"I don't think that Drax fella will be very

popular," he said loudly. Finbar Flash abruptly stopped the interview and bustled to the raised stage area at the back of the pub.

"Good evening, ladies and gentlemen," he smarmed in his phoney voice. "I'm here to welcome you all to this public meeting about the glorious future of your island. Drax TV is recording the event for transmission on all our networks."

When Finbar Flash realised everybody was ignoring him, he grabbed a microphone and shouted into it.

"*I WOULD BE GRATEFUL IF YOU COULD HELP ME WITH MY SOUND LEVELS!*" he roared.

Everybody stopped talking.

"At my count of three, everybody please burst into applause," he continued.

Some people clapped half-heartedly, a bit puzzled at his request. Róisín folded her arms and booed under her breath.

"That's not very good," Finbar Flash roared. "Now let's pretend that Inish Álainn has just won the All-Ireland Hurling finals."

The room broke into tremendous cheering. Finbar Flash gave a signal to Katy the assistant and to the camera crew.

With that, a big bulky man squeezed into the bar.

It was the islanders' first glimpse of Sir Dignum Drax. His two assistants, Stinchcombe and Slinker, who were dressed all in black, marched in behind him carrying a video screen. They were followed by a skinny, sly-looking man with wavy grey hair combed over from one side of his head. Some of the locals recognised him as the Minister for Local Development who worked for the government in Dublin. The applause died away.

"What's that slieveen doing here?" Róisín asked, pointing to the Minister. "He's never developed anything for us in his life!"

But most people were too busy staring at Sir Dignum Drax.

Drax was a big man, as wide as he was tall. He walked with a slight limp and leaned heavily on a stick. He wore a stiff pin-stripe suit and on his fingers were big, flashy rings like knuckledusters. Cassie could have sworn he had more than ten fingers. His hair was dyed coal-black and his eyebrows looked like oversized furry caterpillars crawling across his forehead. He wore dark glasses but underneath them one of his eyes was covered in an eye-patch. His nose was bulbous and his lips were blubbery and thick. He looked rich and sleek and commanding and everybody was a little bit afraid of him. Except perhaps for Róisín.

The Minister was the first to speak.

"It gives me great pleasure to announce a bright future for Inish Álainn."

"Well, it was until you turned up, you miserable old goat!" Róisín heckled. The Minister ignored her and carried on. "Sadly, in the last few decades, the world has moved on and the island has become a bit sleepy." There were a few boos at this. The Minister coughed. "But that is all going to change. Thanks to Sir Dignum Drax!"

Sir Dignum Drax was getting impatient. He stood up and pushed the Minister back into his seat.

"Hurry up, I haven't got all day," he barked. "This will become a tourist paradise and everyone here a millionaire thanks to me. Watch this." He glared at his two assistants who lined up the videotape.

"Behold, Inish Álainn, Island Paradise!" he exclaimed, pressing a button. On the screen a picture of the island came up. It looked like there'd been an earthquake, a volcanic eruption and a tidal wave. The place was a wreck, with all the buildings demolished and there wasn't a tree or a bush growing, let alone a blade of grass. The islanders gasped.

"Not that one, morons," Drax shouted at his assistants. Then he glared at the audience. "Technical error," he barked.

Another picture of the island came up on the screen. This time it was shown as a posh tourist resort with fancy buildings, a golf course and apartment blocks. Mr Mulally's bar was shown as "Ye Olde Shillelagh Pub". The small wooden jetty was replaced by a big marina, full of massive yachts like Drax's. There was a big satellite dish where the Post House had stood on Stag's Cliff. A leisure centre replaced the castle. Fairy Fort House had become luxury flats and the Fairy Field a carpark. Not one house was recognisable.

"I give you Inish Álainn, millionaires' paradise, celebrity playground!" said Sir Dignum Drax. "And all in the native style." He attempted an Irish accent at this point rhyming 'style' with 'oil'. Everyone watched him with stony faces.

"You're forgetting one thing," Mr Mulally said. "The weather."

"Less of a problem than you think," said Sir Drax, dismissing him with a wave of his fat hand. "I am currently working on a top secret invention to control the weather. It need never rain again on Inish Álainn. All that and a handsome payment for your properties." Drax bared his sharp, pointy teeth in a grimace that probably was the nearest he ever came to a smile.

"You just want us to sell our souls to you," Tadgh, the librarian, piped up.

Drax laughed a deathly nasty sound. "I don't just want your souls – I want the whole shoe!"

Nobody thought this was funny, except Muiris, who repeated "Soul, shoe, very good!" until Róisín poked him in the ribs.

Drax was getting impatient again and drummed his large fingers on the Minister's head. Finbar asked all those who agreed to accept Drax's offer to put up their hands. Nobody moved. Drax stamped his foot.

"We can do this the hard way or the soft way!" he stormed at them. "The truth is, with the purchase of McColl castle I already own you all anyway." With that he rose and swept out of the room, followed by his servants Stinchcombe and Slinker, the Minister, Finbar Flash, Katy the assistant who looked embarrassed, and the film crew. Chairs were upturned as they rushed out.

Everyone in the pub was in a right state. They jumped up and all started talking at once.

"What does he mean, he owns us all already?"

"Who does he think he is?"

Hats flew off heads and people ran around like headless chickens. People clambered to get outside and were just in time to see the helicopter taking off. They shook their fists and booed. All they could see was Finbar Flash hanging out the side window of the helicopter, filming them from the air.

The place was astir with talk and argument.

"Huh!" scoffed Róisín. "Turn Inish Álainn into an island paradise! It is one already."

"But the Flesk stream runs from the castle on to my land," worried Stephen Guilfoyle. "He might cut it off and I'd have no water for my animals."

"If the government take away my licence to sail the ferry, no one will be able to go back and forth," worried Podge the Captain.

"And if the ferry doesn't come, no one will buy my Aran jumpers," moaned Mrs Moriarty.

Everyone looked very sad and bothered.

"I don't understand how he can just come and say he owns everything," said Muiris. "Surely there are rules against that kind of thing?"

Róisín clapped him on the back so hard he started coughing.

"You're a genius," she said. "Of course, it is against the law. He's just seeing what he can get away with and thinks we're too stupid to find out."

Tadgh clapped his hands and smiled. "I know a man of the law in Killarney – he's a solicitor called Tim O'Leary. He helped the folks on Valentia Island a few years back in a similar situation."

It was decided that Tadgh should go to Killarney on the mainland to see if Tim O'Leary could help the islanders.

"And we can always have a protest just like you see on the television," said Róisín.

"Poo test," repeated Nancy.

Everyone cheered.

Mention of the television reminded them all that the report about the island was on Drax TV.

"I thought you didn't have TV on the island," Cassie said.

Mr Mulally explained they only used it to watch hurling matches and in special emergencies. He switched it on to the Drax network. The reception was atrocious. It looked like there was a snowstorm on the island. Everyone booed when Finbar Flash came on, standing outside the pub holding a microphone. He spoke to camera.

"Today, Inish Álainn, a sleepy backwater, learned of its brilliant new future as a top tourist destination, thanks to the extramungous generosity of the brilliant Sir Dignum Drax."

A photograph of Sir Dignum Drax smoking a cigar came up on screen.

"*Boo, boo, hiss, hiss!*" went Róisín and the children.

There was a brief bit from Sir Dignum Drax's speech. "I give you Inish Álainn, millionaires' island, celebrity playground!" he shouted.

Then there was a shot of the Minister talking. Finbar Flash's voiceover said, "The islanders will become rich overnight and new families will come to live on the island." There was a picture of Cassie and Nancy playing on the swing and Finbar Flash's voice continued: "These sad children who live here have a miserable, lonely existence."

"Of all the cheek!" Cassie shouted at the television.

It was getting hard to hear what Flash was

saying because everyone was booing by this time.

On the television, there was a shot of Mr Mulally pouring a pint and holding it up to camera. "I think that Drax fella will be very popular." He spoke as if he had hiccups and the picture jumped around.

"I said the exact opposite, that the Drax fella *wouldn't* be very popular!" growled Mr Mulally.

"Bedad you did," said Donnacha, the bodhrán-maker.

"He cut out your words so he did," said Róisín.

"If I ever get my hands on that little git, Finbar Flash," Mr Mulally exclaimed, "I'll throw him in the sea!"

The report finished with the shot of everyone, taken from the helicopter, after they'd charged out of the pub in pursuit of Drax. They were all shaking their fists and shouting. Finbar Flash's smarmy voice said: "The islanders gathered to see off Sir Dignum Drax. No, they are not booing him, but cheering him in their traditional style."

In the pub there were cries of *"Down with Drax! Drax is a cheat!"*

"How can he buy and sell you what you already own?" asked Thomas. "I don't understand."

"Some rich people think they can do what they like," said Connle, "but you three chisellers have to get off to bed."

By now the sun was thinking of setting and they saw Áine slip off with her hood pulled tightly around her face.

The children clambered on to the back of Derry the donkey to make their way home.

When they arrived back at Fairy Fort House, Jarlath was in the kitchen eating a big bowl of porridge. The children tumbled in on top of him, suddenly full of excitement about what had happened.

"That Sir Big Bum is trying to rob the whole island," said Cassie.

"Sir Big Bum really does have a big bum," said Thomas. "In fact it's huge."

"He is very yeuchy," Nancy added.

"Shush," Jarlath said, "one at a time!"

So they told him all about the public meeting. Jarlath listened carefully and shook his curly head. "I've had some bad news myself," he said, looking glum. "I got a letter from the Dean. He's like my teacher, and it said I have to give all my inventions to Sir Dignum Drax because he now owns the university as well. Otherwise I'll be out on my ear. But there's something fishy about it all."

The children looked puzzled.

"That means Jarlath will be thrown out of his big persons' school and it's all a bit suspicious," explained Connle.

"It's a figure of speech," explained Jarlath, "like if you were to pull the wool over my eyes, it means you're trying to fool me – not wrap a ball of wool around my head!"

"It's a funny saying not to be taken literally," said Connle, "like if I was to describe Thomas as a pain in the neck for always picking his nose."

"That's just like our dream," Thomas said, quickly dropping his hand from his nose. "It was full of funny things like that."

But nobody was listening because Connle was telling Jarlath about how Drax said he was going to get rid of bad weather on the island.

Jarlath thumped the table. "That's it! He wants to get his hands on my fog-buster," he fumed. "We'll see about that!"

That night Thomas crept into the bottom of the double bed shared by Cassie and Nancy. It had been a very busy day. It seemed more like a month since they'd had magic porridge for breakfast. Then there was their adventure with the legendary Pike of Glimmering Lake, Jarlath showing them the fog-buster, their strange dream in the field of flowers when Áine and Connle were talking, the great cakes of Róisín and Muiris and lastly the visit of Sir Dignum Drax. It was all very strange but also marvellous.

"We must remember to ask Tadgh about the Legend of the Pike and the Prophecy of Ferdia's Cape before he goes to Killarney," yawned Cassie. But neither Thomas nor Nancy heard her. They were already fast asleep. But little did they know, as they lay snuggled and sleeping in the bed, that the most extraordinary adventure of the day was just about to happen!

CHAPTER 6

The moon rose over Fairy Fort House and a sliver of pale silvery light sneaked in through the curtains. Cassie stirred in the bed. She threw her arm out and felt nothing where Nancy was supposed to be. Oh no, she thought, Nancy must be sleepwalking again. She sat up and saw her little sister over by the window, dancing a little jig with Dog, the Teddy.

Nancy waved to her to come over.

Thomas also roused himself from the bed, rubbing his eyes.

"Listen! There's something going on in the Fairy Fort," Cassie said.

They peered through the curtains and spotted

Connle tiptoeing down the garden path. Suddenly he too broke into a jig. Nancy wanted to call out to him but Cassie stopped her.

Then all at once, both Cassie and Thomas heard the music. It was like tinkling bells and soft summer breezes and it made them tap their toes. Soon they all joined hands, including Dog, the Teddy, and swirled around the room in a crazy jig. Nancy broke away from them and next thing she was dancing up the walls and on the ceiling with Dog, the Teddy, dangling from her hand. The music got more frenetic and then Thomas was also cavorting around the room. He tap-danced across the beds, onto the bedside table and joined Nancy on the ceiling where they whirled round in circles.

"Come down!" Cassie begged them. But the words were only out of her mouth when her feet carried her up the side of the wardrobe. The next thing she knew she too was hanging from the ceiling, her feet tapping madly.

They managed to grab hold of each other's hands and Nancy led them out of the room along the landing. In a mad rush, Nancy pulled them into Jarlath's room on the second floor. They danced over his head on the ceiling. They got a bit of shock when they saw in the moonlight through the chink in the curtains that his eyes were half open. But when he let out a snore like air escaping from a punctured tyre it was hard work for them to stop their giggles.

Before they knew it their feet had carried them down the stairs. They only bothered to open the bottom half of the back door, wriggling under the top half like limbo dancers. They held hands and their dancing feet carried them down the garden path, drawn towards the hypnotic music.

They got as far as the other side of the hedgerow and their legs took them up a haystack just in front of the ring of fairy trees. Then there was a shout, the music stopped and *plop!* They landed in a tumble in the hay.

"Connle, who goes there?" they heard a high-pitched voice squeak.

"Why are you asking me if you already know?" asked Connle. "You fliers are terrible airheads."

There was an outbreak of merry laughter and many cries of "Welcome, kinsman!" and "Good Connle, welcome!".

The children burrowed through the haystack to get a better view. They could hardly believe their eyes! The Fairy Fort was transformed into an outdoor palace. There was a full moon and the whole field was illuminated with lighted torches and tapers. Inside the grassy earthen circle with its ring of trees it looked like a fancy dress party was going on. The Fort was teeming with creatures and little people dressed in the most extraordinary fashion. Most of them were no bigger than small children but some of them were even tinier.

"It's the Little People!" gasped Cassie.

At the entrance to the circle of trees a group of creatures hovered in the air. These must have been the 'fliers' that Connle spoke about. Their robes were as light as cobwebs and the colours kept changing in their rainbow-coloured wings. They were tiny and darted hither and thither like moths. Some of them sat in the air as if on invisible chairs.

A little way off, a group of musical instruments

played all by themselves. The harp was strummed by the wind and a tin whistle played and danced in the air by itself. Invisible hands beat a little bodhrán drum.

In the midst of it all, they could just make Connle out. He was a good bit taller than the others, so maybe he really was Ireland's tallest leprechaun. He was talking to someone who had a pleasant voice but whether it was a man or a woman, young or old they couldn't tell.

"Connle, it is welcome you are," the voice said. "Silver and plump is the full moon, and green and sweet the summer grass. You are welcome, our kinsman, to our Midnight Court."

Connle spoke but his voice sounded more musical than usual. Cassie thought he was putting on airs.

"Though I travelled o'er ocean and mountain, never would I find a sight to gladden my heart as much as the Midnight Court of King Finbhearra of the Sí," he said.

Polite applause broke out and murmurs of approval.

"Gosh, they do like their flowery language," Thomas said.

"Are they talking French?" asked Nancy, who thought any language she didn't understand was French.

"I think they are just saying hello," Cassie said.

Thomas mimed to her to be quiet because the butterfly creatures stirred and hovered towards the haystack. To their relief, the creatures darted back to their posts.

"A good answer, a good answer," said the voice that they supposed belonged to King Finbhearra. "Now riddle me this, young man. What is the most comfortable bed in the world? A bed of soft goose-down or duckling feather?"

"Neither," answered Connle. "It is the bed you are lying in on a cold winter's morning that you don't want to get out of." There was another ripple of applause.

"Well answered, Connle," said a woman's voice. It was light and musical and seemed to make the words dance.

"I thank you, O beautiful Queen Úna of the Sí," said Connle. All the fairies applauded.

"He's really sucking up to that Úna whoever she is," whispered Thomas to his sisters. "What is it she's queen of?"

"The Sí. It's the old word for fairies," replied Cassie. "Shush." The applause had died down as Queen Úna spoke again.

"But it isn't just to answer riddles that you've quitted your own comfortable bed," she continued.

They didn't hear the next bit that Connle said but there were gasps of amazement and calls for him to speak up.

"The signs are threefold," Connle continued. "The Corra flew over the island, the Pike leapt from the lake and three Chingles arrived from the east!"

"They mean us!" Cassie whispered.

A ripple of surprise hung in the air and several voices said, "The prophecy!"

"Yes," Connle said. "It is the Prophecy of Ferdia's Cape. Now that Sir Dignum Drax has arrived and says he owns the whole island, something bad is going to happen but I can't remember what. Nor what to do about it."

King Finbhearra interrupted. "Silence! What care we who owns the soil, we who are Lords of the Invisible? We have seen all the tribes come and go. These events are no concern of ours. It is long since we have meddled in the affairs of men. And not even the little ones believe in us any more."

Nancy opened her mouth to say that she did believe in fairies but Thomas stuffed it with straw.

"But these are the signs foretold," pleaded Connle.

"Now, Connle," the woman spoke, "there is no need yet for alarm. My husband is right. Our lives are no longer woven in with the big folk, like in olden days. And you have the aid of the Bright One whose kingdom is of the day."

"But this monster man wants to buy the Fairy Fort and turn it into a carpark!" Connle was almost shouting.

"That is serious," said the King, "but in all the

ages no one has dared to meddle in our domain. We cannot act without knowledge. You are charged to stop talking about this."

"Now come, dear cousin Connle," said the Queen, "and join our fairy feast. What is the best drink in the world, water from a cool mountain stream, the golden mead of Amercan or the juice of the fruits of the blackberry?"

"It's the one that's handed to you," Connle snapped. The little folk cheered, as if to humour him.

"And what is the best dish in the world?" continued the Queen. "Honey from the heather bees, the sweet cakes of Lammas, or the hazelnut from Cnoc Áine?"

"Well, in truth, I cannot answer," said Connle sounding defiant, "because I've never tasted the hazelnut from Cnoc Áine."

There was silence before the Queen spoke.

"This is not a satisfactory answer," she scolded.

The children bristled in the haystack, annoyed at the treatment of Connle.

"They really are too contrary," hissed Cassie. "It's not fair."

Thomas glared at her and mimed slitting his throat.

"You must have an answer of your own favourite dish," grumbled the King to Connle.

"In truth, I don't like to say," muttered Connle. "It sounds like boasting." There was the crackle of tension in the air.

"For the last time before we turf you in the Flesk and ban you from our feast for insolence, answer!" The Queen's voice shook with anger.

The silence hung in the air like an unexploded bomb waiting to go off.

"Seize him!" cried the King.

Suddenly a voice rang out.

"I know the answer!"

It was Thomas.

There was a commotion and a great racket as the flying fairies zoomed over to the haystack.

"Oh no, we are done for," Cassie cried as the three of them were pulled out of the haystack, snared in a giant net of cobwebs. It looked like it was made of spun sugar but the threads were like fine steel and they couldn't break free. The flying creatures transported them right into the centre of the trees where they were gently dropped to the ground. The children held tightly on to each other. There was rush matting under their bare feet, woven in a spiral pattern and it felt like silk under their toes.

Before them sat Queen Úna and King Finbhearra of the Sí or Fairy Folk. They weren't much taller than Nancy but such was their majesty and their stately bearing that the children hung their heads in front of them. They had delicate, pointy features and slanty eyes. They might have looked enchanting if it wasn't for the sour expression on their faces, as if they were sucking lemons.

When Connle saw who was in the fairy net, he put his head in his hands.

"Merciful hour," he groaned, "what a disaster!"

The King wore a waistcoat of flowers woven together as if embroidered. His trousers were of woven grass. On his bald head was a garland of whitethorn blossoms, his cloak was of glistening rowan leaves and his shoes were made of tree-bark.

The Queen looked ageless. Her hair was raven black, and in it she wore flowers and pearls. Her dress was of flowers like a summer meadow and in her hand she carried a hazel staff with a bunch of hazelnuts at the crook.

But they didn't look cute or homely. More like stuck-up models in Aunty Angel's glossy magazines.

Around them the children felt a thousand pairs of eyes gaze at them. They noticed that everyone else was also dressed like a plant or a flower.

"These are the Chingles?" the Queen said sternly. "Why aren't they in bed?"

Nancy let out a wail. Two of the winged creatures were trying to take her Dog, the Teddy. The Queen commanded them to let her be.

"Quiet!" the King shouted. "I want to know the answer to the riddle. Speak, little fellow, or you can join Connle in the Flesk."

Thomas quaked beside Cassie and Nancy and was afraid that he would wet himself with fear.

"The tastiest dish in the world is Connle's porridge," he managed to say, "because it tastes just like everybody's favourite food no matter what it is."

There was deathly quiet. The King looked puzzled. The children trembled. Connle hung his head in shame.

"Connle, you are instructed to make us a bowl," pronounced the King.

Connle disappeared and did as he was bid, coming back in record time with a steaming bowl of porridge. It seemed like a big pot to the fairies. Connle handed King Finbhearra a spoonful. The King wrinkled up his nose, took a little bite and broke into a big smile.

"Like the sweetest honey from the heather bees of Cluain Meala," he sighed with pleasure. He handed the spoon to the Queen who tasted with great delicacy.

"That tastes better than the sweet cakes of Lammas. Praise to Connle!"

Then the King clapped his hands with delight.

"Well, that is a good answer," he said beaming. "Little man, you are welcome to stay for our fairy feast."

"Only if my sisters can stay too," Thomas said stubbornly, "and Connle of course."

"For your thoughtfulness you are thrice welcomed," said the Queen.

"Does that mean we can stay?" asked Cassie, feeling braver now and getting a bit impatient with their stuffy speech. She was about to add "And why can't you just say what you mean?" but Connle shot her a warning glance and she held her tongue.

"Oh glorious one," Connle butted in, "Cassie, Nancy and Thomas do not understand olden speech."

Cassie bit her lip. Connle must have read her mind again and stopped her getting into trouble!

The Queen raised her hand and blew away the cobwebs that bound them. The children stood there holding fast to each other, still dazed by all the carryings on. A group of fairies brought them little chairs made out of rushes. The children sat down and the fairies carried them, chairs and all to a little raised platform beside the thrones of the King and Queen. The invisible orchestra started up again and King Finbhearra sang them a welcome.

"*Welcome, thrice welcome, Chingles from the East.*
Come join the little people for their feast!
We care about the small things you might pass,
The raindrops on the windowpane, the dew on the grass.
The spider in his web, the steam from the kettle.
The frost on a branch, the tarnish on metal.
When you notice these things, you make us smile.
And you may even see us for a short while.
We like riddles and stories and stings in the tail.
And dancing and singing.
But come break of day, we are gone in a twinkling.
So now, here's your chance,
Take hold of your partner and join in our dance!"

And with that, the children were swept up by

a group of young fairies and twirled around and around in the air. Then the music became faster and the fairies split into circles of different sizes, one within another, like layers in an onion. They danced around each other, one ring going one way, the next ring going in the opposite direction. Then the music would go faster and the circles change direction. Soon, they were all whirring around like wheels within wheels. It was like being inside a hurricane and the children whooped for joy. Then the music ended abruptly and everyone fell to the ground. The grass was soft and springy where the children fell and they lay there, panting.

A group of fairies introduced themselves to Nancy.

"I'm Cam," said a yellow-haired little slip of a girl. "I live among the buttercups." She was dressed in the yellow flowers of the buttercup.

"And my name is Dris," said another with a purple face. "You will find me in the bramble. People say I am a cross-patch but what do they know?" he said crossly. But then he smiled pleasantly at Nancy. "The autumn is my time when the purple fruit blooms on the blackberry bush."

Nancy was enchanted by her new friends but Cassie and Thomas couldn't help noticing that there was a lot more action coming from behind the hawthorn trees. They sidled off and caught Connle swallowing a small glass of something in a great hurry.

"Bedad, Delaney, that would put hairs on your chest!" Connle handed the glass back to a small, wizened man who immediately refilled it with murky-looking liquid from a copper cauldron hidden behind a stone. Delaney wore a tall black hat that slouched over his eyebrows and there were two leather pouches on a belt around his waist.

"Always glad to oblige, Connle, though I was worried you might give the game away when Their Royal Highnesses asked you for the best drink." He slurred his words and smiled lopsidedly.

"I know full well that the royals like to keep the sacred water from the well of Segais for themselves as they don't want the likes of us to get too clever." Connle smacked his lips and downed the glassful in one go. "So when will it start to take effect?"

"Well, they say the sacred water only makes you cleverer if you were so in the first place."

Connle looked at him, bewildered.

"You just drink up before Slieveen, that thieving clurachaun, turns up," said Delaney, hurriedly refilling his glass.

Then Delaney caught sight of Cassie and Thomas and offered them a glass.

Connle suddenly snapped to attention. "Ah no, Delaney, you're forgetting they are mortal children."

Delaney smiled at them. "I've got something better," he said, reaching into one of his pouches. He took out a silver coin and handed it to Cassie. Her eyes widened with greedy pleasure. He took a gold coin from the other and folded it into Thomas's hand. They eyed each other's gifts. Thomas might have a gold coin but Cassie's silver one was bigger, so they were both satisfied.

"Are they real money?" Thomas asked.

The leprechaun nodded and bowed to them. "Delaney at your shhervish," he laughed and then stood on his head and spun on his cocked hat, like a top. When he got back to his feet, he was even more unsteady than before.

"Do you really have a pot of gold at the end of the rainbow?" Thomas asked, fingering his gold coin. But he didn't get an answer because Delaney was distracted by the sight of someone trying to steal a glass of liquid from his cauldron. He pounced and caught a skinny, sly-looking fellow dressed all in green by the scruff of the neck.

"Slieveen, you whelp, I'll tan your hide and make you into a pair of boots, if I catch you robbing my drink again!"

"And right you would be too," pleaded the green fellow. "It's a poor clurachaun I am compared to your lofty leprechaun loveliness."

Delaney let him drop and he landed splat on the ground.

"And Connle, I'm amazed you think that dirty

dishwater is sacred water," said the clurachaun as he stood up and tidied himself down.

"Tis not dishwater!" said Delaney.

The clurachaun leaned over and pushed Connle's glass from his hand.

"Well, if you're so clever now, how come you didn't know I was going to do that!" he said in triumph.

Connle picked up the glass and looked puzzled.

The clurachaun then scrutinised the children through his sly, slitty eyes.

"And what have we here? The famous Chingles? Let's see your coins!" He was a wheedling, slimy fellow and he gave them the creeps. Cassie signalled to Thomas and they held tight to their money.

"No," said Cassie stoutly. "You'll only rob us."

Slieveen laughed at them. "Hold on to them all you like. But you'll soon see what happens to your fairy gold." He slouched off and they were astonished to see him riding away on a goat.

"I see you've met Slieveen," a voice rang out.

A plump, well-fed chap dressed all in red and with a red face appeared out of nowhere.

Cassie and Thomas jumped in alarm. "And who are you?" demanded Cassie. "Didn't your mother ever tell you not to jump out at people?"

"It was the other way round." He disappeared and then reappeared behind Cassie, plucking her silver coin from her ear and handing it back to her, before she'd even realised he'd taken it. "She taught me how to do it."

They looked at him, amazed.

"I'm Rua O'Rogan, the Fear Dearg or Red Man. Some say I'm a practical joker but really they love me because I liven things up."

"Now that does sound like a tall tale," said Cassie, reprovingly.

"Well, how about this one," he continued, unperturbed. "You are looking at the only laddo here who has ever ridden the Pooka."

"And what's the Pooka?" Thomas asked.

"He can take many forms," said Rua O'Rogan. "In these parts he's a big lazy lump of a horse with a long sleek mane. Always causing trouble.

Before me the only other fella who did it was Brian Boru and him the High King of Ireland, if you please. They say the Pooka made him two promises. That he would never attack an Irishman except when he was drunk or going out with evil intent."

"Sounds like he would have been kept busy," muttered Cassie.

A voice came from behind the hawthorn tree. "Don't believe a word out of that fella's mouth."

They were astonished to see a talking horse.

"I'm the Pooka," he neighed and held up his hoof for them to shake. "That Rua O'Rogan is the biggest spoofer in Ireland. The only words I'd believe out his mouth are 'and' and 'the'."

Far from being insulted, Rua O'Rogan patted the Pooka in a friendly fashion.

"Oh look out," said Rua, gesturing towards someone who was approaching from the edge of the field. "Misery loves company."

"Look at the state of yer one, the Banshee," tutted the Pooka. "I don't know why she has that

123

oul' comb because she never uses it. And her clothes are in flitters."

The children glanced over at an old hag but when she emerged out of the gloom they were surprised to see that she was a young woman with a delicate face and the slanted fairy eyes. She took a comb from her pocket and tried to run it through her matted hair but gave up.

Rua O'Rogan was all smiles as if she was his best friend.

"It's weird the way she does that," said the Pooka. "One minute she's an oul' washerwoman and the next a bit of all right, even if her hair's a mess."

"That's good coming from a talking horse," Thomas remarked to Cassie.

The Banshee glided over, blinked at them and drank three glasses of Delaney's sacred drink in a row.

"It's your favourite," Delaney said to her. "Spring water from the well of Cailleach the Hag."

The Banshee smacked her lips.

"I thought you said it was sacred water from Segais' well!" exclaimed Connle.

"Well, it's a bit like your porridge," wheedled Delaney. "It's whatever you want it to be."

Connle looked at his glass in disgust and empted it on the grass.

The Banshee's attention turned to the children.

"What family are youse?" she asked them. Her voice was high-pitched and tremulous, as if she was about to cry at any moment.

"McColl Nelson," Cassie said.

"Oh, the McColls," she sighed. "Not much business for me there. You are all too young and healthy."

The Fear Dearg nodded sympathetically. "There's not much business for you anywhere these days, not like the old days. When the people were poor and sick and miserable and had nothing to eat and were always dying. Those were the good old days."

"I might have to think about taking human form." The Banshee sighed again. "I can pass as a singer."

"I bet you didn't know that nearly half the female singers in Ireland are Banshees," the Pooka said to the children.

"What rubbish!" said Cassie.

"Well, obviously you haven't listened to them all," said the Pooka.

"Maybe you should stick around and see what this Sir Dignum fella gets up to," said Rua O'Rogan to the Banshee.

"He will require the services of the Dúlachán," she sniffed and disappeared back into the night.

"It's a terrible job she has all the same," said the Pooka, "keening when people are dying. No wonder she's fond of the drink."

"And who's the Dúlachán?" asked Thomas.

"Don't talk to me about that fella! He's actually a cousin of mine but not somebody you'd like to meet." The Pooka sounded annoyed.

"That Pooka would talk the hind legs off a donkey until you ask him a direct question," Cassie whispered to Thomas, "and as for that Red Man!" Rua O'Rogan whispered something to the Pooka and they both sniggered.

"You're not supposed to whisper in company," Cassie said.

"Well, you shouldn't do it then," retorted the Pooka and sniggered through his nostrils.

Nancy came over with her little fairy friends, Dris and Cam. They all burst out laughing at Cassie and Thomas.

"So I see you've been caught by the Fear Dearg," Cam giggled, pointing at Thomas's behind.

He turned round, puzzled. He had a donkey's tail! Cassie found this especially amusing.

"You can laugh," Thomas barked at her, pointing at her head.

She looked at her reflection in the side of the cauldron. Oh no, she had donkey's ears!

The Fear Dearg had disappeared. They heard his laughter coming from the hawthorn tree. Connle bustled over and demanded that he change them back to normal. The Fear Dearg sulked but did as he was told.

"No one can take a joke any more," the Pooka said.

When Connle's back was turned the Fear

Dearg reappeared and whispered in Cassie's ear.

"Are you sure that spoilsport is really your friend? Make sure he doesn't land you in it with this Drax fella. If you ever want to find out Connle's secret, ask him his age." He winked and was gone.

The Fairy Queen glided over as if on wheels.

"Will you come and join our feast?" she asked them.

All at once, a huge table appeared out of nowhere groaning with dishes of fruit and cakes, buns and sweets. There were gold goblets containing juice the colour of red berries and silver platters groaning with fruit. Thomas reached for an apple. Cassie picked up a goblet and put it to her lips and Nancy popped a ripe blackberry in her mouth.

Suddenly Connle rushed over and dashed the glass from Cassie's hand and tore the apple from Thomas, crying, "No, no, you must not eat fairy food!"

He grabbed hold of Nancy and made her spit out the berry. Nearly all of it came out in a pulp although her mouth was stained purple. He told her to spit out as much as she could which she did with such enthusiasm that she got sick and everything tumbled out: the remains of the blackberry, porridge from the morning's breakfast and lumps of undigested fairy cakes from Róisín's tea. Far from being disgusted, the fairies were fascinated, thinking it was a wondrous trick. Some of them even gave Nancy a round of applause and clapped her on the back, hoping that she would spew out some more.

The Queen shooed the gawping fairies away and another fairy appeared with a pitcher of water and washed the vomit away.

"We beg your forgiveness, kinsman Connle," said Queen Úna. "I fancy little harm has been done but by the laws of our kingdom she may have to come back for a short visit, else we'll claim her for good."

"Fair Queen, I offer myself in her place," Connle said in great distress.

"She has tasted, if only briefly, of fairy food and it is Nancy who must return," the Queen said, "and maybe next time you come you can bring us more of your porridge."

The sky began to lighten in the east.

"Ah, we must away," the King said.

In the blink of an eye, the fairy folk and their Midnight Court disappeared. The only sign of disturbance was a lump of straw lying at the bottom of the haystack. The children yawned. Thomas bent down and picked up a blade of grass that contained a dewdrop.

"I'm thinking of you, fairies," he said, "and I'm thinking you are all mental." There was a gust of wind and a sound like anger.

"Don't tease them," whispered Connle. "They haven't much of a sense of humour."

"I wish we could just dance back up to our beds," Cassie yawned, suddenly tired.

"Dawn has broken, so the fairy magic that allowed you to dance is no longer," Connle said. "I'm afraid we will have to creep up the stairs." Connle led them to the back door. But just as they were inching their way across the kitchen there was the loud ringing of an alarm-clock.

"Oh no," Connle said for the twentieth time, "I'm done for!"

The next moment, Jarlath burst through the door. They stood frozen in surprise.

"Why, you are all up already," Jarlath yawned, rubbing his eyes. "Let's hurry before the fog disappears."

For a moment, they looked at him with blank faces. Then Cassie remembered. "We promised to get up early to find out if the fog-machine worked."

"Ah yes," Connle said with relief, "and the children were so excited, I don't think they've slept a wink."

"Why, look at you!" Jarlath said to the children, amazed. "Your feet are all wet and your pyjamas are grass-stained and what is that in your hair?" He plucked a piece of straw from Nancy's mop of curls.

"We were so excited we ran outside to see if the fog was still there," Cassie said quickly.

Jarlath beamed at them. "Well, let's crack on! You are my laboratory assistants in a noble experiment."

They pulled on their Wellingtons, put their raincoats on over their nightclothes and set off down to Jarlath's workshop in the Glen. They rode in a little cart behind faithful Derry the donkey. Connle walked beside them, dead on his feet, with Jarlath leading the donkey by the reins. He chattered on about 'centrifugal forces' and 'combustion' and ology-this and equation-that. They didn't understand what he was saying and they weren't listening anyway. He was nearly as boring as their father's book about the European Union that he sometimes used as bedtime reading when they were naughty. They would have fallen asleep if it hadn't been so cold. The air was chilly in the early dawn and the fog smelt of seawater.

At his workshop barn, Jarlath unfurled the hose from his fog-buster and bade the children and Connle to hold it. He pressed a button and it whirred into life like a mad snake.

"Release!" he ordered.

They let go of the hose and it took on a new lease of life, like a snake dancing for a snake-charmer. With much belching and smoking the fog was sucked into the hose, then spluttered out through the back end of the machine as steam. So instead of cold fog they were surrounded by warm steam. But Jarlath seemed encouraged even if they could see no improvement except that steam was preferable because it was warmer. He scratched his head and muttered something about adjusting the equation.

Connle seized his chance. "Jarlath, if you need to do some more work on your big sum, I'll be getting the Chingles home to bed. I mean getting the children home."

Before Jarlath could think of something else, the children climbed back on the cart and they set off down the lane.

Back at the house, Thomas felt in his pocket for his gold coin but when he took it out he was dismayed to discover it was just a lump of coal. Cassie checked hers and discovered that all she had was a pebble. Slieveen the clurachaun was right about fairy gold.

"I don't think you can really trust the fairies," Thomas said to Cassie.

"And what about Connle?" Cassie whispered. "Do you think we can trust him?" She told him about the Fear Dearg asking her if Connle was on their side and about him having a secret. "Wouldn't it be awful if Connle wasn't really our friend!" Cassie sounded alarmed.

"It's not true," said Thomas, sticking his bottom lip out. "That Red Man's out to make trouble."

They both yawned.

"We better find out as soon as we can," said Cassie, sleepily. "Otherwise we're in a whole heap of trouble!"

CHAPTER 7

The children were exhausted and slept well past noon. They woke up so late they had their magic porridge for lunch. But in between every mouthful of porridge, Cassie and Thomas kept giving Connle searching looks. After they'd finished eating, Connle led the children out to the hall and sat them at the bottom of the stairs.

"Okay, spit it out," he said to Thomas and Cassie. "Why do you keep giving me funny looks?"

"The Fear Dearg, Rua O'Rogan, asked me if you were really our friend. A-a-and w-w-well," Cassie stuttered, embarrassed, "you must admit, it is strange, you knowing the fairies and all."

Connle patted her gently on the arm. "It's

okay, Cassie, you have a right to know. I want you to look very closely at these pictures of the McColl family down the centuries."

There was a series of old-looking pictures on the wall going up the stairs, like in a gallery. The first was a very old drawing of a large family dressed in cloaks. Connle said it was from the Middle Ages, over five hundred years ago. Standing at the edge of the picture was a little man in a waistcoat and knee-length trousers with silver buckles on his shoes. He looked very like Connle except his hair was wild and straggly like he never combed it, ever. Connle pointed out a woman with a sharp, intelligent face and white hair in a bun.

"That's your great-great-great-great-great-great-great-great-great-great-great-great-great-great-grandmother McColl," he said.

A few steps up, there was an oil painting of another family. All the men and women wore big curly wigs and the women were dressed in ball gowns. To the left of the group was a footman in a black waistcoat and knee-length green trousers. He looked awfully like Connle too, except he was wearing a wig.

Next, there was a Victorian photograph, which Connle explained was from the 19th century, over a hundred years ago. It was faded brown and appeared to be surrounded by mist. There were loads of children in the photograph dressed in the stuffy clothes of the time. Peeping out from the back was a little man in a waistcoat with great big mutton-chop whiskers.

Next there was a photo from the 1930's of their Grandfather McColl as a boy and his brothers and sisters. Once again there was a man who looked very like Connle.

"So your family has always been friends with our family," Thomas said.

"You could say that," Connle said.

The last photograph had been taken well over twenty years ago. They recognised their mother who was just a few years older than Cassie in it and the twins, Holly and Ivy who must have been about Nancy's age. The baby in Connle's arms, they figured out, was Jarlath. Connle was wearing a Hawaiian shirt and his waistcoat looked just as patched and worn as it did today. He looked exactly the same age then as now.

"There's the Hall of Fame," Connle said.

"Why, all your ancestors look exactly like you, right back to very olden times," said Thomas.

"How old are you?" Cassie asked suspiciously.

Connle sat on the top of the stairs.

"You've asked me the one question I have to answer," he said. "I'm very old."

"Are you as old as that first picture?" asked Cassie, her eyes widening with wonder.

"I could be," he said.

"Then that is really you in all the pictures!" Thomas said, incredulous. "That's cool."

"Are you a fairy?" asked Cassie.

"Well, it is hard to explain," sighed Connle. "I'm only half a one – a *leath sí*, also known as a *gruagach*. My mother was a fairy and my father was human."

"Is she dead?" Thomas asked.

Cassie sat beside Connle on the top stair and Thomas settled on the one below. Nancy ran along the landing and in and out of the bedroom playing some game with her teddy. Cassie was dying of curiosity.

Connle explained that his parents now lived in the magical land beyond the sea called Tír na nÓg. The bargain was his father became a fairy but that Connle had to return to the human world. He was told he was born in Scotland and abandoned in a reed basket in a doorway. As luck would have it he was found by the old lady in the first portrait, Granny Clíona McColl who was also originally from Scotland. She had to leave because people accused her of witchcraft. She came to live in Ireland but then she was banished to the island – again because some people said she was a witch.

"Was she really a witch?" Cassie asked.

Connle scratched his head. "If that is what you call a wise woman who understands things on heaven and earth," he replied. "She took me in and raised me as her own. And I've been with the family ever since. It is hard because you humans live but a short time but then a new lot arrive and it is just like old times." A big plump tear rolled down his cheek. He blew his nose and continued. "Well, your great-great-great-great-great-great-etcetera-grandmother was a powerful woman. She built McColl castle and restored peace to the island. It was during her time that the old warrior called Ferdia caught the Pike in his cape and was told that the signs on the standing stones foretold that there would be peace on the island until the Corra flew over the land, the Pike rose from the lake and the Chingles arrived from the East."

"And you think that's us!" Cassie gasped. "And we've seen the Corra, the big black ugly featherless bird."

"And the Pike rose from the lake," said Thomas.

"So it sounds like we fit the bill," said Cassie.

"That's right," said Connle, "and that is why Granny McColl asked me to stay around so I can help you. But I've grown a bit lazy and forgetful over the centuries. Even I was beginning to believe that it was just a saying. There was another part of the prophecy but I can't remember it."

"I bet it is something to do with Drax," Cassie said. "Does anyone else know what it might be? What about Áine?"

"Áine only knows as much as I do." Connle seemed to be about to say something but then thought better of it. "Please don't ask me about Áine. I'm under *geas* not to talk about her."

"And what is that?" Thomas asked, puzzled.

"It is like a promise," Connle said.

"Maybe Tadgh will know about the prophecy," Cassie said. "It seems he's the only one around here who knows anything."

"We are supposed to visit him this afternoon," Thomas said, "and we have loads of things to ask him."

Connle hesitated. "Tadgh is very clever right enough but you have to promise me you won't reveal any of the secrets I've told you. Not about Granny McColl or the fairies or the Pike. I'll be well and truly banned from the Midnight Court and they are my only relations."

They looked down into the landing where Nancy was still playing a game with Dog, the Teddy.

"We can keep a secret but Nancy doesn't understand," Cassie said. "We'll just have to say that she has a vivid imagination, like my mother always says about us."

"Just like your mother did herself," Connle said fondly.

"I'm sorry I half believed that stupid Red Man," said Cassie humbly.

Connle gave her a hug. "Rua O'Rogan is a trickster and loves causing trouble. You'd be surprised how many tricksters there are out there, so look out for them. They won't all be wearing red."

They looked at the clock. It was nearly half past four. They would have to rush if they wanted to arrive at Tadgh's on time.

"I don't want to go to Tadgh's," Thomas said. "He's boring."

"I think you might be in for a surprise," Connle said, hauling him off the step.

"What happened to Granny McColl?" Cassie asked.

Connle shook his head. "I really wish I knew,"

he said sadly. "When she died, she didn't really go – she haunted the castle for a couple of hundred years and then one day she just disappeared." But there was no time to discuss this because they had to rush to get to Tadgh's.

Connle dropped them off at Tadgh's in the donkey and cart and said he'd pick them up in a few hours. Tadgh's house was amazing. He lived in a round tower that had been built in the 8th century, to keep out invaders and pirates, by the monks who used to live on the island then. The key was hidden behind a trick stone halfway between the base of the tower and the front door, which swung round when it was pressed. They had to climb up a ladder to get to the front door and there was also a rope ladder inside the door for emergency exits. Tadgh explained that the doorway was up high so the monks could pull the ladder up after themselves when the invaders arrived. Then they would throw rocks and boiling oil on anyone who tried to follow them. Cassie said they didn't sound like very nice monks. But Thomas remarked that the invaders didn't sound very pleasant either. Once inside the stone doorway there was a spiral staircase with hundreds of steps running right through the centre of the tower, leading to surprisingly large rooms on each floor. In some of these old rooms were treasures and dusty old books that Tadgh had collected.

He was a tall thin man and he often had to stoop under the doorways. But even though he wasn't young he was as fit as a fiddle and bounded up the stairs two at a time. They learned that Tadgh used to be a professor at a university and an explorer. His father's people hailed from the island and now he'd come back to run the library. Connle was helping him write a history of Inish Álainn.

"His forefathers have passed on stories from generation to generation and Connle is such a good storyteller, it is almost as if he was there himself," Tadgh said, as they reached a narrow little room where he nearly had to bend in two to get in.

"He was!" Thomas burst out.

"A very good listener when he was a child!" Cassie added quickly, pinching Thomas hard.

"Yes, I m-m-mean he w-w-was a very good listener," Thomas stuttered and kicked Cassie on the shins. They glared at each other. Luckily Tadgh didn't notice because he was helping Nancy into the room.

The room was filled with glass cases and cabinets filled with all manner of extraordinary things including masks and skulls and strange jewellery and swords. There were wooden figures with hideous faces and stone carvings that looked like monsters. The children were fascinated. To think they thought Tadgh would be boring! Tadgh explained that he'd collected them from all over the world including Africa and South America. He used to travel around the world finding out about magic and witchcraft. He opened a drawer in a cabinet and took out a small old-looking silver bottle with a stopper in it.

"See this here," he said, holding the bottle up to the light. "This is a witch in a bottle." He handed it to Cassie and she nearly dropped it in fear.

"I'm a wish," Nancy said.

Tadgh laughed and chucked her under the chin.

"Let me see! Let me see!" Thomas said.

"Careful now!" Tadgh took the bottle and held it for Thomas to look at. "This comes from the 18th century. It was an old country superstition that they could catch a witch in a bottle. Then they buried it under the front doorstep. Some workmen found it years ago up near McColl Castle and gave it to me."

"Is that the old castle Sir Big Bum now owns?" asked Cassie.

"Yes, it is," Tadgh answered. "Or thinks he owns."

Tadgh explained that he was travelling over to Killarney later that day to see the solicitor, Tim O'Leary. Then he was going on to Dublin. He had a list called a petition with the names of everybody on the island protesting against Sir Dignum Drax's plans. Cassie and Thomas added their names to the list. Nancy couldn't write so she drew a picture of a flower.

Tadgh wanted to prove that Sir Dignum couldn't have' bought the castle from the government because it didn't belong to them in the first place. Tadgh said that it was supposed to be recorded in a will that Granny McColl intended it to be owned by the whole island when she built it. But the will had been lost.

"Maybe the fairies know," Nancy said. Thomas and Cassie looked horrified and held their breaths.

"Maybe they do," Tadgh laughed, "but I don't know where to find them".

"They were in our Fairy Field last night," Nancy said with great confidence. "Would you like me to ask them?"

Tadgh laughed and patted Nancy's curls.

"She's always telling stories," Thomas said.

"I am not!" Nancy said stoutly. "They were little and they talked funny and I got sick."

"It was a dream," Thomas insisted.

Nancy's bottom lip trembled. "Wasn't! I sawed them and you did too!" She stamped her foot.

Cassie and Thomas exchanged stricken looks. They had to do something fast. Cassie grabbed the witch in a bottle. She screamed to distract attention from Nancy. Tadgh swung round.

"*Aagh!*" Cassie wailed. "I thought it was going to jump out of my hand!" Tadgh smiled and took it from her. He put it back safely in the cabinet.

"Did you ever find out about the flag flying over Sir Big Bum's boat with the snake coiled around the cross?" Cassie asked, quickly changing the subject.

Thomas found a sweet in his pocket and gave it to Nancy to shut her up.

"Follow me," Tadgh said. They climbed up another few flights of stairs. As they rose up the tower there were increasingly good views of the island through the little windows. They could see the steam rising from Jarlath's workshop, the ferry crossing the harbour and Conán and Macdara rolling barrels down to meet it. And there was Muiris whizzing back to Stag's Cliff on his bicycle with an empty mailbag.

At the very top of the tower Tadgh showed them his telescope for looking at the stars. They squinted down it but could see nothing in broad daylight. Tadgh told them that he was on the lookout for a comet that he'd read about in an old document.

"There is a story about a fireball in an old legend and according to my calculations it should come back this year."

"Our daddy is looking for a comet too," said Thomas, "but he's gone to Sweden to find it."

"I can do a vomit," Nancy said and Tadgh laughed. "I showed the fairies –"

"What exactly is a comet?" Thomas interrupted

"Well, it is a mysterious lump of water and dust that flies around in space. It looks like a ball of fire with a tail. But they are powerful things. One is believed to have crashed into the earth 65 million years ago and killed all the dinosaurs."

"The comet isn't going to crash into us, is it?" Thomas asked, his eyes opening wide in wonder.

"Oh no," Tadgh laughed. "This was just an old fairy story about a giant who believes he can replace the sun when the comet comes back."

Cassie looked at him with interest. "Was that Balor that Connle was telling us about who wanted the Star Splinter?"

"The manuscript didn't say but it's very likely," Tadgh answered. "I'll ask Connle about his story." He explained that the monks wrote down many of the stories and they often changed details, added new bits or left other parts out. So there were always many different versions of stories.

They entered another room at the top of the tower, filled with old maps and old papers, which Tadgh explained were the manuscripts. Many were covered in signs and squiggles. He showed them a similar drawing to the symbol on Sir Drax's flag.

"It is certainly of Irish design," Tadgh explained, "though perhaps not Celtic. It is my own belief that it might be Formorian."

"Oh no, not another school lesson," Thomas groaned. "Does no-one round here understand the meaning of holidays?"

"Shut up," said Cassie. "I want to know what it is."

"It's the monster," growled Nancy.

"Don't mind Nancy," Cassie said. "She calls everything she doesn't know a monster."

"Well, she's right in this case," said Tadgh. "Legend had it that the island was frequently invaded by horrible giants called Formorians." Tadgh leafed through a book and showed them a picture of a one-legged giant with one eye in the centre of his forehead. "From their base in Tory Island off the coast of Donegal, they used to terrorise everybody and demand payments including two thirds of the children, the corn and the milk cows at Hallowe'en."

"That's Nancy's birthday," Cassie said.

"So is Balor, the giant who went to Glimmering Lake and who made the worm from his own snot, one of them?" asked Thomas.

"That's right," Tadgh said.

"You know the prophecy on the old standing stones by the lake about the Corra, the Pike and the Chingles?" Cassie asked. "Who are the Chingles?"

"A total mystery," Tadgh said. "It is neither an English nor an Irish word. It could be 'children' and got muddled up over the years. Or it could be an Irish word that hasn't been translated properly. Chingles, shingles, seangaels. Sean-something?" Tadgh was half talking to himself. "Sean Gaels means 'the Old Irish'."

"And is there a second part to the prophecy?" Cassie asked, impatient to get to the point.

Tadgh paused and pointed to a dusty volume labelled *The Book of Prophecies* high up on a shelf.

"It might just be in there. I remember now that the symbols on the second stone say something about a shadow being cast across the land unless the Chingles do something . . . now what was it . . . ?"

But he didn't finish his sentence or take down the book because a large foghorn shattered the afternoon calm.

Thomas ran to the window.

"Look, look!" he shouted at the others and pointed excitedly out to sea. Sir Dignum Drax's powerful yacht was drawing up to the shore on what was known as Boogan Beach. A hatch at the front of the boat opened and large machinery was driven on to the beach. It was just like an invasion. First off was a huge mechanical digger.

It ploughed into the sand like a hungry beast, staining it with oil. The next off was a cement mixer, followed by a miniature crane, known as a cherrypicker. The vehicles rolled off the beach onto the narrow boreen, flattening the hedge and knocking over stone walls as they trundled on. A pony that had been grazing by the hedge reared up in fright. Small birds rose from the bushes. The noise was deafening. Suddenly, a familiar donkey appeared out of nowhere pulling a giant haystack on a cart.

"It's Connle with Derry!" Cassie screamed. "There's going to be an accident." When the donkey saw the digger, he reared up on his hind legs and tipped the whole haystack into the boreen.

Sir Drax's sidekick, Stinchcombe, was the driver of the digger. He banged on his horn and tried to plough into the haystack but only succeeded in covering himself totally in hay and clogging up his engine. Stinchcombe blasted his horn in a temper but it was no use. He was stuck. Furious, he got out of the cab of the digger.

"Don't think this will stop us!" he roared in Connle's face so loud that they heard him in the tower, on the other side of the lake. "You will get a real taste of Sir Dignum Drax's power soon enough!"

"You don't know what you are up against!" Connle shouted back.

"Neither do you, *gruagach*," Stinchcombe sneered.

Cassie and Thomas exchanged alarmed looks. How did Stinchcombe know that Connle was a *gruagach*, a half-fairy as he had explained to them that morning? She wanted to ask Tadgh but he had spotted the ferry halfway on its journey from the mainland and he was rushing around getting ready to catch it.

"Oh, please tell us more about the Prophecy of Ferdia's Cape before you go!" Cassie pleaded.

"I can't," Tadgh said, grabbing his bag made out of deerskin and stuffing manuscripts and the petition into it. "I'll have to dash to the ferry. It will have to wait until I come back."

He led them all down the stairs and hid the

key to the door in the stone halfway up the wall. Before he left, he put the ladder in a little wooden shed close by the tower.

Connle and Derry arrived just as Tadgh was leaving.

"What was it that fellow called you?" Tadgh asked.

"Nothing I would like to repeat," Connle said with dignity.

Tadgh loped down the path on his long legs. "I could have sworn he said *'gruagach'*," he said over his shoulder and he laughed. "Is there something you are not telling me – about your fairy blood?"

"I couldn't even begin to tell you all the things I don't tell you!" Connle called after him, with a twinkle in his eye.

But Tadgh wasn't really listening; he was on his way to the ferry, his long legs eating up the road.

Derry, the poor donkey, had been so traumatised by the encounter with Stinchcombe and the machines of Sir Drax that Connle led him to graze in a field to calm down. Then Connle carried Nancy home on his back. On the way, they kept bumping into other islanders who had been disturbed by the ruckus in the boreen.

"It looks like Drax is ready to start his building work to redevelop the island," Stephen Guilfoyle, the farmer, said to Connle. "I'd say they were heading towards the castle."

"Just as well your donkey stopped those machines," said Donnacha, the bodhrán-maker, who they bumped into further down the road. "Things could have turned nasty."

"I hope Tadgh hurries up with the petition to the government," said Mrs Moriarty, the craft-shop owner, who was knitting at the gate of her cottage. In fact she was knitting a gate. "It looks like that Drax is unstoppable." At least all the islanders were now united in their opposition to Drax.

Connle looked worried.

"Cheer up," said Cassie. "You certainly showed that Stinkbomb."

"Yes, for today," said Connle, "but we can only

hold them back for a short time with tricks and accidents. If only I could remember the second part of the prophecy, I might know what to do."

"Maybe it is in Tadgh's book," Cassie said.

"But he has gone away now," Connle sighed.

They trudged up the pathway.

"Perhaps you could just go and look in his book," Thomas suggested.

Connle was horrified. "Oh, I couldn't do that," he said. "And, children, I don't want you getting mixed up in this any more. You got me into enough trouble with the fairies. You have to promise me you won't do anything stupid."

"We promise," Cassie and Thomas said with reluctance.

Cassie tugged Thomas's jumper and they dawdled a bit behind Connle and Nancy who had fallen asleep.

"Meet me at the bottom of the garden," she hissed at Thomas. "I have a plan."

CHAPTER 8

Connle cooked them a beautiful dinner. It was laid out on the plate like a garden in bloom with grass of peas, trees of broccoli and yellow carrots cut in the shape of flowers. Afterwards, Connle allowed the children to play in the real garden before bedtime. Jarlath was working late at his fog-machine.

Nancy was engrossed in a game of tag called 'Strawberry Jam' with Dog, her teddy, and Connle. Cassie and Thomas loathed that game but it was Nancy's favourite. Cassie beckoned Thomas down to the bottom of the garden near an aspen tree whose silvery leaves blew in the wind. She told Thomas to pretend they were looking at the flowers so they could discuss her plan of action.

"I've been thinking about all that's going on," Cassie said. "Do you remember that dream we had when we fell asleep in the flower meadow? And do you remember what Jarlath said about 'figures of speech' when explaining what being 'out on your ear' meant? I think we dreamt what Áine and Connle were discussing. And I think Áine deliberately put us asleep."

"I'm all ears," Thomas said. "All ears, do you get it? That's a figure of speech meaning I'm really listening to you."

"That's right. It's like a light has gone on in my head. That's another one," Cassie added.

"So when we saw Jarlath with his head in the clouds, what that meant was that Jarlath is a bit dreamy and doesn't know what is going on?" Thomas reasoned.

"Yes," continued Cassie, "and when we saw Stinchcombe winding all that knitting yarn around Jarlath's eyes, it means Drax is trying to fool him or trick him by pulling the wool over his eyes."

"Yes but even Jarlath has sussed that Drax is trying to get his hands on his fog-buster by threatening to have him thrown out of the university," Thomas said. "They must think Drax is up to something else as well."

"Let's think," Cassie went on. "When Connle stopped us from going into a lion's den, he was trying to protect us from something, not really lions. He thinks we might be in danger. What about all the fish in the air?"

"A fishy business," said Thomas.

"And there's more to Sir Dignum Drax than meets the eye. He does only have one eye," Cassie observed, "as well as a big bum."

"In our dream Drax wanted the Star Splinter. Could that be the stone the Pike had? And still has because it hasn't turned up in Nancy's nappies."

"But in the story that Connle told us about Finnen and Glimmering Lake, he said it was Balor who would come back for the Star Splinter . . ." Cassie and Tomas both looked at each other in astonishment.

"What if they are all actually linked?" Cassie continued.

They both gasped.

Thomas's words came out slowly. "You mean Drax could have something to do with the Prophecy of Ferdia's Cape?"

"Maybe Drax is working for Balor?" But as soon as she spoke Cassie knew it was worse than that.

She gripped her brother by the arm. "Are you thinking what I'm thinking?" One look at Thomas's face, white with fear, confirmed her worst suspicions.

"Could Drax really be Balor?" Thomas shook his head as the realisation sank in.

Cassie nodded in agreement. "Áine and Connle won't tell us the whole story because they are trying to protect us. Connle's forgotten anyway," whispered Cassie, nervously glancing up the garden to make sure he was still playing with Nancy. "So there's only one way to find out: go back to Tadgh's. But we promised Connle that we wouldn't."

"We only promised Connle not to do anything stupid," Thomas said. "And I don't think it's stupid to try and save the island."

Cassie smiled at Thomas. "You know, sometimes you are a very clever boy!"

"If we really are the Chingles and Drax really is Balor, then we have a right to know what we're letting ourselves in for," Thomas said grimly.

～❧～

That night Cassie and Thomas were very eager to go to bed. Connle was a little surprised but said nothing. They still had to wait for Connle and Jarlath to retire for the night, and lay awake listening for their moment. Jarlath was late home and they heard his voice yak-yakking for ages. Finally, he shut up and trundled up the stairs. The illuminated hands on Thomas's watch said it was midnight. Nancy was fast asleep, occasionally talking in her sleep about Dog, the Teddy. They could hear Connle and Jarlath snoring in turns. Connle honked like a goose and Jarlath whinnied like a horse.

Silently, they crept out of bed and tiptoed down the stairs as carefully as a cat stalking a bird. Creak went the floorboards, groan went the door to the kitchen. Outside, they heard the howling of a dog. They held their breaths as they pulled their raincoats on over their pyjamas. They'd never noticed before just how loud the material crinkled and the zips sounded like planes taking off. Their Wellingtons made more noise than a hippopotamus having a mud bath. A sound like gunfire nearly gave them a heart attack. But it was only the hoot of an owl. The back door with its two halves was as squeaky as a cave full of bats. It shut behind them like a volley of gunfire.

Finally they made it outside and heaved a sigh of relief. The night was black as tar and there was a stillness in the air that frightened them more than the noisy house. Their breath was ragged and raw in their lungs. Then the wind started up and it felt like it could take a layer of skin off their faces. Each of them secretly wished that the other would lose heart and want to go back. But neither of them gave in. It was only when they got outside that they realised that their bicycles were locked in the shed and Connle had the key. It was too far a walk for them to be back in bed before everyone woke up and Derry, the donkey, was still in the neighbour's field recovering from his fright. Then Thomas remembered seeing old bicycles in the old shed at the end of the garden.

They crept down to the shed using their torches to light their path and there were the two rusty bicycles that used to belong to Holly and Ivy, their twin aunties. They were the old-fashioned bikes called Choppers with very low saddles and high handlebars but they'd never been so happy to see a bicycle in their lives. With much heaving and sighing, they managed to extricate them from the piles of old buckets, worn-out pots, rusty old irons and other assorted rubbish mouldering in the shed.

Quick as a flash, they jumped in the saddles and set off, the wind hitting them like a smack in the face. There was a bright moon, so they could make out the twisty turny boreen that led to

Tadgh's tower. At one stage Cassie thought she heard horses' hooves but they were faint and miles away in the distance. Then she reckoned that it was probably just the clatter of the bicycles on the stony road. The exercise heated them up and their eyes soon became accustomed to the night. There was something thrilling about cycling down a boreen by moonlight. It really was the most daring thing either of them had ever done!

When they got to the round tower, they began to relax a little but then they discovered that Tadgh had locked the shed where he'd put the ladder.

"Oh no," said Thomas through chattering teeth, "it's all been a waste of time."

"Now let's think," Cassie said, walking back to the tower. "There was also a rope ladder inside the door." They scanned the wall up to the door of the tower.

"I think if you help me, I'll be able to climb up," Thomas said.

He pointed to crevices and gaps in the face of the wall. Cassie gave him a leg up and then held the torch while he clambered up, as agile as a monkey.

"Go on, my son," she muttered under her breath, remembering what her dad said when he watched Arsenal, his favourite football team, play.

Thomas counted the stones from the base and located the trick stone halfway up that turned in when pushed. He pressed it and it swung round, revealing the hiding place of the key.

Soon he was fumbling at the door. At one point he nearly dropped the key and it was such a relief for Cassie when she heard him push in the heavy door. He shone his torch down at her.

"I'm King of the Tower!" he said. "Grab hold of this!" He threw down the rope ladder. She climbed up and was soon by his side. She had never before been so pleased to see Thomas in her whole life.

It was too risky to put any lights on, so using their torches they wound their way up the tower, sticking close to the outer wall where the steps were widest. It was like being in an endless corkscrew. Even though it was unlikely anyone would hear them, they still whispered nervously to each other. Cassie remembered that Tadgh kept his reference manuscripts at the top of the tower.

The books they'd looked at earlier were lying around the room. The one about the Formorians was still open on the picture of the one-legged giant and they shuddered when they saw it.

They had to search the shelves for the *Book of Prophecies* and then scramble around for the stepladder. It was a large book and it took both of them all their strength to haul it off the shelf. There was so much dust flying off it, Thomas had a sneezing fit.

Cassie thumbed through the pages . . . the prophecy of the black cat, the prophecy of the seagull . . .

"Look under F for Ferdia," Thomas whispered.

Cassie ran her finger down the index. There was the Prophecy of Ailill, the Prophecy of Beelzebub . . . she hurried on through C, D, E and F. Finally she found it: *"The Prophecy of Ferdia's*

Cape." Cassie read what it said aloud. "*The Prophecy of Ferdia's Cape, see also Prophecy of Finnen's Lake. This is a prophecy peculiar to the island of Inish Álainn off the west coast of Ireland. Ferdia was a village elder in the 16th century who caught the legendary Pike of the lake in his cape. The Pike offered him a wish if he put it back. Ferdia asked for a translation of the Ogham on the standing stones by Glimmering Lake, thinking they promised the secret of great wealth. The Pike told him the first stone said there would be peace on the island until the year of the comet when the featherless Corra bird flew over the island, the Pike rose again from the lake and the Chingles arrived from the east. No one knows the origins of the word 'Chingles'. It might be a corrupt version of 'children'.*"

"But we know all this," Thomas said disappointed.

"Wait, there's more," Cassie said, turning the page. "*The second standing stone said the one-eyed one will return and reduce the island to dust unless the Chingles c —*" She stopped reading. "Drat, drat, drat! Thomas, the page is torn. I don't know what the last word is – except that it begins with C."

Thomas surveyed the torn page glumly.

"Drax is definitely the one-eyed one," said Cassie, shivering. "He must be Balor. Yes, there are just too many coincidences."

"He's going to kill us and destroy the island and we don't know what to do!" Thomas moaned.

They suddenly felt very tired and scared, all their earlier bravery blown away by the realisation of what they had to face.

They passed by the telescope on their way out of the manuscript room.

"I wonder if that comet Tadgh was talking about is on its way," Cassie said.

They tried to reach the eyepiece of the telescope but it was too high. The stars shone through the skylight. Thomas dragged over a chair for them to stand on so they could reach the telescope. It was a heavy old-fashioned piece of furniture so Cassie gave him a hand.

And then they heard it. A sound like a lone

wolf in a valley except deeper and scarier, followed by horse's hooves.

"Oh God, he's coming to get us now!" Cassie screamed.

The hairs on the back of their necks stood up and they both had goose bumps. For a moment they froze and clung to each other, too scared to move.

"Just concentrate on breathing in and out," Cassie whispered.

It was what their mother always said to them when they were afraid. This seemed to help and they were able to confront their fear. They held hands and crept to the bottom of the stairs. They threw down the rope ladder and Thomas locked the door behind them with trembling hands. Then they scampered down the ladder as fast as they could, jumping halfway to the ground. The moonlight illuminated the tower. Oh no! They'd forgotten about needing to pull the ladder back up. Thomas started to go back but Cassie held on to him.

"It's too late," she said. "We'll have to hope

Tadgh thinks he was in such a hurry that he forgot to pull it in."

Neither of them realised that they'd left the key in the lock.

They raced to their bikes and pulled them out towards the boreen. But they were in for another shock. The sound of horse's hooves clattered like thunder all around them. It was impossible to know where the sound was coming from. They dropped their bikes in panic and ran to find a hiding-place.

A massive black horse with sulphurous black eyes materialised towards them in the road. Astride him was a rider covered in a dark cloak. He held a lantern in his hand. Thomas grabbed Cassie and they dived into the ditch. They cowered behind a blackthorn bush as he came closer. The horse's hooves clanked and the horse reared up in the air. As he towered above them, they saw it was no lantern the rider held in his hand but his own head, the eyes blazing like lights. Their hearts nearly stopped. The horse came down heavily on its front legs and turned his scorching eyes towards them.

The children held tightly on to each other and waited to die.

But just as the head was about to speak, another cloaked figure on foot appeared and shouted harshly at the horseman. The horse once more reared up, bounded off and was gone.

"Please don't kill us!" Cassie cried as the cloaked figure drew nearer.

"It's all right, Cassie and Thomas!" It was a familiar voice.

"Áine!" they cried.

They ran to embrace her. But when Thomas shone the torch near her face, she drew back and pulled her hood to cover her face.

"My eyes are sensitive," she said. "In any case, keep the torch off so the Dúlachán doesn't return."

"That was the creature that Róisín said she saw and the Pooka talked about," Thomas said. "He's horrible."

"He was about to speak when you saved us," Cassie said. "Had he come for us?"

"I do not know," Áine said. "You must be careful, children. Evil things are out at night."

"But we just wanted to know what the prophecy was about," Cassie said. They told her what they had discovered.

"We'll talk about it in the morning," Áine soothed them.

"But Drax is already invading the island with his machines and Stinkbomb called Connle a *gruagach*!" Cassie pleaded. "No one else is supposed to know that!"

"And they want Jarlath's fog-machine," added Thomas.

"Later," Áine spoke softly. "We must get you home."

She bade them close their eyes. Just as she did so, Thomas caught a glimpse of her face in the moonlight. She looked old and worn. He thought nothing of it because he was beginning to feel about a hundred years old himself, so tired was he in his bones.

But Cassie turned stubborn and backed away. "I want to know what is going on," she demanded even though she was still shivering with fright. "All these riddles and hints and clues. We know there is danger and we know it has a lot to do with us."

Áine gripped Cassie gently by the hand. "When it is time," she said, "you shall know everything, Chingles from the East."

They closed their eyes and her cloak covered them.

The next thing they knew it was morning and Connle was calling them down for their porridge. Cassie opened her eyes but she couldn't see a thing!

"Oh no, I've been struck blind by the Dúlachán!" she wailed.

CHAPTER 9

Nancy who was up already ran into the bedroom and jumped on Cassie and Thomas in their beds.

"Get up, sleepy heads," she lilted in a sing-song voice. "Everywhere is froggy!"

Cassie opened her eyes. For a split second she thought she was back at Tadgh's tower shivering behind the hawthorn bush as the headless horseman passed by. But no, she was safe at Fairy Fort House in a bedroom full of fog. She hugged Nancy.

"Oh, I thought I had gone blind!" She rubbed her eyes and smiled with relief. "But what is this strange fog?"

Thomas clambered out of bed and tried to remember all the things that had happened the night before. "Was that a dream last night?" he asked Cassie. He yawned with tiredness and there were big black circles under his eyes.

"Look at the bottom of your pyjamas," Cassie said. They were flecked with mud. They really had been out in the dark.

"Oh why do we have to be the ones to save the island?" Thomas yawned again.

"I don't know," Cassie snapped.

"I don't want to be a stupid Chingle," Thomas complained. "Just because Nancy can't speak properly, everyone's got this stupid idea."

"You're just a scaredy cat," Cassie sneered.

Thomas stuck out his lower lip in a pout and looked very glum indeed. But their worries about the possible destruction of the island and the fear that they were all going to die would have to wait because they were very, very hungry.

Down in the kitchen, Jarlath was pacing about in great excitement. "This fog is perfect for trying out my fog-buster," he said.

Thomas nearly tripped over his uncle but, obsessed with his invention, Jarlath barely noticed him. Thomas sat down at the table and, yawning loudly, buried his head in his hands.

"I think that devil Drax will start demanding my machine if he sees how good it is. But I've got to try it. Have I ever explained to you the difference between mist and fog?" he asked the children.

"I don't want any more school lessons." Thomas was in a bad mood.

Jarlath shrugged and pulled on his anorak. He was in such a hurry that he didn't realise that he still had his pyjamas on. But he soon ran back into the kitchen. Áine was coming up the pathway.

"Perhaps you should learn how to dress yourself before teaching us anything," Thomas said cheekily to Jarlath.

As Áine came in the door, Jarlath turned as red as a traffic-light and ran from the room.

Thomas was relieved to see that Áine must have had a refreshing night's sleep, as she'd looked so worn out the night before.

"Children," she said in her musical voice, "I need to talk to Jarlath."

Jarlath stuck his head around the door. This time he was dressed properly, or as properly as Jarlath was ever dressed, in baggy shorts and a T-shirt on back to front.

"I have a special favour to ask of you," Áine said to Jarlath. "I would like to teach the children about plants and herbs. I'll come back later today if that's all right with you."

Cassie looked at Thomas. This was something to do with last night.

"Yes, please!" chorused the children.

Jarlath looked doubtful. "I don't know. Only this minute Thomas told me he didn't want any more lessons."

Thomas's face was a picture of frustration.

"It just shows you how much he has to learn," Cassie shot back.

Jarlath hesitated. "I don't want to put a strain on poor Thomas. He's starting to pout again."

Thomas looked daggers at him.

"Okay," Jarlath said finally, breaking into a smile.

Cassie gave her uncle a hug but Thomas just mumbled a faint thank-you.

Áine thanked him warmly.

"I'll go back to my house now," she said, "and fetch my things. No reason why we can't get started this morning."

"I'll come with you," Jarlath said. "I was thinking of walking the long way around the island to check how thick the fog is."

"I thought you were in a hurry!" Thomas piped up to Jarlath who glared back at him.

"That would be lovely," Áine said.

"Before you go," Thomas spoke to Jarlath in an innocent voice, "what's the difference between mist and fog? I'd really like to know."

Jarlath just laughed and set off down the boreen with Áine.

"Honestly, grown-ups!" said Thomas. "They are so contrary."

Connle was upstairs trying to clear the fog from the house by closing all the windows and curtains. The children went to the bedroom to tell him about Áine's return later in the morning.

He raised his eyebrows when they told him of Áine's purpose but he said nothing and proposed they make a cake for later.

That morning, Thomas and Cassie only had two arguments over whose turn it was to lick the bowl of melted chocolate and over whose fault it was that the custard ended up on the floor. And Nancy only burst into tears once when Thomas teased her that Dog wasn't invited to Áine's lessons. They didn't dare discuss what had happened the night before because Connle was watching them like a cat following the every move of a mouse. When Nancy was having her mid-morning nap, Connle questioned them about Áine's keeness to give them lessons.

"It is a great honour she is showing you," he said. "She must have something to tell you."

Cassie shot Thomas a warning look but it was too late – he'd already started speaking.

"Yes, she said to us last night that she would tell us more –"

Cassie glared at him and kicked him in the knee. He roared.

But Connle clapped his hands and pulled the truth out of them like a snake-charmer hypnotising a snake. They told him everything about their midnight journey to Tadgh's tower. Connle put his head in his hands.

"I'm really done for now," he groaned. "Imagine you young ones out all alone and meeting the Dúlachán, and me snoring in my bed after waiting five hundred years to protect you!" Two big fat tears ran down his cheeks and his sorrow was worse for Cassie and Thomas than if he'd shouted and screamed at them. They tried to soothe him.

"At least we know more about the prophecy now," said Cassie. "Us Chingles have to do something that begins with the letter C when the one-eyed one returns. And Drax has one eye. And we know he plans to destroy the island." She stopped. It didn't sound very comforting and everything she said was making it worse.

"We'll say it was all our fault," said Thomas, putting his arm around Connle. Big blobs of tears ran down Connle's cheeks like raindrops on a windowpane.

"I just wish sometimes I could talk to Granny McColl. She's the nearest thing to a mother I ever had."

Cassie and Thomas hugged him and started crying themselves. They realised that everyone sometimes needs their mother even if they are five hundred years old. But they also cried from fatigue and a gnawing fear of what was ahead of them.

Connle heaved a huge sigh. "Never mind. Maybe this is the way it is meant to work out." He fished in his pocket and took out a little blue bottle and gathered their tears into it to mingle with his own. "They say the tears of children have magical properties," he said. He blew his nose in his hankie and cheered up a tiny bit. "Áine will know what to do." He put the blue bottle back in his pocket.

As if on cue, Áine walked in the back door. "Why are you all in tears?" she asked, taking out a hankie and drying their eyes in turn. They told her how upset Connle was at their escapade. Áine hugged him and he heaved a huge sigh of relief.

"It was a dangerous act but they did it for the right reasons," she said, smiling kindly at them.

They asked about the Dúlachán.

"The Dúlachán is a creature who appears when there is supposed to be a violent death. He does not speak except to pronounce the name of the person who is to die. He passed us by last night but we don't know who he was coming for," she explained.

"All the evil things are stirring," said Connle. "And now this rotten fog. It is the worst we've had on the island for at least three hundred years."

They heard Nancy calling Connle from upstairs and he left the room, leaving Áine alone with Cassie and Thomas.

"I've been thinking about the prophecy you read at Tadgh's," Áine said. "*The one-eyed one will return and lay waste to the island unless the Chingles c–* . What could that word be?"

"Cheer up?" Thomas suggested glumly.

"Chuckle?" wondered Cassie. "Or cry or complain? But we do all those things already and

I can't see how they would be much use against an evil giant."

"Change their behaviour?" offered Thomas.

"Now that would be a hard thing to change," Áine teased.

"We don't want to change," said Cassie. "We like the way we are already."

"It would be impossible for us to be good all the time. There is a boy in my class who is a goody-goody and he is a creep," Thomas said.

"Thomas is already changeable," Cassie said. "This morning he was like a bear with a sore head!"

Áine's eyes lit up. "That's it! You've got it!" she exclaimed. The children looked at her mystified. "No, it's not about changing your moods," Áine's voice rose with excitement. "I think the sentence went on to say 'change shape'."

They looked at her blankly. Maybe Áine was mad.

"I'm not mad," Áine said reading their thoughts, "but we are talking of things not normally understood. You children are already able to travel between worlds. Like when you sleep, you all inhabit the same dream. And you travelled into the fairy world. Most people cannot do that."

"But we can only do it sometimes," Cassie said, "like when we hear music or are asleep."

"And it's not a good time to fall asleep if you are being attacked by a monster," observed Thomas. "And as for the fairies! You can't rely on them."

"That's what I'm here for," said Áine. "To teach you to use your powers when you need them. I'm going to teach you shapeshifting."

The children's eyes lit up with curiosity.

"Shapeshifting is an ancient skill," Áine explained. "In the past, people called shamans were able to transform themselves into animal shapes. Sometimes they did it on what we call the astral plane, sometimes in this dimension."

"Sometimes Cassie eats like a pig," said Thomas.

Cassie looked daggers at him. "And you are as stubborn as a goat."

"But I'm never a bear with a sore head," Thomas said gruffly.

"Now, children," Áine just had to look at them to stop them quarrelling, "let me give you a demonstration."

She instructed them to move their chairs together and she held out a small apple that she had cut in two and told them to eat. As they bit into it, they were filled with a surge of strength that felt almost magical. Every nerve in their body felt alert and all their senses became super-sensitive. Their perfectly normal kitchen became as lively as a fairground. They picked up smells they'd never noticed before. Under the cooking smells their noses were tickled by the odour of wood and metal and even of the earth under the floorboards. They heard a mouse scratching behind the skirting board.

"*I'm a little mouse, living in our house,*" joked Thomas.

"If I was a cat I'd eat you!" teased Cassie.

"Not if I was a moose, living in our hooose," replied Thomas, pleased with his joke.

The mouse answered with a shrill squeak that made them jump.

They picked up Nancy's breathing in the bedroom upstairs. Their eyesight became pin-sharp. They saw motes of dust swirling in the ray of sunshine through the window, each one like a miniature planet. They noticed microscopic crumbs on the floor that Connle had just swept.

"Wow!" said Thomas. "This is like being inside a microscope!"

"It's better than a film!" exclaimed Cassie.

Áine took a small bodhrán drum from her bag and gently beat on it with a stick wrought with swirling carvings. As she drummed she said some words in Irish that sounded like a prayer. Then she intoned, over and over again,

"I am the Bright One,
Queen of the Day,
Help me to guide,
The Chingles on their way."

They found themselves slipping into a trance. Their eyes felt heavy. They weren't sleeping but it was as if they were in a waking dream.

"Come with me," she said in a hypnotic voice. "We are travelling in a small boat to an island."

It felt as if they were leaving their bodies and were really in a boat together, with Áine gently rowing. They floated serenely on the lapping water.

"Ahead of us is a cave," Áine continued. "Let us enter." They got out of the boat at the shore and tiptoed into the cave. It shone with crystal. Through the cave they came to a lush meadow. The smell of flowers intoxicated them, the scent more beautiful than they'd ever encountered before. At the end of the meadow there was a waterfall with a beautiful pool. It was like a dream or a vision that they were all part of. Each of them could see it in their mind's eye. Cassie felt as light as air and Thomas as if he could float. All their senses were tingling.

A beautiful stag with a crown of seven tines was drinking at the pool.

And then the stag spoke to them!

"Drink the water," he said, "and you can take my shape." The stag disappeared.

In the dream, Áine bent down to drink and before their eyes she changed into a deer! It happened in a split second and they gasped in amazement.

Áine's voice came into their heads. "Change, Chingles, change! Take the shape of a deer!"

Cassie and Thomas scrunched their eyes tight.

Cassie tried and tried. She felt the terror of falling that she'd had when learning to ride a bicycle. It was as if she was hurtling into a yawning chasm but at the same time shrinking, like a ball squeezed tight. And then *poof!* It was as if she was turned inside out. She looked at herself in the water but instead of a deer she was a little kitten. Her fur bristled and she recoiled from the pool. She knew exactly how cats feel about water.

Thomas's heart pounded so hard that he thought he would burst a blood vessel. His head was filled with a buzzing noise. There was a pressure as if something burst inside him and all his bones and muscles were rearranged. But then he began to contract, like air let out of a tyre.

Next thing he too was a different shape but smaller as if he had been squashed. He could

189

hardly see through his little eyes. Tall straight trees blocked his sight. No, they weren't trees but blades of grass. Fear shook his little body and his long tail vibrated. His sense of smell was keen and he lifted up his hand to rub his nose. But he saw that his hand was now a paw and felt that instead of a nose he had a snout with whiskers.

"This is too weird!" he said, rubbing his furry hand on his snout. But it got weirder. The words were in his head but his tongue wasn't working properly, as if his mouth was numb. He tried to speak again. But nobody replied. He realised why. The sound that came out of his mouth was "Eek, eek!" But he could certainly smell and his whiskers twitched with fear.

He picked up a strong musky scent and glimpsed his enemy peering down at him with green eyes. In a split second he knew he was a mouse and his little mouse heart rattled his insides with dread.

Cassie watched the little creature and waited. His coat looked so shiny. She wanted to pounce on him more than anything in the whole world. The fur bristled on her back and her claws drew out in readiness. All she had to do was grab him by his long tail. She reached out her paw but something held her back. She was still Cassie and she knew she wasn't supposed to eat her little brother, no matter what shape he was!

"Move away!" she cried. "Don't let me hurt you!"

But what Thomas heard was a deafening MIAOW! He scurried as fast as he could and sheltered behind a rock.

Oh dear, Cassie thought as she played with a blade of grass, neither of them was anything like a deer.

Thomas shivered in fright behind the rock, uncertain what to do.

"Change, Thomas," Áine's voice commanded.

There was a popping and fizzing in Thomas's head, as if all his brain cells were being rearranged. His limbs shuddered like he was having an electric shock.

He fell onto all fours and thrust out his head. A new shape was growing inside him. But it was as if a bomb was going to explode in his stomach and he was about to burst. It was like the moment before throwing up, knowing that there would be a sharp stab of pain and then relief. It was more terrifying and more exciting than a rollercoaster ride and flying in an airplane put together! Then the explosion in his insides stopped and he knew he had changed shape. He was dying to see what he was!

One look in the water showed him that he was a big, misshapen deer. On closer inspection, he saw he wasn't the world's ugliest deer but a moose! He was big and powerful with a crown of antlers and strong powerful jaws. His big eyes on the side of his skull saw what was going on not just ahead but at the sides and behind him as well. He was curious about his feet and was stunned to see hooves when he looked down.

Oh my poor little feet. He thought. Oh well, bye, bye for now!

Through his large nostrils, he detected a faint rustling in the grass. His ears were able to twist back and forward and he heard a small animal panting. Then he picked up the scent.

"You won't be able to hurt me now!" he shouted at Cassie. But what came out was a deep roar.

Cassie, the kitten, scampered off in fright.

"Interesting changes for a first attempt," laughed Áine, the deer, "but you're not supposed to fight each other."

Cassie scampered around, enjoying being a kitten. She licked her whiskers and miaowed a few times. Thomas growled and munched some grass.

"Cassie!" Áine called trying to get her attention. "Try again to imagine yourself as a deer."

Cassie tried and tried and tumbled in the grass. But her urge to play kept getting in the way. But as she turned and scampered something inside her body was trying to leap out. It was the feeling she got when she'd had a growth spurt and all her clothes were too tight for her. She was a balloon that was about to burst!

She stretched out her arms and they were long and slender limbs with hooves instead of hands. Her legs and arms felt long and fluid and she stood up on all fours, shaking her short tail. She was a little doe, a baby deer.

The world was full of movement through her doe eyes and her senses were highly tuned. She felt the slightest physical sensation, the ripple of the wind on her chestnut-red fur, the closeness of Thomas and Áine in their different animal shapes. She made a soft barking noise and suddenly felt very, very thirsty. She trotted to the pool, lapping the cool water with her long tongue. It was the sweetest, coolest water she had ever tasted.

Suddenly, Cassie felt a rush of energy in her limbs. She knew she could run for a very long time and raised her head high and alert. She pranced gracefully over to Thomas and playfully nudged his moose belly.

Then she leapt from the pool and she was off, at a swift run across a long meadow. Thomas understood the game and followed her. Surging along on his powerful moose legs, he soon caught up with her. Both of them were a bit new to four legs and wobbled now and then but their joy at their new powers was uncontained.

A forest appeared at the meadow's edge. It was so thrilling! The wind ruffled Cassie's fur and she felt as if she was flying. Thomas headed for the forest. Soon he would be jumping over fallen branches and enjoying the shade of the overhanging trees.

But just as they neared the forest's edge, a dark shape flew up from the trees and a squawking cry tore the air. Through her doe eyes, Cassie saw a large creature with leathery wings and a scrawny neck. Her heart knocked against her ribs. It was the Corra and it was making straight for them.

With his swivel eyes, Thomas saw it too and let out a growl, rearing up on his hind legs. They could feel the wings of the monster bird beating them back from the forest. Then the Corra rose high in the air, getting ready to swoop in attack!

There was only one thing for it. They had to get back to the pool. Cassie saw Thomas's moose shape ahead of her. She didn't dare look back but could feel the Corra darkening the light above her.

"Áine, Áine," she cried out but all that came out was the frightened bark of a deer.

The sound of beating wings came closer and

closer. Their breaths were ragged but they ran with all their might. Cassie let out a cry as she felt the beat of a wing on her back.

But then they saw Áine run from the pool and in a split second transform into a soaring eagle. Her plumage was magnificent and tawny and her talons were powerful and fierce. The eagle swooped towards the Corra who let out a horrible cawing sound. But the shadow of the Corra backed off.

The eagle flew overhead, protecting Cassie and Thomas.

If I can just reach the water and change into a fish, I'll be safe, thought Cassie.

The danger of their situation made them change very fast. Thomas leapt into the water as if hurling himself off a cliff. And once more he had the sensation of being turned inside out. But instead of becoming a fish he'd turned into another creature.

He was an otter. His smooth silk coat kept him warm as he pushed through the water with his webbed toes, using his tail as a rudder.

At the pool, Cassie glanced back for a moment. Áine as an eagle was circling through the air, beating back the Corra who snarled but didn't dare attack.

Cassie felt panicky and exhausted but with one great effort threw herself at the water.

She landed plop! As a jellyfish. It was a funny feeling, like she was made of bubbles. She could smell and taste but she couldn't see although she knew the difference between light and dark. She floated helpless, worried that the Corra could plunge towards her.

Áine's voice came to her rescue. "Think of yourself as an umbrella," she said. Áine must have changed from her eagle shape.

Cassie tried to shut herself slowly and managed to push the water away. She created a jet propulsion, the water moved in one way as she moved in the opposite direction.

She sensed the presence of Áine and Thomas near her. She trembled and shuddered in the water and certainly felt like she was made of jelly.

Thomas's whiskers bristled in fear around his round otter's face but he didn't dare get too close to Cassie because he knew her trailing tentacles could sting him. Together but not too close, they hid behind some rocks sheltered by reeds. They prayed that the Corra wouldn't find them.

A flash of silver flicked in the water. It was Áine in the shape of a salmon.

"We can now rise as birds from the water," Áine said.

They saw Áine's silver back course through the water but as she broke the surface she turned back into an eagle.

It was an extraordinary sight. She moved so quickly that the salmon became a blur and one animal shape merged into the next.

"Rise to the air," she commanded.

Thomas, the otter, leapt up. All of a sudden he felt himself grow wings and he caught a current of air. He had turned into an eaglet, a baby eagle, but his flight was unpredictable and he soon skiddered down to earth. Even though he was a young bird, he had sharp and powerful claws and his large eyes had excellent vision. He saw the stag they'd met earlier chasing the Corra back towards the forest.

"That's good, Thomas," Áine said. "You are getting there."

Cassie tried to follow but jellyfish aren't very good at leaping so she was stuck.

Áine hovered over. "Take the shape of a water bird – quickly in case the Corra returns," Áine the eagle said.

Cassie's fear concentrated into a single point. She was no longer a blob but felt herself as a solid bird's body. She was confident and moved on the water like a small boat. She had managed to change into a puffling – a young puffin like the ones they had first seen on the ferry journey with Jarlath. She floated on the water for a second and tried to fly. It took all her energy and she bumped along for a bit until she took wing and flew. Even through her fear, it was a brilliant feeling.

"Now let us land and come back as ourselves," Áine commanded. Thomas and Cassie tried to change in a flurry of feathers. As they rolled and settled, wings once more became arms and feathers smooth skin. Instead of their beaks, once more they had ordinary noses.

"Now let us join hands," Áine urged. "Hurry, hurry!" She muttered some words again.

Back in the kitchen Áine clapped her hands. The children opened their eyes. Cassie and Thomas blinked at each other across the table.

"That was amazing but terrifying!" said Cassie. "Bet you're glad you're a Chingle now, Thomas!"

"Who said I wasn't glad?" Thomas said. "But why was the Corra attacking us?" he continued before Cassie could contradict him.

"The Corra is your enemy. He was trying to scare you from entering other worlds but you stood the test," Áine said.

"And who was the stag?" asked Cassie.

"That was the Lord of the Shapeshifters," said Áine, "because you Chingles have been chosen."

"But all those changes into animals, how did that happen?" Cassie's head was bursting with questions.

"The first lesson of shapeshifting is to transform in your mind's eye. You entered the soul of your power animals. But you had a helping hand with the sacred apple. That enabled you to do quickly what takes others years of practice."

"And you changed too. Who are you really?" asked Cassie.

"All in good time," Áine said mysteriously, "all in good time. You will be tired now from the inner journey. I think you should rest."

The children yawned and suddenly felt exhausted. Without further protest they went upstairs for a nap.

Connle came downstairs with Nancy who was still half asleep.

"The Corra tried to scare us off in our journey to the inner world," Áine said. "I fear we have less time than I hoped for."

"This fog must come from Drax," said Connle.

"It might have something to do with the approach of the comet." Áine looked worried. "We may not have enough time to teach the Chingles how to shapeshift."

"Then we will have to find a short cut," Connle pronounced. They looked at each other for a moment.

"The Sacred Grove – we'll go there this afternoon," Áine said. "It's our only chance."

CHAPTER 10

Following their nap, the children were enjoying their lunch with Áine and Connle when Jarlath burst through the back door. They were so intent on eating their starburgers, lots of tiny burgers in the shape of stars with a moon made of cheese and a sun of carrots, that they didn't pay him much attention. His face was black and his clothes were damp and oil-stained but he was triumphant, as if he'd won the lottery.

"Children, children," he called, "you must come and see my magnificent machine."

"But it's too foggy," Thomas muttered, his mouth full of half-mashed burger.

"There won't be a fog for much longer – just

do what mammies always say and wrap up warm."

When they'd finished eating, they pulled on their raincoats and Wellingtons.

"There was one funny thing," Jarlath said. "I found the old rusty Chopper bicycles that Poison and Prickly, I mean the twins Holly and Ivy, had when they were young, just outside Tadgh's tower."

Cassie and Thomas turned scarlet.

"We borrowed them the other day," Thomas said, thinking fast.

"Yes and they were so rusty we left them there and walked home," Cassie added.

"But I don't remember you getting them out of the shed," Jarlath tutted but he was distracted by Nancy demanding to travel on the handlebars of his bicycle.

Cassie and Thomas looked at each other in relief. Just as well he knew nothing of their trips to fairyland and their experiments with shapeshifting!

The fog was still thick and heavy and in some places they could hardly see as far as their noses. The light of their bicycle lamps looked yellow in the gloom. Things weren't much better at Jarlath's workshop. The fog-machine was positioned just outside the barn doors. Jarlath started to stab buttons and there was a great chuntering and clattering. There was a small bang and the children leapt back in surprise. Black smoke came out of the machine, turning the fog black. Everyone started coughing. Jarlath pressed another button, and then slowly at first, then in a swirl, the fog started to disappear around the workshop. Water dripped from the machine and gathered in a puddle.

"Eureka!" Jarlath cried. "Breakthrough! I've cracked it." He ran around like a madman, embracing them all in turn. He lifted Áine clean off the ground with a hug and twirled her around. Then he remembered himself and apologised profusely for getting carried away but her eyes were shining and she laughed to see him so happy.

"Jarlath is definitely soppy on Áine," Cassie whispered to Thomas.

"I hope they don't start kissing or anything horrible like that," Thomas said. "Yeuch!"

"Think of all those germs," Cassie said, miming getting sick.

"At least they are both weird," Thomas said. "I thought Áine was normal at first but she is getting weirder by the day." He too pretended to get sick. Nancy joined in, enjoying the game. They all collapsed into hysterical laugher.

"What are you laughing at?" Jarlath asked.

This just made them laugh even harder until Cassie had a stitch in her side and Thomas was gulping for air. When they'd calmed down, they set off with Áine to the castle. Cassie and Thomas dawdled on their bikes and pretended to be various animals. Even though they didn't change shape, they enjoyed the lingering after-effects of keener senses. The fog was beginning to lift but it was still gloomy and cold.

As they reached the brow of the hill, a great explosion rocked the island! They raced to the top of the hill and saw that people were running from the four corners of the island towards McColl Castle to see what the commotion was.

As the fog cleared from the castle, they soon

saw what was going on. Drax's men were bulldozing the castle! They hurried as fast as they could to the scene of the crime.

What was left of the castle was now a pile of rubble. A crowd had gathered to watch the last wrecking-ball demolish the front entrance. The rest of the castle was just a heap of stones with rotten roof-beams sticking out of the debris.

"You, you, vandals!" Róisín shouted at the men who were all dressed in black under their fluorescent jackets and wore black balaclavas under their yellow hard hats. She shook her fist at Stinchcombe who was in charge. Stinchcombe, who was fat around the middle with a small pointy head and thick podgy arms, was showing plans to a group of workmen.

"Clear off, peasants," he sneered. "This is a protected site. Be thankful that Drax hasn't yet got around to demolishing your smelly homes." He turned his back on them.

"Don't rise to him, Róisín," Muiris said to his hotheaded wife.

"You impudent pup!" she shouted at Stinchcombe

and aimed her umbrella at his fat bottom. She scored a direct hit and Stinchcombe roared in pain. Howling, he gave a signal to the crane driver and poor Róisín was picked up in the pincers and dangled above the islanders. Muiris was very upset and shouted for Róisín to be put down. Stinchcombe laughed and had her lowered to the ground where she was dropped into the mud.

"That will teach you, you interfering old biddy," he sneered. All the workmen roared with laughter.

Róisín was flustered and startled but was still defiant. "You stupid, ignorant, ignoramus! You great big fat *amadán*! There are powers on this island greater than you. You will not get away with this."

Stinchcombe waved a paper in her face. "This permission from the government in Dublin says that I can. Clear off the lot of you or I'll get the police over to arrest you."

The workmen moved forward and hustled everyone away. Connle and Áine walked a little to one side to talk in private.

"We'd better wait until tomorrow to visit the Sacred Grove," whispered Áine. "There are too many of Drax's people about."

Jarlath was anxious to get back to his workshop because he wanted to make sure his fog-machine was safe with so many of Drax's workmen crawling all over the island. Áine walked back part of the way with the children.

"Drax is moving faster than I had hoped," Áine said. "You are looking for explanations. I permit you to ask me three questions, so think what they will be."

Cassie and Thomas went into a huddle. Cassie asked first.

"Are we definitely the Chingles and the only ones who can save the island?"

"According to the prophecy, yes," Áine said, "but you will have many helpers. That was two questions, Cassie, but I'll let you off."

"How on earth are we going to stop Drax destroying the island?" asked Thomas. "We are just children and he has machines and bad men and a huge yacht. Is it to do with shapeshifting?"

"A mouse can outwit an elephant," Áine said. "We will have to use our cunning. Just as you both asked me more than one question." She smiled at them. "Perhaps the way to defeat him is through the power of the weak."

Áine was talking in riddles again. But for a brief moment they didn't feel so small and defenceless.

"You have one question left and no cheating this time!" Áine wagged her finger at them.

Thomas and Cassie discussed it. Thomas wanted to know the true identity of Áine and Cassie wanted to know more about Drax and if he had special powers. But Nancy piped up with a question.

"Can we poke the bad man in the eye?" Nancy asked with passion. Cassie and Thomas sighed. Nancy had gone and spoiled their ideas.

"Nancy, with the wisdom of the very young, has asked an important question. Drax is not an ordinary man. We will need the help of special powers to defeat him. And that is what we will seek tomorrow," Áine said.

With that she left them, asking to meet them first thing in the morning.

That night in bed, Cassie and Thomas practised their shapeshifting exercises. They shared an ordinary apple and Nancy beat a saucepan lid with a spoon. They made up their own chant.

"All the powers that are strange,
Help the Chingles change!"

They sat holding each other's hands and tried to concentrate. They tried to send energy to every pore in their body but nothing happened. Disappointed, they gave up and went to bed.

But when they fell asleep, they dreamed themselves back by the poolside in the meadow that Áine had taken them to on their inner journey. The soft springy grass tickled their legs and they turned cartwheels and tumbled for joy. The whole scene was bathed in a strange white light and everything felt fresh and new.

Then Nancy tugged Cassie's pyjamas. "Who is that strange man?" she asked.

Under a great oak tree was a man seated on a mossy bank. He was dressed in green, a deerskin cloak around his shoulders. A blackbird sat on his right shoulder. On his head was a crown of antlers and he held a silver dagger in his left hand. They approached him with caution but didn't feel afraid. There was something familiar about him. From a bag at his side he took a hazelnut and cracking it open, offered half the kernel to the blackbird. He ate the other half himself. He took another nut from his bag and held it out to the children. Nancy and Thomas reached forward but Cassie held them back.

"No, remember what happened with the fairies." Then she said to the strange man, "We aren't supposed to eat food in the Otherworld."

His sharp, handsome face broke into a smile, lighting up his piercing eyes. He spoke and his voice was deep and warm.

"I am Lord of the Shapeshifters," he said, "though I have many names. Some know me as Cernunnos. Others as Uath Mac Immomuin or Herne the Horned One. "

Before their eye he transformed into the magnificent stag Cassie and Thomas had met on their inner journey with Áine. He knelt down and the three of them climbed on to his great back. He sped off. Beautiful birdsong rang out from the trees and the foliage on the branches was a richer green than they'd ever set eyes on. They ran and ran through the ferny undergrowth.

They stopped only at one small tree covered in spiky branches with white flowers and small red berries.

"This is the hawthorn tree," the stag said. "The berries are poisonous to most but sacred to shapeshifters. Remember this tree."

Then they sped back to the meadow.

"Stay awhile and play," commanded the stag and disappeared. Their bodies felt charged with electricity and soon they were tumbling and gambolling in the springy grass. They found that by thinking of animals they could change form. Cassie kept laughing and turning into the wrong things like a mouse when she wanted to turn into a cat and a rabbit when she wanted to be a wolf. But Thomas was getting quite good at it. Even Nancy started to join in. She liked turning into strange things like a milk bottle and a scarecrow and at one point she even turned herself into a stone.

They played a shapeshifting version of 'O'Grady Says' taking it in turns to call out different animals.

"O'Grady says be a duck!" called out Cassie. Thomas turned into a duck with swan's wings and Nancy turned into a rubber duck.

"O'Grady says be a hare!" shouted Thomas. Cassie turned into a rabbit and they got very worried when they didn't see Nancy but then they noticed she had indeed turned into a hair. A black curly hair like the ones on her head.

Then the stag reappeared. Without thinking, Thomas in his own shape leapt on his back. The stag jumped into the pool. Cassie shouted to Thomas to look out. Nancy ran to her and they watched in agony, fearful of what had happened to their brother. But in a split second, Thomas emerged in a blur, except this time he was riding a salmon. The salmon leapt from the pool and in mid-air changed back into the stag with Thomas still clinging to his back.

The stag trotted over to the girls and knelt down. Thomas slid off his back, his eyes shining.

"That was brilliant!" he exclaimed.

The stag transformed back into his human shape of Cernunnos. He carried a horned serpent in his left hand. Nancy and Cassie shrank back but Thomas held his ground. Cernunnos touched Thomas on each shoulder with the serpent.

"You have the mark of the shapeshifter," he spoke.

Cassie and Nancy embraced Thomas, relieved that he wasn't hurt. But he was fine and Cernunnos smiled at them. For a brief moment, he covered them with his deerskin cloak. The world went dark and they returned to sleeping in their beds.

The dew was still on the grass when Áine arrived the next morning to take them to the Sacred Grove, which was part of the castle's grounds. On the way they told her of their dream of Cernunnos. She told them it was a good omen.

"And why did he touch me with the serpent?" Thomas asked.

"You passed the test of staying on his back," Áine explained. "Shapeshifting is your gift."

Thomas was very pleased but Cassie sulked, annoyed that she hadn't distinguished herself. Áine tickled her under the chin.

"You have your own talents and each of you has a part to play," Áine said. Cassie cheered up.

"I don't mind," she said. "Thomas is better than me at shapeshifting. Mummy always said he was very changeable."

Áine laughed. "I do believe you are growing up!"

When they got to the castle, there was no sign of Drax's workmen but a big fence had been erected all around the grounds and a sign said: 'Property of Drax. Keep Out. Trespassers will be prosecuted.'

Áine was livid. "How dare they!" she said through clenched teeth and for a moment it seemed to the children that her face flashed red and her hair was licked by fire.

Suddenly, a big gust of wind blew the sign over.

"Sign is all gone!" Nancy said. "We can go in now."

Áine beamed. "Why, Nancy, you are exactly right."

Áine produced a hazel wand and touched the lock on the gate. It sprang open immediately. They marched in through the ruin of the castle and headed down to the Sacred Grove.

The Sacred Grove was in a narrow valley where the trees grew along the hillside in a clump around a well. As soon as they entered, the place felt sacred and important like a cathedral. They also had the peculiar feeling that they'd walked into somebody's living-room. There was something private about the way the trees were huddled together, their branches all delicately touching each other.

"This is the Sacred Grove," Áine said. "Some say these trees were once the loyal band of warriors of the King of the Isles. When they died, they were buried together and some of the essence of the warriors is embedded in the trees. But we do not know. These are truly mysterious trees."

As they got closer, Áine bade the children stay and she approached the trees alone.

From where the children stood, it looked as if the trees were turning towards Áine. Cassie looked at her brother and sister.

"I think I'm seeing things," she said. "I could have sworn they moved."

"It's not just you," Thomas said rubbing his eyes. Then all three of them gasped. The trees had turned into spirit beings that were a mixture of human and tree!

Where the trees had stood there was now a group of tall, stately tree-like people who clustered around Áine. But they were all continuously in transformation from tree to person and back again. So in the blink of an eye they looked human, then made of wood and branch, then a mixture of both and then back again to a person. Some of them looked fierce and warlike but others were gentle and wise-looking.

The tree beings listened intently while Áine

spoke about Drax and their need for help in defeating him. When Áine finished speaking, the tree people murmured among themselves.

For once in their lives, the children were too dumbstruck to make any comment. Áine joined them with a smile of relief on her face.

"They have agreed to help us," she beamed, "but we must be respectful. They are very private and secretive and will talk to you separately."

A high light voice reached their ears. "Nancy, come!"

Too young to be afraid, Nancy trotted over to the silver-barked birch tree.

"I am Beith, Lady of the Woods," the tree spoke in a voice like a tinkling musical instrument. For a moment the tree transformed into a beautiful woman with silver hair and delicate features and then was a mixture of tree and woman. For one second she became a maypole, then flickered into a ladder and then the branches knitted into a baby's cradle. Then the boughs encircled Nancy.

"Use my bark against the one-eyed man," the tree told her.

Nancy peeled a piece of silver-coloured bark off the tree.

A tough wiry-looking tree then bent towards her and let out a whistling sound. He became a warrior holding a shield bearing a symbol of one straight line and four horizontal lines.

"That's Fearn, the Alder," Áine whispered to Cassie and Thomas. "It means Nancy is going to need protection." Cassie and Thomas looked at each other with concern. Fearn's hand stretched out towards Nancy and turned into a branch.

"Take my catkin," he said, in his voice like a reed instrument, "for protection in fairy realms."

Nancy skipped back to her brother and sister with her silver bark and dark brown catkin as if she'd just been to see Santa Claus.

"Look," she said, "the funny trees gave me presents."

Cassie looked at Nancy's catkin and the piece of silver bark that had a carving notched into it like a cross with only one arm. She tried to hide her feelings but she wasn't convinced that they'd be much help for anything.

Next Cassie was called by the willow tree in a

voice that trembled like running water. Suddenly, Cassie felt quite nervous as if she'd been summoned by the Headmistress in school.

"I am Saille, the tree of enchantment," the Willow said. The tree flickered from young girl to old crone and her roots seemed to be in water. The moon appeared in her branches.

"I see you are not sure of our gifts," said the Willow.

"I was expecting magical weapons, I suppose," said Cassie quietly. This bizarre tree person could certainly see right through her.

Saille spoke gently in her hypnotic voice like running water. "We give you gifts more powerful than weapons. Yours is long sight for the battle to come." An arm came down that changed into a branch and a silver catkin fell into Cassie's hand. It was soft and furry to touch.

"I don't understand," Cassie said in a voice she hoped was meek. She remembered Áine's warning about being respectful and tried not to think negative thoughts in case the tree suspected that she was ungrateful.

"You will be aided by visions." Saille's voice

was like a whispering brook. "You do well to struggle with your doubts." Unnerved by the tree's mind-reading abilities, Cassie was about to return to the others when another tree beckoned her. It had straight branches rising from the ground and soft velvety leaves with a ragged edge.

"Child, I am Coll, the hazel tree, the tree of your mother's family, the McColls. It is good that you question what you see." Coll's lively voice had an edge of amusement. "That is the way to knowledge."

Coll transformed into a bright-eyed man with a keen, intelligent face. Then he held up his arms and they changed into branches, heavy with hazelnuts.

"Here's knowledge in a nutshell, food of the gods. I will help you in the flowering of your skills, daughter of hazel. For you a gift of nine nuts." Cassie held out her hands and the nuts fell into them. She gazed at the nuts in their frilly leaves and thanked the tree warmly. She still felt uncertain when she returned to the others but something told her the wise old trees understood.

"This gift will help you to interpret the visions given by Saille, the Willow," Áine explained. "When you need to understand what you see, nibble a nut."

Thomas was getting restless watching the others get all their gifts and he was relieved when a clear male voice rang out for him to join the trees. It was the apple tree and as he came nearer, it took on the shape of a young warrior.

"I am Quert," he said, "the tree of shapeshifters." Then the tree moved through a bewildering series of changes. He became a magician, a serpeant, a beautiful maiden, a mad-eyed lunatic. The tree changed from having bare branches to blossoms to heaving with juicy red apples. A ripe red apple fell into Thomas's hands. Its glossy skin felt charged with energy and he was very tempted to bite into it. A laugh came from the tree.

"You will know when the time is right," he said, "and not before. It is a special gift for your time of greatest change. Good luck, young warrior."

Thomas waited, expecting another tree to

summon him but there was a pause and then the trees started to talk among themselves. It sounded like wind rustling through branches and the creaking of boughs mixed with light and deep voices. Puzzled, Thomas was looking anxiously back at Áine when a beautiful young woman appeared before him, white blossoms in her hair.

"Patience, Thomas," she smiled at him and she had the beauty of early summer. "I am Uath of the Hawthorn."

She lifted up her arms, which became boughs. The branches were filled with dark red berries. Then a flash of lightning ripped through the tree and she was a beautiful young woman again. Thomas realised that it was the same tree that Cernunnos had pointed out in his dream. A dark shadow passed over his heart and he was filled with dread at the dangers that clearly lay ahead of them all. Then the tree spoke again. "Courage, Thomas. When the time is right, my help will be revealed to you but remember my kind can protect you from lightning strikes."

Somewhat reassured, Thomas returned to the

others and Áine went to the huge oak tree that was so large it would have taken twenty people to surround it.

"We thank you, noble Dair, King of the Forest," she said.

The tree turned into a powerful man dressed like a hunter with a crown of oak leaves around his head. He spoke with a deep voice, like the rumblings of the earth itself. "Courage for the battle to come."

The children sat on the grass, in awe of the living trees. Their meeting with these strange tree people had happened so fast it was hard to take it all in.

But then Cassie whispered to Thomas, "I got nine nuts and you only got one apple."

"But my apple is the best," Thomas replied with his nose in the air, "and I don't even like hazelnuts. They stick in my teeth. So there!"

Nancy tickled them with her catkin from Fearn the Alder. "Mine is the best," she said with great confidence.

Cassie whispered quite loudly to Thomas,

"She's too young to realise she's only got a piece of bark and a tiny catkin."

But Nancy heard her and exclaimed, "Mine is the bestest!" She struck Cassie with the bark. More out of surprise than hurt, Cassie let out a big cry.

Áine turned round sharply. "Children, you mustn't fight among yourselves!"

They all looked guiltily at her, Nancy most of all who looked like she might burst into tears.

A deep rumbling voice came from Dair, the Oak.

"Children, come to me," it said.

He gathered them into his arms and before they knew it they were high in his branches. It was an amazing feeling as if a current was running through their bodies. They felt on fire and ready for anything.

"The apple is no better than the acorn nor is the acorn better than the hazelnut," said Dair, the Oak, in a deep voice that seemed to come from the earth itself. "You three are like the Sacred Trees. No-one is better than any other. You must work as one to defeat the one-eyed beast. He is dangerous and will stop at nothing. Remember my acorns when you need courage and strength."

The branches of the Oak gently dropped them to the ground. The children were spellbound. But mixed up with their amazement were feelings of worry. All of the trees spoke of a great battle to come. Here among the big strong trees they felt brave and full of fire but what would it be like when they finally had to face Drax?

A wind rose up and a gentle rain began to fall. They sheltered under the tree boughs. While they waited, Áine set to making jewellery. She deftly knotted the silver-birch bark into a leather thong that she wore around her neck. Then she took off a beautiful beaded bracelet from her wrist and offered to add on Cassie's silver catkin. Cassie generously offered it to her little sister so Áine skilfully threaded on the catkin from Fearn the Alder. She presented the jewellery to Nancy who was thrilled with herself. Thomas and Cassie had to admit that Nancy now certainly had the handsomest gifts. Áine instructed

Thomas and Cassie to keep their gifts safe in their pockets.

"Come on, children," Áine said as the rain cleared, "we'll go back to your house now."

They didn't want to leave the Sacred Grove but did as Áine bade them. As they walked out, Cassie fingered the silver catkin in her pocket. She felt a sense of panic and foreboding and saw a picture of a burning fire in her head. She looked back at the Sacred Grove. For a moment the trees flickered as people and smiled at her and then were once more trees again.

"Come on, Cassie," Áine called.

Cassie hesitated. It probably meant nothing, she thought, and decided not to say anything. Outside the grove, the rain fell heavily from the sky. She was getting wet. She put the thought out of her mind and ran to join the others.

She was soon to regret that she didn't pay attention to the prompting of the Willow.

CHAPTER 11

T hat night Cassie tossed and turned in the bed as if she was on fire. She could feel the prickle of heat on her skin and gasped for air as if she could not breathe. She sweated and strained against the covers, tossing against Nancy and murmuring in her sleep. As dawn was breaking, she sat up straight in her bed and knew in her bones that something terrible was going to happen. She roused her sister and brother.

"We need to go to the Sacred Grove," she whispered.

Nancy was so sleepy she smiled at her sister with her eyes closed, got up and then promptly got back into bed. Thomas grumbled a little bit but did as he was told.

When she'd managed to get the others to put some warm clothes on, Cassie tiptoed into Connle's room and shook him gently on the shoulder. He looked so peaceful lying there in his stripey nightshirt and wearing a tassled hat like they did in olden days. He awoke with a start.

"Cassie, you frightened the life out of me – what's up? Are you ill?" He placed his hand on her forehead. "You'd better get straight back to bed. You have a bit of a temperature."

"I'm fine," she panted, feeling anything but. "I've had some awful dreams. It is something to do with the Sacred Grove. I think we need to go there." Connle fetched her a drink of water and ushered her back to her room but she stood unmoving at the foot of the bed. Thomas and Nancy were lying on their beds fully dressed but half asleep.

"We must go," Cassie pleaded. "I have a funny feeling."

Connle looked at her intently and saw a light burning in her eye.

"All right," he said. "I'll go and fetch Áine and see if anything is happening. You stay here and get some more sleep."

Cassie watched until Connle disappeared down the boreen. Áine's house was even further away than the Sacred Grove and waiting for Connle to return would waste too much time. She knew it was bad to be disobeying Connle yet again but she felt a fire within.

She shook Thomas and Nancy awake and they set off towards the castle grounds on their bikes with Nancy sitting on Cassie's handlebars.

The island looked beautiful in the pale early morning. The dew was on the grass like little glass beads and the birds were singing. Jarlath's fog-buster seemed to have cleared away most of the fog. Thomas thought of the fairies and felt a gentle breeze on his cheek, like a kiss. The sky was overcast but there was a light patch in the clouds in the east where the sun was trying to break through.

At the castle grounds, they stowed their bicycles out of sight. There was no sign of

Stinchcombe or the workmen but they'd forgotten about the big fence. It was topped with barbed wire and was much too high for them to climb over. They were almost about to give up when Nancy noticed a gap under the fence where an animal must have burrowed through. They slipped under the fence and ran to the clearing.

Just as they got to the Sacred Grove they heard harsh voices and the sound of machinery starting up. Cassie froze for a moment, unsure what to do. They were going to be in the most awful trouble when the workmen found them. Worse still they were bound to get Connle into trouble. The machines sounded as if they weren't far away. "Quick, let's go to Dair," she said, pointing to the Oak.

They climbed into the branches of the huge oak tree. Through the branches they saw a line of men advance towards the grove. They were wearing protective clothing and holding chainsaws like machine-guns. Security guards lined the perimeter of the fence.

Then the children saw Stinchcombe waddling

towards them with a can of spray paint in his hand.

"They are going to chop down the Sacred Grove!" Cassie screamed into the tree.

The voice of Dair answered her. "Children, flee from harm. This is not your battle."

The children were too frightened to move and watched the lumberjacks walk through the grove, like an invading army. Stinchcombe stepped forward. On each tree in turn he painted a big red X. Nancy began to sob quietly.

A big burly man stepped forward. Through the leaves they could see he had a red stubbly chin and mean eyes under his hard yellow hat. He pulled the cord of his chainsaw. It leapt into life like a snarling beast just waiting to bite into the flesh of the trees. He approached the slender, silver bark of Beith, the Birch.

"Oh, no, they are chopping down Beith!" Cassie cried, thinking of the beautiful silver-haired woman they'd met just the day before. But her words were drowned in the angry growl of the chainsaw.

Beith, the Lady of the Woods, fell fast and clean. A team of men advanced and dragged the silver trunk into the centre of the grove and chopped it into smaller logs.

Next it was the turn of Fearn, the Alder, which housed the spirit of the tough wiry warrior. When they cut into the trunk, blood appeared to ooze out and there was a high-pitched keening sound. The lumberjack paused briefly, thinking he had cut himself. But then he noticed it was the colour of the sap flowing down the bark. When he realised he wasn't injured, he carried on.

"Sacrilege!" a voice shouted out. It was Róisín.

The children looked towards the fence. A group of islanders had gathered and were trying to push it down. Áine and Connle pushed through to the front. Two giant security guards with snarling Alsatians blocked the way behind the fence.

"Clear orf," shouted Stichcombe, "or we'll charge you for the show!"

The islanders booed and shook their fists.

The children cowered in the mighty boughs of Dair, the Oak. But it was to no avail. The lumberjacks advanced towards Saille, the delicate Willow. As the lumberjack raised his chainsaw and pulled the cord, the sky turned dark and for the briefest moment, the moon appeared in the sky. A harsh breeze sprung up. For a moment the children thought Saille might release some enchantment. But it didn't happen. The shiny metal teeth of the chainsaw bit into the Willow's bark as if it was butter.

At the wire fence Áine tried to talk to the security guards.

"You are breaking the sacred laws," she pleaded. "These trees are special."

"Naff off," snarled the security man.

Áine's face darkened. A strange flash came from her eyes and it was as if the security men were temporarily blinded. At that moment, the islanders found a rip in the fence and pulled it apart with their bare hands. Áine and young Macdara and Conán from the pub climbed in through the gap and ran past the security men.

The children watched, terrified. The security men recovered and set their dogs on the invaders. But Áine was able to stop the dogs attacking with one look.

Connle pulled Áine to one side. "Be careful!" he said. "Do not expose your power."

Conán and Macdara raced to the apple tree and threw themselves around it holding each other's arms. Áine was blocked by the massive lumberjacks. Two more security men grabbed her and were about to dump her back outside the fence when Stinchcombe intervened.

"Hah, let her watch," he crowed. "She is no match for the might of Drax." A frustrated Áine struggled to control herself.

"Some day you will rue those words!" Her voice was low and serious but Stinchcombe just laughed in her face.

It took four security men several attempts to pull Conán and Macdara apart. The children cowered in the Oak, frightened by the rough treatment meted out to the islanders who dared oppose the will of Drax.

Róisín, however, protested loudly.

"We will avenge you, Quert," she shouted as the lumberjack chopped down the apple tree. The golden boughs crashed to the ground. Several apples rolled away but the boots of the tree-cutters smashed them into smithereens. Thomas's heart was heavy when he thought of the lively warrior he'd met yesterday with his boughs full of apples. The Birch, Apple, Alder and Willow trees were gone but there was still the Hazel, the Hawthorn and the Oak. All the while, the people outside the fence tried to shake it down.

Cassie looked up the road and gave a little whoop of joy. Jarlath was advancing in his fog-machine. It wasn't very fast but it was sturdy and strong and soon it had mangled up the fence as if it was tinfoil. The islanders streamed in over it. The security men with the dogs managed to halt their progress but then Jarlath burst through in his fog-buster and they backed off.

The lumberjacks and the security men were in a mess and Stinchcombe lost control of the situation. Seeing her chance, Cassie scurried down the Oak tree and climbed up Coll, the Hazel tree. Róisín, Muiris, Mr Mulally the publican and Donnacha the bodran-maker formed a circle around it. Connle ran towards the Oak, chased by a big lumbering lumberjack.

"Look out behind you!" Thomas shouted down to him.

"Merciful hour!" shouted Connle, as he caught sight of Thomas's head through the branches. The lumberjack was nearly on top of him but suddenly Connle rolled into a ball and crawled through his legs. The big ugly fellow didn't know where he'd disappeared to.

"We're sorry," Thomas said to Connle as he climbed into the tree. "We had to come."

Connle huffed and puffed and the lumberjack snapped at his heels but he managed to reach the branches where the children were hiding. The lumberjack was too big and clumsy to shimmy up the trunk and tried to shake the branches.

"I'll get you yet, you monkey!" He shook his fist at Connle and skulked off to get reinforcements.

"Now what do we do?" Connle said to the children.

"We are having a poo test," Nancy said.

"You mean protest." Thomas squeezed his little sister's hand.

"Oh no!" wailed Connle. "Cassie's right in the thick of it!"

From their position in the branches they could see everything that was going on. A line of security men advanced towards Uath, the Hawthorn, first. Another two with dogs guarded the Hazel to stop any more islanders joining Cassie. And the lumberjacks surrounded the Oak. In the middle, Stinchcombe ran around like a headless chicken. It was chaos. Birds screeched and dived overhead and squirrels ran from the branches.

"Watch out, Jarlath!" Cassie shouted to her uncle.

Three security men ran towards Jarlath and tried to drag him from the fog-buster. One of them managed to clamber on to the cockpit but Jarlath flicked a switch and the fog-release tube whipped round like an elephant's trunk and lobbed the man off. Over at the Hawthorn, the islanders tried to hold firm as a line of security men shouted in their faces.

"A crane is coming through!" Thomas shouted.

Sure enough, a big yellow machine lumbered into the grove. A lumberjack climbed into the cage. Stinchcombe stood by the machine with a megaphone.

"Stand back," he shouted through the megaphone. "Cutting will commence!"

The crane hoisted the lumberjack up towards the crown of Uath, the Hawthorn, and he started to lop branches off the top. Thomas felt a pang in his heart at the thought of the beautiful maiden crowned with white who'd promised to help him in his hour of need. But she was no match for the hard steel of the lumberjack. A prickly branch hit Muiris on the head. They all ran for cover.

"Ha, ha, ha," Stinchcombe taunted them through the megaphone. "Not so brave now!"

Róisín tried to run at him but a security man picked her up and dumped her outside the perimeter fence. She ran to Muiris who was bleeding from the forehead. Soon the Hawthorn looked like a straggly bush and when the crane came down, the lumberjack finished the job.

Now only Coll, the Hazel, and Dair, the Oak, were left. Flushed with the success of beating the islanders from the hawthorn, Stinchcombe advanced towards Coll where Cassie was wedged among the branches. She tried not to think of the bright eyes of the keen, intelligent warrior who'd given her gifts of knowledge.

"Come out, you silly child," Stinchcombe shouted through his megaphone.

Two security men tried to pull Cassie from the boughs. One of them made a grab for her hair. Cassie kicked and screamed and landed a hit on his nose.

Jarlath saw what was happening and lurched the fog-buster into life. But it was stuck in the mud and he ground the wheels to no avail. He pulled all the levers and switches but smoke rose from his engine. He watched in vain as the two security men advanced towards Cassie.

Cassie managed to tie herself to the branches

of the tree with her belt. She spat at the security men like a wild cat. When the first security man tried to untie the belt around her waist, she lashed out, scratching him across the face. She bit the second one's hand when he reached up to her face.

Cassie was fierce but she was no match for two burly security men. Soon, they had her by the waist and hauled her down the tree. Stinchcombe leaped about with triumph when they threw her at his feet. Hot tears of anger were in Cassie's eyes.

"Oh, if only my master, Sir Dignum Drax, could see you now, you pathetic snivelling creature!" Stinchcombe taunted her through the megaphone. Stinchcombe was too stupid to know that she cried not because she was hurt but over the destruction of the Sacred Grove.

But Cassie wasn't defeated yet. She jumped up, dodged through the security men and climbed back into Dair's boughs again.

Finally Jarlath's fog-buster lurched into life and the hose cuffed Stinchcombe on the head. He yelled like a baby.

"We'll get you for this," Jarlath shouted from his machine, as three burly security men dragged him into the mud. As if in agreement, his engine snorted and exploded, making the security men leap into the ditch with fright. But the battle was lost. Muiris, Jarlath and Róisín were dumped on the other side of the fence as if they were bin-liners full of rubbish. Soon, the only tree left in the grove was Dair, the Mighty Oak, and all eyes turned to see what was going to happen.

Jarlath and Áine tried desperately to push through but there was no getting by the snarling dogs and security men this time. Up in the branches the children and Connle watched as scores of burly men in yellow jackets loomed towards the tree.

"Why can't the trees use their magic to save themselves?" Cassie asked Connle.

"It's not their way," Connle said. "Their powers are in their gifts and can only be used by others. We must be patient."

A voice spoke deep from within the tree: "*Save yourselves for the battle to come!*"

Cassie looked at Connle, Thomas and Nancy. Without speaking, they all joined hands. Stinchcombe was standing at the foot of the tree, megaphone under his arm. They heard him talking to his workmen and the two climbers.

"Those wretched brats are up there," he said. "I suppose we'll have to be careful. But don't overdo it," he instructed his men.

Nancy hissed at them.

"I know there's more of them than us," Cassie muttered, "but we won't make it easy for them."

Thomas remembered Dair's instruction about his acorns and had an idea. He pulled some acorns from the branches and *Ping!* – one landed straight on Stinchcombe's nose. He fell straight into the arms of the nearest lumberjack.

"I've been shot," Stinchcombe moaned. "They have a gun!" A hail of acorns rained down on the workmen and they retreated as if they were under fire.

But soon the children ran out of acorns they could reach. The workmen crept forward, carrying shields.

Suddenly a big ugly fellow with a wart on his nose and a great big straggly beard appeared through the branches. He was in the cage of the crane. Thomas took aim and an acorn landed on his forehead. But the great ugly mug was so thick-headed it might as well have been a fly.

"*Behind you!*" a voice shouted out from the gates. The children turned around.

The two climbers had scaled the tree and were swinging towards them. The tree shook with the commotion and there was much grappling and shouting. Nancy bit one of the climbers who had a face like a weasel. The ugly lumberjack in the crane caught hold of Connle and shook him out. Now only the children were left.

Swoosh! Before they knew what was happening, the climbers threw a net over them and they were trapped as if they were giant butterflies. They screamed and shouted but it was no use. Stinchcombe had won and they were lowered to the ground.

The islanders cheered for Connle, Cassie, Thomas and Nancy as they were deposited outside the fence. Áine and Jarlath wrapped them in a big hug. But Cassie in particular felt a pain in her heart. Hot tears sprang to her eyes.

"We are going to get them for this," she sobbed.

Dair was so large it took thirty workmen an hour to hack him down. Mr Mulally secretly took photographs on an ancient-looking box camera. He managed to take out one roll of film before a security man stopped him and smashed the camera. It was terrible to see such a noble, strong tree reduced to timber and splinters, logs and tinder. Cassie felt as though her heart would break. Áine tried to comfort her.

"I knew this was going to happen," Cassie sobbed, "and I didn't know what to do."

"Hush," Áine said, patting her gently on the head, "there is nothing we could have done."

"But if only I'd realised what the feelings I had last night meant," Cassie said, blowing her nose.

"The gift of long sight is a hard one," Áine consoled her. "You did well to warn us. And next time we will be able to act."

A lament arose from the islanders. The sky darkened even though it was early in the morning.

"We should try to rescue seeds and fruits so we can plant again," Áine said.

The felled trees were all now cut into logs and piled in what had been, for thousands of years, the Sacred Grove. Stinchcombe held a can of petrol and a lighted torch. He was going to make a bonfire of the remains of the trees. Jarlath could take no more. He made a lunge through the fence, followed by Muiris, Róisín, Thomas, Conán and Macdara. They got to the logs and pulled out branches, berries, apples, acorns and hazelnuts. Then Stinchcombe recovered and beat them back with his lighted torch. He threw petrol on the broken branches and logs.

First there was a crackling sound and then a great blaze. The flames licked through the wood and there was a harsh sound as if someone was dying. The children watched and thought they saw, not smoke rise from the flames but the spirits of the trees: Willow, Hazel, Alder, Birch, Hawthorn, Apple and Mighty Dair, the Oak. These were their friends whom they'd only just met and now they were gone.

It seemed like hours before the fire burned itself out. Several times, the workmen tried to damp it down with water but it burned on furiously. Most of the islanders left but Áine, Jarlath, Connle and the children waited until the very last ember had burned itself out. Stinchcombe picked up a handful of ashes and blew them at them.

"Be off now, you fools," he scoffed. "So much for your Sacred Grove!" Finally the workmen left and Áine sneaked back in under the fence and gathered up ashes from the fire into her scarf.

Thomas felt bitterly disappointed that the trees were so powerless before the machines of Drax.

"Don't be sad," Áine consoled him. "Some day new trees will rise from these ashes," she said.

But Thomas couldn't help worrying about how easy it had been to destroy the Sacred Grove. He remembered Dair's words about saving themselves for the battle to come and felt a deep sense of foreboding.

"I don't suppose I'll ever see my fog-machine again, and just as I was getting the better of the fog!" Jarlath sighed. The workmen had chained it down and there was no hope of getting it back. As they looked around they saw that the fog was indeed returning.

"Well, there's only one thing for it," Jarlath said. "I'm going to build an even better one!"

Back at home, Connle made them diamond and pearl cakes out of spun icing sugar to cheer them up. But they all felt very sad about the destruction of the Sacred Grove.

"It's just so awful," Thomas said. He couldn't shake off his deep disquiet. "Drax will stop at nothing."

"Why do horrible things have to happen?" asked Cassie.

Connle looked thoughtful and scratched his head.

"Oh, I wish Granny McColl was here to explain it all," he sighed. He sat down beside them. "Well, I'm a lot older than you," he said, "and I've seen many things happen. And I'll tell you one thing.

The bad ones don't always win. They do for a time and they think they own the world. But they don't. There's always another day."

"Dair said we had to save ourselves for the battle to come," Thomas said. "This was bad enough. I dread to think what's ahead of us."

"I hope I don't have another sleepless night," Cassie yawned.

But there are worse things than sleepless nights, as she was about to find out.

CHAPTER 12

Cassie didn't get her wish of a peaceful night's sleep. That night, a great storm assailed the island. Lightning rent the sky and thunder echoed like the crack of doom. The storm raged for three days and when it died down the island was still covered in fog. Without Jarlath's fog-machine, it was much worse.

The ferry couldn't sail back and forth and people were even afraid to leave their houses. All over the island, people felt a curious sickness as if the fog had got into their brains and their bones. It was hard to move about or do anything. Muiris and Róisín didn't deliver letters and Mrs Moriarty stopped knitting for the first time in her life. Nobody came to the pub and Mr Mulally stayed in bed. Even the children, who were normally as jumpy as a bag of jellybeans, were just a little bit listless and tired. And there was no sign of Áine.

The fog was so steamy and soggy, Jarlath was convinced that Drax's men were using his captured fog-machine, which could generate fog as well as eat it. On the fourth day, the air was so thick you could hardly see your hand in front of your face. Jarlath got into a right lather about it. He was determined to visit the site to see if they were misusing his invention. He was also worried about Áine and said he would call in to visit her. He set off on his bicycle even though he could hardly see where to put his hands on the handlebars.

Cassie and Thomas were fighting more than usual and were like two rats in a cage. Even the normally good-tempered Nancy was fretful and cross. Only Connle seemed to remain the same. He made the children's porridge even though they didn't seem to appreciate it and spent more time flicking it at each other than actually eating it. When Jarlath arrived back from his mission, Thomas was trying to give Cassie a Chinese burn and she was howling. Then she got her arm free and boxed Thomas around the ears.

Jarlath was so down in the dumps he didn't pay any attention to them and just slumped in a chair. He looked even more bedraggled than usual. He only had one sock on and he was soaked through from the fog. His curly hair looked like a floor-mop on his head. He put his head in his hands. Nancy came and sat on his knee.

Connle put a big bowl of porridge in front of him but Jarlath showed no interest. Cassie and Thomas realised something really was up.

"Is it your fog-machine?" Connle asked.

"I managed to fool a workman into thinking I was one of them," Jarlath said, "and he told me they were using my machine to increase the fog. But that's not the worst thing," he sighed.

They asked him what it was.

"Áine didn't want to see me," he said, downcast. "She told me to go away because she has a cold and didn't want to come out. She wouldn't even open the door."

"If she's sick, she probably doesn't want to see anybody, poor girl," Connle said casually but the children noticed he was more concerned than he was letting on.

"I don't think she likes me any more." Jarlath sounded very sad indeed. Before Cassie and Thomas would have had a joke at Jarlath's expense but they saw he was really upset. He looked like he was trying not to cry.

"And there's something else," he said. "My equation is all rubbed out. Now I'll never understand the significance of the number 9." He gave a big sniff and fumbled for his hankie. "I have nothing," he said, his voice breaking.

Nancy gave him a hug.

"It's all that Drax's fault," Cassie said, kissing Jarlath on the forehead. Jarlath sniffled into a hanky. "Sorry, my eyes were leaking." He opened his arms for a group hug. That seemed to cheer him up.

"I'm going to get even," Jarlath said.

"And I'm going to get even evener!" Thomas said, stamping his foot. His uncle's courage lifted his spirits. They weren't done for yet.

"Why don't I call over to Áine with some healing foods?" Connle suggested.

"Only if we can come too," Cassie piped up, seeing a chance of escaping from the house. The prospect of getting out gave them a surge of energy and they ran upstairs to put on warm clothes. Nancy tagged along after them.

"You can't come," Cassie said firmly as she struggled with the buttons on her cardigan. Nancy's head was stuck in her jumper and Thomas pulled it off his younger sister's head, teasing her by dangling it over her.

"You are only a baby and you'll get in the way," Thomas taunted. "Babby Nancy wears a nappy to bed!"

Nancy's lip trembled but she went to Cassie and pulled her by the cardigan.

"Please can I come? I'll be good," Nancy beseeched in her sweet little voice.

But Cassie was having none of it and snapped

at her. "Honestly, Nancy, you'll have to learn you can't come everywhere with us. You'll slow us down." Nancy tried to cling to her but Cassie pushed her roughly and she fell back against the bed. Nancy cried in anguish.

"Shut up. I hate you!" Cassie shouted crossly.

Nancy's howls brought Jarlath up the stairs. He dashed in and picked up the distraught little girl.

"Were they bullying you, you poor child?" Jarlath soothed her.

Cassie glared at her and Nancy didn't dare speak.

"We want to go with Connle and she can't come," Thomas pouted.

"Get out of my sight, the pair of you!" Jarlath snapped at them angrily. Cassie and Thomas scampered down the stairs.

Down in the kitchen, Connle packed a picnic basket with healing foods of nettle soup and honey cakes. As he headed down the path, Cassie and Thomas appeared on their bicycles.

"Jarlath said we could come too." Cassie guiltily

avoided looking Connle in the eye. "Please, otherwise we'll go stark raving mad."

Connle looked to Jarlath who was standing with Nancy in the doorway.

"It's okay," he said, "I'll stay here to look after Nancy." And then he turned to Nancy. "We're better off without that nasty brother and sister of yours." Poor Nancy sobbed as if her heart would break but Thomas and Cassie were so relieved to be let out they pretended they couldn't hear her.

Connle rode on the donkey and held a torch and the children had their bicycle lights. But progress was slow. The fog was thick and eerie. Cassie and Thomas knew that Connle was displeased with them and didn't dare break the silence.

"When we get to Áine's, I'll just have a quiet word with her," Connle said. "We won't go in or anything."

Cassie and Thomas barely heard him. They were beginning to regret their insistence on coming out. The fog felt like being in the lungs of a horrible beast. It was cold and clammy and made them feel very small and alone. They could barely manage to cycle and their consciences felt bad about Nancy.

It took ages to get to Áine's house. The fog here seemed especially thick. It was almost like black smoke. They could scarcely find the door. Connle called Áine's name.

"Go away," they heard her voice but she sounded muffled and strange. "Leave me in peace."

"Áine, I have healing foods to help you," he said softly.

While Connle tried to persuade Áine to take the food, Cassie whispered to Thomas that they should go around the back of the house. Connle was so busy talking to Áine that he didn't notice them creep off. They felt their way around the back and came across a small open window. Without discussion, Cassie gave Thomas a leg up. He was small enough to slither through the window. Once inside he undid the latch of the main window and Cassie clambered in.

It was hard to see inside because the fog was

almost as thick inside as out. They felt their way through a narrow passage. It was lined with growing meadow flowers and the sweet perfume of the blossoms filled the house. The fog thinned out as they progressed softly down the corridor and in a room off it they saw a fire burning in a hearth. The air was thick with the smell of burning herbs.

The room where the fire was burning dazzled them. It was filled with a large oak bed, intricately carved and inlaid with thousands of crystals that caught the flicker of the fire. The walls were studded with precious stones and crystals and the whole room shimmered with reflected light. All around were bottles of dried herbs and potions. Cassie and Thomas crept further inside.

"What are we supposed to do?" Thomas whispered in Cassie's ear.

They could hear Áine down the other end of the hallway murmuring to Connle.

"Let's just make sure she is really okay," Cassie said.

Áine was slumped by the front door in a black

cloak, as if she had crawled there on her hands and knees. They walked a little way up the hall and called her name. But when she turned round they froze in shock. It wasn't Áine at all but an old woman! For a moment they were confused and rubbed their eyes as if they were seeing things. Maybe it was the fog that was befuddling their eyesight.

Then the stranger shouted and covered her face.

"She's been trying to fool Connle that she's Áine!" cried Cassie.

"What's going on in there?" Connle called through the heavy brass door. "Cassie, Thomas, are you in there?"

"Connle, it's a trick!" Thomas shouted.

"Do not seek Áine here," said the strange old woman.

"Who are you?" demanded Thomas. "Where's Áine?"

Connle started to bang at the door.

Cassie and Thomas ran at the stranger and tugged at her cloak.

"What have you done with Áine?" Cassie shouted.

"Connle!" Thomas yelled as he tried to open the brass door. "There's an old woman here who's pretending to be Áine!"

The old woman tried to shake Cassie off and stuck out her foot in an attempt to prevent Thomas from opening the door but he dodged her easily. With much heaving and puffing Thomas finally pulled the door open and Connle burst in, nearly toppling over as he came over the threshold. The strange old woman dropped the cloak from her face and slumped against the wall.

"Quick, let's get her inside," Connle said, an edge of panic in his voice.

"Tell us where Áine is first!" Cassie shouted at the stranger who held up her hand to her face in confusion.

"Just do as I say!" commanded Connle, pulling Cassie away.

Reluctantly, Thomas and Cassie helped Connle carry the strange old woman into the main room and laid her down on the crystal bed. Connle fetched her a glass of bubbling liquid that was on a small table beside the bed.

"Why are we helping her?" asked Thomas, perplexed. "What has she done with Áine?"

"She will answer for herself," said Connle.

The old woman sipped and seemed to recover a little. The children were able to get a good look at her now. She was old and worn-looking but also beautiful.

"Who are you?" Thomas asked. "Where is Áine?" His heart was in a knot of confusion and concern.

The stranger recovered her voice. "Your loyalty to Áine serves you well," she said in a voice both strange and familiar. She opened her eyes and a flash briefly lit them up.

"You know who I am," she said.

"Are you Áine's mother," Cassie asked, "or her grandmother?"

The stranger smiled.

Then Thomas remembered the glimpse he'd caught of Áine the night at Tadgh's tower when she rescued them from the Dúlachán.

"It is you!" he gasped. "*You* are Áine."

The children looked at her as if they had seen a ghost.

The old woman smiled and nodded.

"But what has Drax done to you?" Thomas asked, totally bewildered.

"Is she going to die?" asked Cassie, her eyes welling with tears.

"Not if we can help it." Connle gently wiped her tears away.

Thomas held Áine's hand.

"Do not tire her," Connle said. "She is weak and should not leave the crystal bed." Áine waved her hand and muttered something in Irish.

"Sit down," said Connle to the children, "and I'll explain." He pointed to crystal chairs near the fire.

The chairs looked like they might be cold but when they sat on them, they felt bathed in a golden glow. It was like a warm bath without any water. For the first time since the fog came, they felt warm and glowing.

"Áine is no ordinary woman," Connle told

them. "She is from a race of gods called the Tuatha dé Danann who came to Ireland long ago in the mists of time. Áine is the Goddess of the Sun."

Cassie and Thomas were amazed.

"So how come she has turned into an old woman?" Thomas asked. "I suppose she is very, very old."

"As old a time itself. Áine has taken human form to fight Drax," Connle continued. "All day when the sun shines, Áine is a bright and beautiful young woman. As the sun dies in the heavens at night, she becomes old and worn. Then she has to come and rest in her crystal bed. But then every dawn she is reborn and becomes a young and beautiful woman again."

"So that is why she always goes home before nightfall," Cassie said.

"And why she wouldn't let us see her face at Tadgh's tower," Thomas added.

"Drax has released some terrible enchantment. He's using Jarlath's fog-buster to make it worse," Connle went on. "Áine cannot fight this fog, the fog of despair. If it does not lift she may sicken and die."

"So it's not Jarlath's machine that is doing all this?" Cassie asked.

"Drax may be using it," Connle shrugged, "but he has mixed in some menace of his own."

The children were overcome with worry for Áine and ran to the bed. Cassie kissed her on the cheek.

"Please forgive us, dear Áine," Cassie said. "We're going to get that Drax."

Thomas stroked her lovely face that was still kind and gentle, even though old.

Áine opened her eyes briefly.

"Remember the gifts from the Sacred Grove," she said weakly and then lapsed back into her sleep. Connle covered her with her cloak and left the healing draught at her bedside.

"We must leave her," he said.

It was with heavy hearts that they kissed her and left the house, pulling the heavy brass door behind them.

"Imagine, Áine's a goddess!" Cassie said to Thomas. "Wait until Jarlath finds out."

"Not a word to anyone!" Connle warned and he made them promise that they would keep the secret.

Outside, the fog seemed to be getting even thicker. It was grimy and acrid in their throats and they could hardly breathe. They couldn't see beyond their noses and constantly bumped into hedges. Even Derry, the donkey, was confused. At one stage Cassie nearly ran over a stray sheep. The poor animal was even more frightened than they were. They soon realised that they were lost. In the distance they heard cattle mooing and the oinking of pigs.

"That's odd," Connle remarked. "It sounds like all the animals are wandering from the farm."

Occasionally there were shouting noises and cries but the fog muffled and deadened every sound. A tree rustled nearby like whispers on the breeze.

"That tree is trying to say something to us," Thomas said. They shone their torches through the fog and they could just about make out the ghostly grey bark of an aspen tree, marked with black diamonds.

"Go, go . . ." the leaves whispered.

"It is the quaking tree," Connle said. "Eadha, what is your message?"

The words were ghostly in the wind. "Go to the lake . . ." The leaves trembled and fluttered. "The veils between the world are thin."

"But how are we to find our way?" Cassie wondered.

Connle suddenly gave a little shout of joy and patted around in his pockets.

"Áine told us to remember the Sacred Grove," Connle said. "I think we have a guide." He fished a forked hazel wand out of his jacket that he'd rescued from the bonfire.

"This is a divining rod," he explained. "It will lead us to the water." The branch began to twitch in his hands, indicating the direction of the lake. The route was leading them across fields so they abandoned their bikes by a gate and left Derry in the first field they passed through.

They followed the hazel rod cautiously at first, then more boldly as they realised the guide was strong and true.

As they drew closer to Glimmering Lake, they saw powerful searchlights tearing through the fog. There was a great commotion going on and they knew Drax's dreaded henchmen were round about. The searchlights lit up huge mechanical diggers and great big cranes at the side of the lake. When they got quite close, they ducked down behind some prickly gorse bushes.

"They are dredging the lake," Connle whispered.

Through the darkness, they heard Drax's strong and terrible voice.

"I must find the Star Splinter," he shouted, "or you will all suffer!"

"But we've gutted all the fish in the lake," Stinchcombe answered in his nasal weaselly voice, "and there's no sign of a pike or a stone."

"Keep dredging," Drax shouted even louder. "The time is near. I must have that stone!"

Drax's henchmen swarmed all over the lake like flies.

Suddenly Connle and the children heard a flock of birds rise into the sky beating their angry wings.

"They are confused by the lights in the dark," Connle said.

A bird was captured in a beam of light. It was black and featherless like some prehistoric creature from the age of dinosaurs.

"It's the Corra again," Connle gulped. "A bad omen. Something is stirring the monster from the deep."

A shout came up from the workmen at the lake.

"We've got the Pike. We've got the Pike!!"

All the searchlights turned towards the lake. Through the criss-cross of beams, Thomas and Cassie watched as a giant net rose from the water. Within it the great fish writhed and slithered. All the machinery went quiet.

Then Drax's cruel voice cut through the air. It gave the children goose bumps.

"I'll deal with this fellow myself!" he roared.

The net was lowered and Drax lunged at the

Pike, grasping it in his big fat hands. But the fish thrashed from his grasp and tried to dive back towards the lake.

"Go, Pike, go!" Thomas whispered.

"Pull in the net," Drax commanded.

"Oh no," Cassie said as the fish was once more lowered into Drax's grappling hands.

Drax held the Pike and looked it in its cold eyes. "Give me the Star Splinter!"

The fish once more tried to break free but Drax had a firm grip.

"Here's a knife," Stinchcombe said eagerly. "Slit his belly."

"I've got a better idea," Drax laughed – a horrible snarling sound. He opened his mouth wide and lunged at the fish, clamping it in his teeth. But the scales of the Pike turned into chainmail and he cracked his teeth on it. Drax pulled the fish out of his mouth by the tail and spat out several teeth. He then beat it senseless on a rock. Enraged, he took a knife and plunged it into its soft underbelly, rummaged around and feasted on its guts. He spat out the bones with disgust.

"It is not here," he said angrily. "Someone must have got there before us. We will dynamite the lake later to make sure."

Thomas and Cassie gasped. They heard Drax's footsteps approach in their direction. He stopped and they heard him sniff and grunt.

"I bet those horrid children and that nasty mongrel, Connle, have something to do with this. I'll make those Chingles from the East wish they had never been born!"

Thomas, Cassie and Connle tried to creep as close into the gorse as they could, even though it was stinging their skins. Thomas had to bite his hand to stop himself shouting out at Drax. He was angered by the insult to Connle. They were almost afraid to breathe, so close was Drax. But then there was a great whirring sound as an engine started up and Drax walked on.

But they weren't safe yet. They heard Drax round up several of his guards. He instructed them to comb the place for any sign of intruders. Cassie, Thomas and Connle looked at each other in alarm.

"Someone think of something fast!" Cassie whispered as she spied two ugly guards bearing down in their direction. They were seconds away from being captured!

CHAPTER 13

At the very moment they expected Drax's men to find their hiding place, they were lifted up in the air. A dumper truck had scooped them up, bush and all, by accident as it drove away from the lake. Whoever was driving couldn't see them from the cab. It was cold and bumpy, like an unpleasant fairground ride but it was also the last place that Drax and his men were likely to look for them.

They came to the crossroads beside Tadgh's tower where the right-hand turn led back to their own house and the truck came to a halt. At Connle's signal they jumped out, landing softly in a patch of heather. They burrowed down into the bush, praying that the driver hadn't seen them. It wasn't as stingy as the gorse but it was prickly enough.

They heard Drax's other machines approach and lumber to a halt and then they heard his voice booming in the distance.

"Search every inch of this island, starting here! That wretched bookworm thinks he's so clever running off to the mainland to prove I've broken the law. Hah, we'll see who is clever!" he roared.

"They won't be able to get in," whispered Thomas. "The door is too heavy to break down."

They heard crashing and banging and the searchlights came on again.

Then Stinchcombe's weasel voice cut through the air in triumph.

"Ha, ha, someone has kindly left the key in the lock!"

"Oh, no," said Cassie, "that was us!" She wanted to blame Thomas but she knew it was equally her fault. They saw a flutter of white paper come out of the window.

"Poor Tadgh's books," Connle moaned.

After much rattling and banging, Stinchcombe and his henchmen emerged from the tower.

"Did you find it?" Drax demanded.

"There are lots of smelly old books and masks and things," answered Stinchcombe, "but no Star Splinter."

Drax huffed and puffed like an angry bull.

"And there was a telescope at the top of the tower," added Stinchcombe.

"Oh, the bookworm has been looking out for the comet," Drax laughed, "but I alone know the hour of its coming. And then I shall be master of the skies!"

"The only thing of value was this silver bottle," Stinchcombe said.

This made Drax furious. "A bottle, you stupid nincompoop, I suppose if I asked you to find me a bottle you'd bring me a diamond!"

The next thing was the bottle came flying past their ears. Connle nimbly caught it and put it in one of his many pockets. "I'll give this back to Tadgh," he whispered.

"There was a great big book open on prophecies," they heard Stinchcombe say. "At the one about Ferdia's Cape."

"Ha, ha," said Drax, "yes, I will have a date with my little friends. Then we'll have some fireworks. Perhaps it is time we got better acquainted." And with that all the machines started up again and took the fork in the road towards their house.

"They are going to our house," Cassie gasped, as soon as the machines had gone past. "We've got to get back to Nancy and Jarlath as soon as we can. They wouldn't be there if it wasn't for us fighting with Nancy. I'll never forgive myself if something happens to them."

Cursing the fact that that they'd left Derry, the donkey, and the bikes behind, they rushed off after Drax and his men on foot. "Wait!" said Connle. "This way! We'll cut across the fields again! It's faster."

They had just clambered up a rocky hill and could see the lights of their house below in the distance when the sound of horse's hooves alarmed them. The hooves made a fearsome rat-a-tat on the stony road like machine-gun fire. The children and Connle froze as they heard the horse pull up right outside their house and there was no mistaking that this was his destination.

It was the Dúlachán. His black-cloaked headless figure was visible in the light of the doorway and he held his head in his outstretched hands like a lantern. The eyes were green and sulphurous. He opened his mouth and his tongue was a flame of fire. He uttered one awful word.

"NANCY!"

The shout echoed all around the island. Their blood ran cold as if an icy hand had squeezed their hearts. The horse reared up on its hind legs and clattered away again on thunderous hoofs. The Dúlachán cracked his whip. It looked like a human spine. At the same moment, they saw the shadowy shapes of Drax and his henchmen arrive at Fairy Fort House.

Both Thomas and Cassie let out a wail of despair.

"Shush, children, we have to be strong,"

Connle's voice trembled with the effort of trying to be brave. "We'll have to head over the bog. It's the quickest way to the house and there's less chance we'll be seen. It is dangerous but we have no choice."

They scrambled down the little hill and set off across the bog at its foot.

Cassie and Thomas tried hard not to weep. The bog was treacherous. The ground was spongy and wet and one false move and they would be sucked down into the slurpy earth. But Connle knew the lie of the land and guided them through the heather along firmer patches of ground.

At one stage, Thomas nearly lost his shoe but Connle said, "Oh bog, be good to us in our time of need" and amazingly, Thomas was able to pull his foot out, shoe and all.

The air was misty and cold and every so often they thought they saw formless shapes rising before them.

Then suddenly Cassie started giggling.

"Stop that, Thomas. How can you make me

laugh at a time like this!" She could barely get the words out between her giggles.

"I'm nowhere near you," Thomas was annoyed. But then he too broke into hysterical laughter. "Connle, Connle," he managed to wheeze out, "stop!"

Cassie and Thomas were getting so worked up Connle had to grab hold of them.

"It's the Bo men. They are weird ghostly creatures that haunt the bogs and marshes. Some say they are made up of all the crankiness and bad humour that escapes from people. They'll tickle us to death out of spite!" He tried to shake some sense into Cassie and Thomas but invisible hands were tickling them into hysterics. Thomas fell to the ground and jerked about and Cassie had to hold her stomach because she was getting a pain from laughing so hard.

"I wish we knew how to make them stop," Connle wheezed through clenched teeth as he tried to stop himself laughing but it was impossible. The Bo Men had found his funny bone.

All three of them were finding it harder to breathe and their bodies were wracked with pain.

"Somebody please help us!" Thomas gasped, laughing his head off.

At that, a white shape cantered through the mist and they heard a whinny.

"Well, what have we here?" came a familiar voice. "I see you've met the hilarious Bo men. I don't think."

"Pooka!" Connle shouted. "Make them stop."

The Pooka shook his mane. "I blame that Dúlachán. I know he's my cousin but he's a real misery guts. He's giving ghost horses a bad name."

"Please, we are trying to save Nancy from Drax. The Dúlachán has pronounced her name!" Connle squealed, as if it was the funniest thing in the world.

"I just knew it!" the Pooka seethed. "Him and his headless rider thinking they are it! I've a good mind to run round shouting 'Dúlachán' like the voice of doom. I'd love to get one over on him."

"If you help us we might be able to save

Nancy," Cassie sobbed with laughter. "That would spite him."

The Pooka seemed oblivious to their desperation and hesitated as if there was all the time in the world.

"Mmm. I suppose if she was saved that would show everyone what a big fraud he is," he mused.

"Please help us!" giggled Thomas.

"You have to tell them jokes," the Pooka said finally, "and make them laugh instead. That should be easy for a gang of comedians like yourselves. I don't think."

"Knock, knock!" Thomas spat out.

"What are you playing at?" Connle chuckled.

"Knock, knock," Thomas managed to breathe out.

"Who's there?" Cassie giggled back though it took her about a minute to get the words out between the laughs.

"Phyllis," said Thomas.

"Phyllis who?" Cassie replied.

Thomas started giggling again but eventually managed to say, "Phyllis a bucket of water."

"Oh that will have them rolling in the aisles," the Pooka scoffed.

There was a low rumbling sound and it felt as if the shapeless forms in the bog were wobbling. Then there was a strange chuckle.

"It's working," gasped Connle. "Quick! Think of another joke."

While the Bo Men were laughing in their strange fashion, the children had time to get their breaths back.

"Knock, knock!" said Cassie quickly.

"Who's there?" said Thomas.

"Neil!"

"Neil who?"

"Neil down before the Vampire King," finished Cassie in a rush.

The low rumbling sound continued. They felt the strange breaths of the Bo Men and knew they had made them laugh.

"Well, they'd obviously laugh at anything," sneered the Pooka. "Those are the worst jokes I've ever heard."

"Why did the chicken cross the road?" sang Cassie.

"That joke is so old it should be drawing a pension," said the Pooka.

"To get to the other side," Thomas gasped.

"What's black and white and red all over?"

"A newspaper!"

And so they continued across the bog, struggling to think of jokes while at the same time trying not to lose their foothold. And all the while, the Pooka jeered their efforts. They'd never felt so miserable in their lives. After what seemed like an age of walking they found the ground becoming firmer under foot.

"We are nearly there," said Connle. "The Bo men are afraid of the fairies and won't follow us into the field."

"Well, I hope you were worth saving," the Pooka neighed. "You sock it to that Dúlachán in the eye, otherwise I'll sour your milk for a year!"

He cantered off and they were glad to see the back of him, even if he had come to their aid.

As they climbed over the low stone wall, Thomas shouted one last joke at the Bo men.

"What's fat and stupid and invisible? The silly Bo men of the bog!"

There was a rasping bellow and Thomas ran through the field as fast as he could.

They ran to the house, fearing that they were too late. There was no sign of Drax and his men. The front door looked like it had been kicked in. Inside, cupboards were open and drawers upended. The place had been ransacked. They ran from room to room, shouting *"Nancy, Jarlath, Nancy, Jarlath!"* But there was no sign of them.

Cassie burst into tears when she found Nancy's toy bear, Dog, thrown on the front lawn with his ear torn off.

"Drax may have taken them to the yacht," Connle said.

Thomas was trying not to cry but soon the tears were rolling down his cheeks. Then even Connle joined in.

"It's all our fault for not letting her come with

us," Cassie's whole body was wracked with sobs. "We've killed her!"

"Oh, I hope she'll be all right," Thomas sobbed. "If she comes back I won't ever fight with her again! What will Mum and Dad say? We won't be let stay with Jarlath again and Áine is old and Connle will be sent away!" The words came out in big gulps.

Cassie dried her tears and hugged her brother and Connle fished a handkerchief out of his pocket. When he pulled it out, it was wrapped around the strange silver bottle that Drax had tossed away at Tadgh's tower. The bottle throbbed and glowed in his hand and, amazed, Connle pulled out the stopper.

The children leapt back in fright. A ghostly head, then shoulders, followed by the upper body of a ghostly old woman shrugged out of the bottle.

"Yerra, Connle, *a stor*, don't stand there gawping, ye ken! Look lively and help pull me free," the ghost said in a strange Irish/Scottish accent. Connle was open-mouthed with astonishment. He looked like

285

he'd just seen a ghost! But then he meekly did as he was told. Thomas and Cassie held the bottle while he tried to grab hold of the ghost under the arms. Of course, his hands went right through and he ended up boxing himself on the ears.

"Now, Mr Lummox Brain, just blow gently on the rim!" The ghost sounded amused even if she spoke cross words.

Connle did as she asked, but nothing happened as his breath passed over the rim of the bottle.

"There's only one thing for it," said the ghost. "I'll have to make the children cry."

"No need," Connle said, rummaging around in his pockets. "I have some ready-mixed tears, previously prepared."

From an inside pocket, he found the little blue bottle where he'd saved tears from a previous crying episode. He gave it a big shake and then placed some tears on the neck of the silver witch bottle. There was a sizzle and a puff of steam and, in an instant, before them stood a ghost with eyes more penetrating than they'd ever encountered in a living person. She was just over six feet tall and was very imposing but an amused expression played about her lips. Her grey hair was in an untidy bun and she wore an old-fashioned long woollen frock with a plaid shawl around her shoulders.

Connle beamed with pleasure and pride. "Children, let me introduce you to your great-great-great-great-great-great-great-great-great –"

"That's enough greats out of you, Connle," interrupted their ancestor, "Just call me Granny Clíona." Whatever else she was, she wasn't very patient. Then she turned to Cassie and Thomas who gaped at her in awe.

"Well, look at you, aren't you the very spit of my own wee Hamish and Fiona? I'd give ye a big hug if I could." Instead she blew and ruffled their hair. It was a nice feeling.

So there she was, their famous ancestor, Clíona McColl who'd arrived on the island nearly five hundred years before, exiled from Scotland for being a witch. Later chief clanswoman of the island, mother of fourteen children and finally witch in the bottle in Tadgh's tower. They recognised her from the portrait on the stairway.

She didn't look like a witch, more like a sparky grandmother. True, she had a sharp tongue but so did their mother. Evidently sharp tongues ran in the McColl family.

"Are you a witch?" Thomas asked wide-eyed.

"Och, if a witch is a wise old woman who knows evil when she sees it, then I'm proud to call myself a witch!" Her voice was lilting and she was full of mischievous humour.

Connle looked happier than they'd ever seen him before. She gave him a searching look.

"And you, my little foundling," she said to him, "have you been caring for the Chingles?"

Connle hung his head in shame. "Drax has taken Nancy."

"It's our fault," tears streamed down Cassie's face again. "We wouldn't let her come out with us."

"Shush, my dear, it's no good blaming yourself. You weren't to know," said the ghost of Clíona McColl.

Cassie dried her tears, feeling a tiny bit better.

"You can tell me all about what is going on but there's something I have to do first," continued Granny Clíona. "Connle, where's your tin whistle? Play me my favourite tune."

Cassie and Thomas looked on in amazement as Connle played a jig and Granny Clíona danced around the room. She turned cartwheels and side-stepped across the ceiling, gambolling about the place like a lamb in springtime. She flexed her muscles and shook her legs and whooped with enjoyment.

She was out of breath at the end of it. "I've been waiting nearly three hundred years to do that!" she gasped. Even though they were still worried about Nancy, they were glad to see her joy.

When she had finished dancing, they filled her in on all that had been happening. All about Sir Dignum Drax and his buying the island, the Prophecy of Ferdia's Cape, the destruction of the Sacred Grove, the sickness of Áine and now the kidnapping of Jarlath and Nancy. Granny Clíona paced up and down as they spoke.

"So the prophecy has come to pass," she said,

scratching her chin. "This Drax has come in search of the Star Splinter and you have come from the East, ye Chingles."

"East Croydon," Thomas piped up.

"Áine has been training us to fight Drax," Cassie said, "and we were given gifts by the Sacred Grove."

"I must admit you're a lot younger than I expected. I had it in my head that you'd be old warriors," Granny Clíona shook her head, "but who am I to argue with the prophecy! And you're my own flesh and blood!"

They all felt a bit better thanks to Granny Clíona's cheerful outlook.

"Now, Cassie," she said, "eat a hazelnut and use your long sight."

Cassie cracked open a nut with her teeth, then held the Willow's silver catkin, closed her eyes and nibbled on the nut.

The vision was like a half-remembered dream. She saw Drax's yacht on the water, its great black hull like a killer whale. She could see inside the boat and she saw Stinchcombe walking into the hold at the bottom of the boat. There on a high chair, her sister Nancy was chained, and she was screaming and crying, *"No, no, no!"*

Connle shook her awake and Cassie realised that she was the one who was screaming. It was strange. She felt the feelings, just like when she knew the Sacred Grove was going to burn but this time she had vivid pictures to go with them. She closed her eyes again. In her mind's eye, she roved over the waves. She heard cries of *"Help, help!"* and felt as if she was drowning. She saw Jarlath's curly head. He looked like he was slipping under. Then she saw no more.

"Nancy is imprisoned in the hold of the boat, guarded by Stinchcombe. I saw no sign of Drax. Jarlath was in the sea – maybe thrown overboard." Cassie gulped. "I think he's drowning!"

Connle and Thomas let out a gasp.

"We don't know that." Granny Clíona's tone was businesslike. "You haven't seen it and I haven't heard the Banshee sing. She always lets us know when a McColl is passing over. He'll come to no real harm."

Despite their worries, her confident tone gave the children and Connle some hope.

"Maybe he'll be rescued by the Merrows," Connle said.

"And who are they?" Thomas asked.

"They are Irish mermaids," Connle explained, "but they're not very reliable and –"

"We'll worry about that later – first we have to rescue Nancy," Granny Clíona interrupted. "Now what day is it?"

They gazed at her with blank faces.

"Aren't ye all a grand lot of amadáns!" she scolded.

"I think it is a Saturday," Connle said. "Drax's fog has made all the days blur into each other."

"That was his intention. The comet is very near. Tonight, for the only time in five thousand years, the Star Splinter can be activated to replace the sun. That's why Drax wants it. And whoever controls the light, controls the world."

"So as well as rescuing Nancy we have to find the Star Splinter," Thomas said.

"Correct. Now, Cassie, see if your long sight will reveal the location of the Star Splinter."

Cassie bit into a nut and closed her eyes again. All she could see was Nancy's sweet little face shouting out for someone to save her. "It's no use," she said. "I'm too upset about Nancy."

Connle gave her a hug.

Cassie closed her eyes for one more try but all she saw this time was that all the boats on the beach were wrecked.

"That's valuable information," Connle said when she told them. "We'd better get the currach from the lake, otherwise we won't be able to get near the yacht."

Outside, all was dark and the air was cold and sharp, chilling them to their bones. Cassie felt sick to her stomach with worry about her dear little sister. What would their mother and father say when they found out that she had failed to look after her? Thomas clenched his fist and bit it to stop himself crying again. At least they now had Granny Clíona on their side.

Then, as if she could read their thoughts she

said, "Courage, children. We are McColls and so is Nancy. As little as she is, she won't give in without a fight."

"It might be better if you travel inside the bottle," said Connle, "in case we see anybody. And you could be our secret weapon."

"So long as it doesn't take another 300 years to get me out," Granny Clíona joked and with one big whoosh she was back in the bottle. Connle secured the stopper and stowed her safely in one of his many pockets.

They held hands in the darkness and crept to the bottom of the garden, relying on Connle's hazel wand for direction. They prayed that they wouldn't see the Dúlachán again. But a 'hee-haw' sound made them all jump out of their skin. Something was nuzzling them in the dark.

They heard another timid bray and realised it was Derry, the donkey. Cassie and Thomas threw their arms around the animal with relief and gave him a big hug.

"He must have found his way back from the field," Cassie said. "I bet he sensed Nancy was in danger." Derry brayed as if in agreement, and knelt down so Connle, Cassie and Thomas could climb on to his back.

"We've got to rescue Nancy who has been kidnapped by Drax," Thomas whispered in his ear.

Suddenly, a change came over Derry who had never been quick at the best of times. He brayed loudly in the darkness and sped off at a gallop. It was like being on a rollercoaster. He leapt over ditches, cantered through fields and jumped over hedges, flying through the air like a steeple chaser. It was odd, speeding through the countryside in the dark. They were jostled and jumbled and felt like they were in a spin-dryer as they clung on for dear life. There was no stopping this donkey.

"Bedad, I'll be entering you in the Derby next year," Connle exclaimed in surprise.

"It's only because Nancy is his friend and he wants to rescue her. And that's exactly what we're going to do!" Cassie said, trying to sound braver than she felt.

They knew they were at the lake when Derry came to a juddering stop and they were thrown over his ears, landing in a heap. Torchlight shone in the darkness and they heard heavy boots approach them.

"We've forgotten about Drax's guards," groaned Cassie. "They're going to dynamite the lake today."

The witch in the bottle throbbed in Connle's pocket. He peeked inside the stopper.

"Let me out," said Granny Clíona, "and I'll give them the fright of their lives."

"Halt, who goes there!" they heard the harsh voices of Drax's security men.

Connle opened the bottle and Granny Clíona oozed out smoothly this time.

"*Boo!*" she said, half jokingly.

But Drax's men didn't think it was a joke. They dropped their torches and ran. Granny Clíona followed them.

"And boo again!" she laughed, shunting them in the direction of the bog.

"Please, please, don't hurt us," the men bleated like sheep.

"Oh boo-hoo, poor you," mocked Granny Clíona as they fled over the hedge. Little did they know they were heading straight into the boggy hinterland of the island that spread from the lake to the foot of the hills around Fairy Fort House.

Moments later the children heard low grumbling laughter.

"Sounds like the Bo men have got them," Connle said. "Now let's see if we can find the currach."

"We can't speak to the Pike," Thomas said. "Drax killed him."

"The only one who can help us now is the White Worm," said Granny Clíona.

They picked up the torches abandoned by Drax's men and saw a stack of dynamite waiting to be tipped into the lake.

"Looks like we've arrived in time," Connle sighed with relief.

"Ouch!" shouted Cassie as she stubbed her toe.

They felt around and discovered it was the

currach. They were about to lift it up, when there was a splash and a thud. Something was rising from the deep and the children and Connle were sprayed with water. For a moment, a pale sliver of new moon illuminated the scene.

A huge whitish shape loomed out of the lake. It was horrible, a great big flabby worm tinged with green, the colour of snot with no eyes and a big mouth in its horrible head. They hid behind the boat.

"Listen to me, Chingles from the East!" said the monster; its voice heavy with phlegm like it had the worst cold in the world. "You are the only ones who can stop him!"

"Who or what are you?" Cassie stammered.

"It's the White Worm of Glimmering Lake!" exclaimed Granny Clíona.

"There is more to him than meets the eye," said the Worm.

"Why does no one in this place ever, ever give us a straight answer?" Thomas complained. "I'm sick of all these riddles."

"Sir Dignum Drax has Nancy and we've got to

find the Star Splinter. Where is it?" Connle asked.

"The Star Splinter and the child are one and he will devour her to get what he wants," said the Worm.

And with that there was a splash and the monster was gone.

They stood together trying to take in the awful consequences of what the Worm had told them. Cassie, Thomas and Connle each remembered Nancy's encounter with the Pike at Glimmering Lake with a guilty conscience. Cassie finished off a nut and saw the yacht again where Nancy was imprisoned. There was a faint glow from Nancy's stomach.

Cassie gasped. "Nancy definitely swallowed the Star Splinter that time when we caught the Pike!"

"And she must still have it in her tummy because it hasn't appeared in her nappies," Thomas added.

Connle felt a whistle of air around his head. Granny Clíona was trying to box his ears in the dark.

"Do you mean to tell me you let my great-whatever-it-is-grandchild swallow the Star Splinter!" she shouted, her voice rising with anger and surprise. "You nincompoop!"

"I didn't mean –" Connle moaned.

"Stop!" Thomas interrupted. "You grown-ups are always telling us not to fight among ourselves. We have to concentrate on saving Nancy."

Connle and Granny McColl looked shamefaced and said sorry to each other. Granny McColl slipped back inside her bottle without another word.

There was no time to waste so as quickly as they could they attached the currach to Derry's saddle and set off for the beach. As they passed some of the houses on the island, Cassie thought of all the poor people on Inish Álainn, made helpless by the fog of despair. Of Róisín and Muiris, of Donnacha the bodhrán-maker and Mr Mulally, all caught in that strange half-sleep without hope or energy that was the struggle with despair. Perhaps it was only their witch's blood that saved the children and Jarlath. And she thought that despair was the worst thing that could ever happen to a person. She popped a nut in her mouth, closed her eyes again and saw the black hull of the boat. Through the steel of the hull, she saw Nancy chained to her high chair and Stinchcombe trying to make her drink something. And Nancy shouting and spitting and then suddenly kissing Stinchcombe on the cheek . . .

"She's still alive but for how much longer! Oh I think they're trying to poison her!" Cassie spoke her fears to Thomas in the darkness. But he couldn't hear her as they sped to the beach.

The beach was a sorry sight with all the boats on the island broken up and wrecked by Drax's machines. They were glad of Cassie's foresight that made them bring the currach. Cassie told them of her latest vision of Nancy still alive in the hold. Thomas and Connle absorbed the information quietly and worked as fast as they could. Out at sea, Drax's yacht was all lit up, like a party boat. They pushed the currach towards the edge of the water. Just as they were about to jump in, Thomas noticed something glinting in the sand. He picked it up.

"It's Jarlath's pocket watch," he called.

Connle grabbed it and kissed it.

"Oh poor, poor Jarlath, my best friend," he cried. "I hope he's not in a watery grave!" He felt around for his hanky and took out Granny Clíona's bottle.

As he took the stopper out, her voice growled out. "Quit bawling, ye big heap o' groats! Now listen, I have a plan. Let me fly towards the boat and my name isn't McColl if I can't cause some havoc. Cassie and Thomas, you go in the currach and then sneak on board."

Connle objected, saying he didn't want to let the children go towards danger on their own.

The voice in the bottle answered him, "But who else is going to help Jarlath if he makes it to the beach? Go ask the Boogan in the cave if he knows what has happened to him. And we need you here to guard the beach in case Drax has something else up his sleeve."

"You're right," Connle said. "The watch is

stopped at only half an hour ago. Someone might have seen something."

"Till we meet again," Granny Clíona called as she flew above them. "When I make this sign, Chingles, you will know to come on board." She raised her hands above her head and crossed her clenched fists.

For a moment, they watched her stately form heading out to sea, praying that she would reach the boat in time. Then Thomas and Cassie clambered into the currach while Connle set off to find the Boogan. They had less than an hour to save Nancy from the fate of the Pike!

CHAPTER 14

On board the yacht, "*The Ocean Beast*", Stinchcombe dragged a barrel of castor oil up from Provisions onto the deck. He huffed and puffed as he hauled it with his great ugly hands and nails like talons.

He was used to doing his master's bidding in all kinds of evil deeds but something was bothering him. It was that little child. She could be cross and loathsome and scratchy but she also had lovely curly hair and dimples and the cutest laugh.

For the first time in his life Stinchcombe didn't want the Master to hurt someone. He had to get the Star Splinter out of her before the

Master did. And he shuddered to think what the Master would do when that time came.

The Master was taking a nap before the special time when the comet would be highest in the sky and Stinchcombe had to act now. He had tried forcing the child to eat cakes to make her vomit it up but she spat them all out. He'd tried to make her eat prunes but she hurled them across the room, laughing when she scored a bull's-eye on his nose. Now he thought he'd force-feed her castor oil. If it didn't work, the Master would rip open her stomach, or boil her alive or tear her limb from limb. Worst of all, he might even eat her, like he did the fish. Stinchcombe who had done many a horrid thing himself couldn't bear the thought of it. All because when he'd given her a glass of water she had kissed him on the cheek.

The yacht creaked on the waves and he shivered as a cold breeze licked his face. But the coldness spread to his toes. A sudden whoosh made him look up at the sail. He got the shock of his life!

Against the blood-red sails of the yacht, the white shape of Granny Clíona stood out, bright and blinding. Stinchcombe fell over the barrel onto his back.

"Where is the child?" she intoned.

Stinchcombe knelt, gibbering and quaking.

"Answer, ye who disturb my ghost!"

"Sh-she is in t-the h-hold, ch-chained t-to a h-h-high ch-chair," Stinchcombe stuttered.

"And your master?"

"H-he is pr-preparing for the hour. After the nap, he w-will eat l-live things."

There was the sound of mooing, clucking and baahing from deep within the yacht. All the farm animals from the island were on board and it was clear that Drax intended to eat them all.

"Filthy beast," snapped Granny Clíona. The deck was now flooding with castor oil from the barrel let fall by Stinchcombe.

Granny Clíona bid him open the hatch to the hold. There was a quaking and a stirring deep within the boat and the imprisoned animals ran out on deck.

"What have you done with the child?" demanded the ghost.

"I was t-trying t-to make her sick up the Star Splinter. Otherwise M-master will eat her," Stinchcombe could barely talk for his teeth chattering. He shivered in the ghost's chill.

"Pl-please don't h-hurt me," he moaned. "I was only trying to help."

Cows and pigs and hens rushed around the boat, sliding in the castor oil and creating a great squawking hullaballoo. Several of Drax's men appeared in order to get the animals back in the hold. At the sight of Granny Clíona, most of them took fright, clambered into the lifeboats and headed for the mainland.

Granny Clíona saw the currach bobbing on the water. She gave the signal by crossing her clenched fists above her head.

Cassie and Thomas, their knees shaking, mounted a ladder at the side of the yacht, then hid under the tarpaulin of a lifeboat on deck. Stinchcombe was still shivering in fear and had crawled behind a lifebuoy. The coast was clear.

Granny peeked under the tarpaulin and told the children that Nancy was still in the hold while Drax was in his cabin having a nap before he would eat live things. Nobody voiced their fear about Nancy's probable fate. In three-quarters of an hour when the comet passed through the sky, Drax intended to activate the Star Splinter.

"But we're going to stop him," Granny Clíona spoke firmly; knowing they were thinking of the danger Nancy was in. Granny told Thomas to prepare for shapeshifting. "Let's hope you have beginner's luck," she said. "You have the apple from Quert of the Sacred Grove. You must eat it but, whatever happens, do not eat it until ten minutes to the hour. Make no move until then."

He felt a ghostly kiss on his cheek like butterfly wings beating against his skin. He felt frightened to the pit of his stomach but he willed himself to be brave.

"Cassie, you will have to use your long sight to guide us all," Granny Clíona said and Cassie too received a ghostly kiss. "Do it now!"

Cassie ate a nut.

"I see a storm rising because of the comet," she said.

"I'll take care of that," Granny Clíona replied decisively as if it was no bother at all and with that she flew up to the sail.

As the wind rose, she whirled round the sails, creating a counterforce to keep the boat upright. Around them the sea was choppy but on board, all was still.

Cassie felt for Thomas's hand. "Good luck," she whispered.

He didn't have time to answer because a roar came from the bottom of the boat that made their blood run cold. And then they heard their little sister scream.

❧

Across the water, Connle sat on the beach, feeling lonely and abandoned. He clutched the stopped watch and a fat tear rolled down his face.

"Oh poor Jarlath," he wailed, "he can barely swim!" He didn't share Granny Clíona's confidence that he'd escaped a watery grave. Connle rummaged in his pocket for a hanky but instead pulled out a spare nappy belonging to Nancy. This made him cry all the more.

"Be japers, what's all this fuss?"

Connle turned round. The voice came from deep inside a cave. He shone his torch in and saw the Boogan coming towards him. He looked like a creature made entirely out of seaweed with hair of purple dulse seaweed and a body of bladderwrack. Around his neck was a necklace of limpets and his belt was made of mussels and swordfish.

"It's Jarlath," Connle wailed. "He's drownded and the Chingles are trapped on the boat with that monster."

The Boogan shook and quivered, flecking drops of seawater off himself.

"That evil man has polluted our waters long enough!"

"Have you seen Jarlath?" Connle asked. "Tall chap, curly hair, jumper on back to front, two odd shoes on his feet?"

The Boogan's big watery eyes looked at him blankly. "I did hear a big splash a little while ago," he said, "and I saw a red cap of feathers in the water." His voice was soft like the rush of air from within a seashell.

"You definitely saw a red cap?" Connle brightened up. "Then he was rescued by the Merrows." He embraced the Boogan even though he was all wet and blubbery.

"Well, struth," said the Boogan, "if he's still alive you might have just as much trouble getting him back from the Merrows as raising him from the dead. You know they lay claim to every drowned man they save. And if the God of the Sea, Manannán Mac Lir, finds out that they let one slip, he'll certainly make waves!"

☙

Back on the boat, Cassie and Thomas crept towards the hold as Granny Clíona kept up her circling like a vortex. A dark rumbling sound came from the hold.

"Give me the Star Splinter," Drax roared.

"I want my Dog!" screamed Nancy.

Cassie squeezed Thomas's hand.

"She is definitely still alive and kicking!" she gasped.

They crept slowly down towards the narrow steps leading to the bottom of the yacht. A wave lapped on board, drenching them, and a strong gust of wind blew open the doors to the hold. Before Drax could turn round, Cassie and Thomas crept in and hid behind some barrels.

"Go away! I hate you!" screamed Nancy at Drax.

They were sick with fear but heartened that Nancy seemed unharmed.

"Ha, ha, ha! Not long, my pretty." He held out a horny misshapen hand with six fingers and tickled her on the tummy. "You just keep my jewel warm for me."

Nancy spat at him.

"Couldn't be better," he laughed, "like a Scotch egg. A child egg. I'll chomp you up and have the Star Splinter. Like a peach, ha, ha! Not long, not long."

Above Nancy's head were twenty-five clocks with the time in the different zones around the world. The main clock was labelled 'GMT' and stood at fifteen minutes to midnight. The comet was due to pass in a quarter of an hour.

The clock ticked. Cassie and Thomas trembled, not knowing what to do. As the seconds passed, a change came over Drax. He beat his chest and tore off his captain's uniform. He appeared to increase in size.

"It is nearly time," he roared, "and I am Balor returned to rule the earth as I was meant to do five thousand years ago!"

Before their eyes, Sir Dignum Drax transformed into Balor of the Evil Eye. It hadn't been much of a disguise in the first place. They now understood all the remarks about there being more to him than meets the eye. He wasn't just a fat, greedy, evil media baron wearing an eye-patch but under his fine clothes a scaly, misshapen monster with one eye in the middle of his forehead and six fingers on each hand. He expanded to at least three times his size.

Thomas and Cassie felt rooted to the spot and frozen in terror. They couldn't move with fear and Granny Clíona had told them not to do anything until ten to the hour. Drax was almost bursting out of the hold. As frightened as they were, they wanted to attack him but they knew it might end up with all of them being killed.

With his one good eye, Balor/Drax looked around the room then he turned back to Nancy.

"You are just a spit in the bucket," Nancy shouted, spitting at him. She held up the leather necklace Áine had made for her with the silver bark, the gift of Beith, the Birch. Balor's claw-like hands bore down on her. The blade-like tip of a horrible horny nail sliced the necklace from her. It flew across the hold.

"Don't jest with me," Balor growled. "I am not called Balor of the Evil Eye for nothing. With one look from my eye, I can knock you stone dead." With that, he lifted up his eye-patch and blinked his hidden eye at Nancy. Nancy slumped in her chair, like a rag-doll.

Cassie and Thomas clasped each other in anguish, barely able to prevent themselves from screaming out in horror.

314

They didn't know whether she was dead or stunned.

The clock hand moved to ten minutes to midnight.

"Quick," whispered Cassie, "eat your apple and start your change." Thomas ate the apple. It tasted fresh and clean and he scrunched up his eyes and concentrated with all his might. It was no use. Nothing happened. Cassie whispered in his ear.

"Remember what Áine told you about not trying too hard. Pretend you are floating on your back and the water is doing all the work. All you have to do is let go."

Balor heard the sound. In a matter of seconds he would discover their hiding place. Cassie knew what she had to do, even if it meant Balor might kill her. She had to create a diversion to give Thomas time to change. She came out from behind the barrels.

"Leave my little sister alone!" she yelled. "Don't you dare touch a hair of her head!"

Before Balor knew what had hit him, Cassie

sped forward and bit him on the big toe. His toe was nearly the size of her head and it was one of thirteen of his large hairy, horrible foot. She then realised he had only one big foot with yellow toe-nails like horns, just like the drawing in Tadgh's book. That's why Drax had used the sticks to walk.

A huge, ugly hand swept down and picked Cassie up by the toe as if she was a toy. Cassie shut her eyes as he held her aloft before his baleful eye.

"Oh it's the little wretch's big sister, another of the famous Chingles come to defeat me. Ah bless her!" He moved her towards his mouth and she smelt his poisonous breath as he bashed her off his huge tombstone teeth.

"I can use you as a palate-cleanser," he laughed.

She looked into his throat and saw his vast tonsils like great big bells.

"Stop!" Cassie shouted. "I can be useful to you. I have long sight. I can tell you about the future."

He lifted her out of his mouth and glared at

her. She forgot to close her eyes but luckily his eye-patch had slipped down and was covering his evil eye.

"As if a mere child could be of any use to the magnificent Balor," he sneered.

"We are the Chingles from the East come to fight you as foretold by the Prophecy of Ferdia's Cape!" Cassie tried to sound brave.

"Oh yes and you are doing a fine job. Keep up the good work!" He laughed and she smelt his stinking breath again. With his other hand he picked Nancy up and she was limp and lifeless in his fingers.

"I see you crushed and broken by the strength of a child!" Cassie shouted at him with all her might. She was still trying to buy time to see if Thomas could shapeshift but it was looking very bad. She spoke with venom: "You cannot win, you vile, hideous beast!" She sounded braver than she felt.

"Enough of your time-wasting!" Balor licked his lips. "I'm going to eat your little sister to get the Star Splinter and then both of you will be in my belly," Balor roared with triumph, "and after that I'll find your smelly little brother."

"You are just full of wind, you stupid giant!" Cassie didn't care any more. If she were going to die, she would say what she liked. "You are ugly and evil and everyone hates you, even the people who work for you! They couldn't get off this boat quick enough!"

He swung her and the lifeless Nancy towards his mouth.

"Now which one will I eat first?" he said. "I know, I'll eat you both together."

The clock struck nine minutes to twelve. Cassie thrashed about blindly and called to Nancy.

Balor lowered them both towards his big mouth. Cassie felt big splashes of spittle on her face as he licked his lips. He brought them nearer and nearer, then away again, enjoying Cassie's screams as he played with them like a cat with two mice.

"Even your own snot doesn't like you!" she shouted at Balor.

Crouched behind the barrel, Thomas felt every nerve in his body tingle. His stomach was in a knot and he thought he might be sick. His skin was cold and clammy and his head was heavy and numb with the effort of trying to change. He was sick with worry about his sisters, and his fear of Balor immobilised him. The more he tried to relax, the less it worked. He wanted to cry out in despair. Tears welled up in his eyes. It was no use. He was a coward and a fool.

But then a vision of Cernunnos, the Lord of Shapeshifters, came into his head. He carried the horned serpent in his right hand. Thomas felt the lightest touch on his shoulders.

"Remember Uath the Hawthorn, the tree of shapeshifters," Cernunnos said.

The clock struck eight minutes to. There was no more playing and Balor opened his mouth wide to pop them in. Cassie couldn't bear it and closed her eyes. She smelled his foul breath and brushed against his massive teeth. But then she felt a rush of wind by his nose, followed by a buzzing sound. A fly was circling around his head.

It was an angry, buzzing bluebottle and it landed right on his nose. Thomas had changed! Balor raised his left hand that held Cassie to brush it away. She saw her moment and bit him with all her might on the tip of his nose.

"*Ouch!*" he yelped and dropped her to the floor.

Cassie scuttled away and tried not to cry. She looked up. It was too late. Nancy wasn't in his hand any more! Oh no, Cassie moaned, and felt her heart break.

"I still have the important one," he said, but the bluebottle flew right into his mouth and out again.

The giant's fury rose. He ripped off the eye-patch. Thomas watched through his bluebottle eyes making sure not to look directly into Balor's evil eye. It was hard to know what was going on. With one blink of his baleful eye, Balor turned into a giant spider. Cassie watched, her heart sick, as the monstrous spider wove a huge net to catch the fly.

"He's now a spider, Thomas!" she shouted. "Look out. He's on the ceiling!" Even if Nancy was dead, perhaps Thomas could stop Balor activating the Star Splinter. She tried to guide her brother as best she could but soon the room was a maze of silken cords with the strength of steel. Thomas flew about in a panic, his fragile wings beating frantically.

The spider scuttled as fast as it could on its eight legs and wove with fury. Thomas, the bluebottle, was forced into one corner of the ceiling. It was only a matter of time before the spider captured the fly. Thomas watched the ugly, hairy spider get closer and closer. It clambered over the silken chords with its eight legs, its pincers twitching, ready to inject deadly poison into the fly with his sharp fangs.

Thomas concentrated hard and in his mind heard Áine's voice: "Take on the spirit to take on the shape." He imagined he had large feathered wings and could fly on the breeze. The fangs of the spider came closer. Thomas was nearly done for. He concentrated with all his might. I need better wings to fly from here, he thought. To his relief, the change happened in an instant.

He was amazed to feel his throat open and a blackbird's song issue from his breast.

Suddenly he felt a surge of energy as he realised he could escape on the wing. He ripped through the web with his sharp yellow beak and the cords that had seemed like steel to the fly were just flimsy cobweb to a blackbird. He flew around the hold, trying to find an exit, thinking it was best if he could draw Balor away from Cassie.

"Watch out, Thomas!" Cassie's voice rang out. "Balor is changing too!"

In the blink of his evil eye, Balor changed into a black cat. Cassie shrank back from his sharp claws. Balor watched the blackbird escape, following his flight with his narrow yellow cat's eyes. For a moment, Thomas lost strength and plummeted towards the floor and Balor the cat pounced at the blackbird on the wing.

But the blackbird was too quick and Thomas flew straight and true, out of the hold, across the waves and landed by the banks of the River Flesk. He heard the waters lapping by the bank and, exhausted, dipped his beak in for a much-needed drink.

Cassie watched her little brother escape and

was glad. For a moment he had wrong-footed Balor who snarled and paced around the boat. She jumped in front of her enemy.

"I told you that you'd be undone by the power of the weak!" Her voice quaked and her knees buckled under her but her one thought was to buy some time for Thomas.

"Foolish child, we are only beginning," Balor's foul tones took on a feline nastiness.

Cassie felt something against her foot and picked up her little sister's broken necklace with the bark of Beith, the Birch. Prepared to die, she closed her eyes and held the necklace up in front of her face. Then Balor leapt at her, tearing at her flesh with his claws. She fell to the floor, blood pumping from her cheeks.

Then Balor, the cat, performed a mighty jump right out of the boat across the waves to land inches from Thomas in his blackbird shape. The cat nearly grasped him in his claws. Just in time, Thomas flew into the branches of a hawthorn-tree, exhausted from the chase.

"Keep going," whispered the tree. "I am of

Uath, eat my berry." It was the special tree that Cernunnos, the Master of Shapeshifters, had revealed to him.

Thomas plucked a red berry in his beak. Immediately, he felt a surge of stength.

"Beware," breathed the tree.

The cat was padding silently up the branches, his sharp claws extended, ready to strike. The berry warmed Thomas's insides. As the cat leapt towards him, he took wing and prepared for his next change. The pressure of the effort made him think that his brain would explode. It was hard for him to control his flight and he veered dangerously low towards the ground. He beat his wings madly.

In mid-flight, he felt himself changing and the violence of the change forced him into a nosedive. He landed badly but then he found his feet.

He had paws and a strong, sinewy back and a muzzle. He was graceful and strong and covered in a rough wiry coat. He barked loudly and then growled, a low, rumbling noise. He was a wolfhound with keen sight, power and swiftness.

Balor, the cat, meowed harshly and the fur went up on his back. He launched himself at Thomas, spitting with his teeth bared. Thomas's heart beat in his chest and for a moment he was frozen, unsure what to do. But then his animal instincts took over. The wolfhound caught the cat with a blow on his back quarters.

Balor recoiled from the blow and hissed. They both backed off and squared up to each other. Balor, the cat, was no match for Thomas, the wolfhound. Thomas smelled blood. Now maybe he should move in for the kill.

"Ah you have learned a few party tricks," taunted Balor, "but it takes more than the bite of an apple to take on a master like me!"

At that Thomas lost his concentration and faltered in his attack.

Then before his eyes the cat transformed. It became a wolf with horrible claws and huge jaws filled with sharp teeth. Balor sprang at Thomas. The wolf and the wolfhound fell to the ground, fighting for their lives. Balor, the wolf, started to get the better of Thomas. He could feel the stinging of the wounds where Balor's sharp claws tore his flesh. The wolf was about to bite into the neck of the wolfhound when a thunderstorm rumbled across the island. Hard rain slashed the animal shapes of Balor and Thomas in combat. The comet was drawing near.

Out at sea, the approach of the comet's tail caused the sea to boil and heave. But the boat was kept upright by the efforts of Granny Clíona, still spinning round like a top. Inside the hold, Cassie came out of her daze. In a vision, she saw Thomas's change from a blackbird to a wolfhound. She opened her eyes and felt dizzy and sick. Her cheek stung where Balor had torn into her flesh but she was no longer bleeding. The necklace with the bark of the silver birch must have saved her and she put it in her pocket for safekeeping. She hoped Thomas could keep going and the one thought in her mind now was to reach Connle and Granny Clíona and tell them what had happened.

Cassie's legs shook under her as she walked

towards the chair where she'd last seen her little sister and when she reached it she threw her arms around it. "Oh, it's too late!" she cried. "My beautiful little sister is dead!"

She closed her eyes in despair and then screamed in horror! She saw Thomas as a wolfhound grappling with the ugly, snarling wolf. It was too awful and she opened her eyes so she would see no more. She was so afraid and helpless. She felt in her pocket and found one of her hazelnuts. She cracked it open and nibbled on it, praying for some inspiration, some chink of light in this dark place. Immediately, she felt enough courage to close her eyes again.

She saw Uath the Hawthorn, when the Sacred Grove was destroyed. She remembered Thomas meeting the tree and its promise of protection from lightning strikes! With all her will, Cassie tried to send her thoughts to Thomas.

The wolf tried to hold Thomas in its claws and bite his neck. Thomas struggled with every sinew in his body. But it was hopeless; he just didn't have the strength.

"What use is it resist with both your sisters gone?" Balor taunted him.

Anger rose in Thomas's blood and then a stab of sorrowful pain. Balor was right. What use was it?

But just as he was about to give up, a vision of Cassie came into his mind. He knew that Balor was lying. A mighty crack of thunder tore through the sky and a flash of lightning temporarily blinded Balor, the wolf. Cassie's voice came into Thomas's head, "Fly to the hawthorn!" As the wolf pulled away from him, Thomas saw his chance. He bounded away and sought refuge from the storm back under the branches of the hawthorn-tree.

Thomas wasn't beaten yet. He smelled the river near him. His head throbbed and his stomach somersaulted inside out. But what shape should he take?

The white willow by the water sang out to Thomas. "Swim, salmon, swim!"

Thomas leapt at the river as a wolfhound but landed as a salmon, his silver scales flashing in the water.

The wolf came panting to the water just as Thomas disappeared below the surface. On the bank, the tree branches swung around, trying to knock Balor over. For a moment he was entangled in the branches but then, in the blink of an eye, he transformed himself into an otter and dived into the fast-flowing stream.

Thomas, the salmon, swam downstream, strong and sturdy on his belly, and felt the otter in his slipstream. He knew the otter was fast and sleek in the water and had powerful jaws and sharp teeth. Thomas began to fade. More and more, he relied on the strength of the current to carry him downstream. Exhausted, he swam over to the bank and hid in a tangle of reeds. He had to think what to do. It was no use running away from Balor forever, he thought. He was going to have to stand his ground and fight. But he was unsure what shape he should take. His energy was ebbing away and the changing was so violent it was making him even weaker. His body might be weak but he suddenly felt clear and determined. I will be guided by Cernunnos, he realised, when the time is right.

At that moment Cernunnos's voice spoke to him in his confusion: "Remember how you rode on my back?"

The otter swam past him but in a split second sensed that his prey had eluded him. He swished his sleek body round towards the reeds and saw a flash of silver. Thomas saw the sharp teeth, the evil sulphurous eyes. The otter pounced – and found himself kicked in the face by a stag that was rising out of the water!

In the nick of time, Thomas had found some strength to turn himself into the stag. He panted, his breath coming hard and fast, and shook his antlers. He was a majestic beast and he would run no more. It was only a matter of time before Balor caught him. This was his last chance to kill his enemy. Even if he died, at least his sisters might escape. He held his head high and roared a challenge.

He did not have long to wait.

A shape rose from the water and in mid-air Balor transformed from an otter into a great, marauding boar with a long muzzle and a ridge of stiff bristles along his spine. His huge tusks were aimed straight at Thomas's neck. The boar lunged but Thomas had seen him coming and leapt aside. He was strong and quick. The boar landed in a heap but quickly gained his feet, his large fierce head and shoulders tapering to smaller hindquarters. Thomas felt the blood coursing through his veins and felt the majestic strength of the stag. He pounded the earth with his paws and lowered his crown of antlers to fight. For better or for worse it would be a fight to the death.

On board the yacht, Granny Clíona appeared at Cassie's side.

"Don't give in to the fog of despair, my dear," she said, her voice kind but resolute.

"But Nancy is dead," wailed Cassie, "and Thomas is locked in deadly combat with Balor. I cannot live without them. I used to think I could never live *with* them and wanted to be an only child. But I was wrong. I never thought I'd say this but they are my best friends."

Granny Clíona touched her. It was like gossamer silk or a cool breeze.

"Close your eyes – what do you see?" Granny Clíona urged.

Cassie nibbled on a half-eaten nut, then closed her eyes tightly and concentrated. She saw Thomas as a majestic stag in a stand-off with Balor's deadly boar's tusks.

Cassie opened her eyes and told Granny Clíona of her vision.

"The time of reckoning is approaching and there is still hope," said Granny Clíona, "or our name isn't McColl!"

With what was left of her strength, Cassie climbed up to the deck and headed for where the currach was tethered to the side of the yacht. She moved like a robot following Granny Clíona's orders to untie the rope and leap into the currach. She drew a deep breath, praying she would land safely. But just as she was about to jump overboard a freak wind carried the currach away!

On land, the boar and the stag faced each other head-on and charged like medieval knights. There was a clang of bone on horn when Thomas's antlers collided with the huge tusks of the boar. They pulled apart and braced themselves for the next attack. Thomas was exhausted. But then he thought of poor little Nancy in the grip of evil Balor and anger rose in his veins. This time the boar charged with all its strength but Thomas once more nimbly evaded him and even nicked the boar's thick hide with his sharp antlers. But the injury only made the boar angrier.

Thomas was on his last legs. He thought, I am going to die soon but at least I fought as best I could. The boar barrelled towards him at a hundred miles an hour, his tusks deadly weapons aiming for his heart.

But just as the boar was inches away Thomas thought, no, I want to live and made one last great leap for his life . . .

⚊⚊

Cassie was trapped on the boat! She looked

333

around in desperation for another lifeboat but Drax's men had taken them.

"It's not safe to stay on this boat," Granny Clíona urged her. "Who knows what might happen when the comet passes overhead and Balor might come back at any minute."

"We've got to stop that evil man before he does any more damage!" said Cassie.

"That's the spirit," Granny Clíona replied.

But the waters around the yacht were choppy and dangerous and without a boat Cassie didn't know how she was going to get back to the beach. It was a hopeless situation!

"Come on, Cassie girl," encouraged Granny Clíona. "We'll have to make do with something else."

Cassie felt rooted to the spot, numb with fear and sorrow as Granny Clíona frantically charged round the deck trying to find another craft.

"If only I had my broom, then you could fly with me," sighed Granny Clíona.

Cassie looked up and then she saw it. Her one hope of escape. Drax's helicopter!

CHAPTER 15

Connle paced up and down on the beach keeping watch for any sign of Jarlath and the children. He held Jarlath's pocket watch in his hand and constantly checked it to see if it was working again. The Boogan had told him to hold it up when the comet passed by and it might mend. He also kept a look out at the sky, hoping to catch sight of the comet's fiery tail. Out at sea, the yacht stayed afloat in the centre of a boiling sea. The storm raged near the shore but it was also strangely calm on the beach.

A loud buzzing sound shattered the air. A beam of light came down from the sky and fixed Connle in its glare. He looked up. It was Drax's helicopter! Connle felt a stab of cold fear in the pit of his belly and his legs trembled from under him. He couldn't move with fright. The helicopter jerked towards the shore and Connle's clothes swished around him in the downwind.

Then another black shape loomed above in the sky. It was coal black and had ragged wings and a big red beak. It was the Corra! It launched itself at the helicopter, attacking the cockpit. The helicopter lurched in the sky and began to fall to earth.

"Look out!" the Boogan shouted. Connle crouched into a ball and rolled to safety finding shelter behind a rock with the Boogan.

Inside the helicopter, Cassie was too angry to be frightened. How dare that horrible black bird try to knock her off course! She pulled in the gearstick and launched straight at the giant ugly bird that was looming in front of her. This was the last thing the Corra expected.

A terrible screech rent the air. The bird lurched away, one wing broken, and fell towards the sea. But the impact of the crash sent the helicopter into a tailspin. Cassie fought desperately at the controls to bring it out of its dive. Just as she managed to pull the helicopter upwards, the Corra rallied.

Through the windscreen Cassie saw its terrible horny beak open wide as it lurched at the windscreen. It was trying to gobble her up. For a moment she was eye to eye with the horrible bird and saw the huge fangs in his horned beak. It lunged at the glass, causing the craft to shudder and the glass to crack.

Panicking, she pressed a button on the control panel. The propellers extended and turned into blades. Cassie nosed the craft down, trying to evade the Corra who careered through the air towards her. As the Corra dropped down to her level, Cassie quickly pulled under it and reversed direction, rising in the air, catching it by surprise.

For a moment, Cassie throught they'd plunged into the sea when she couldn't see out through the cracked glass. But then she realised it was the oozing black blood of the Corra that was obscuring her vision. The helicopter shuddered as the Corra was cut to a thousand pieces in the blades. The helicopter took to the air again. But she realised the impact of the crash was causing her to lose height fast.

Down on the beach, Connle peered over the rock and saw Granny Clíona's white shape above Drax's black-and-yellow-striped helicopter, guiding the propellers. He wondered why she was doing that. The helicopter hovered over the choppy waters and threatened to crash into the sea but it juddered to a stop and landed just at the shoreline.

Connle and the Boogan watched from their hiding place as Granny Clíona flew towards them. The helicopter was buffeted by the waves and would be carried out to sea in a minute.

"Quick, the door!" Granny Clíona shouted.

Connle was roused from his shock and ran to the helicopter door. He pulled the handle with all his might and forced it open.

He was amazed to see Cassie on the other side in the cockpit! But he saw from her wounded face that all was not well. She fell into his arms.

"She's gone," Cassie wailed, "just like Jarlath! Oh, that evil, evil man!"

Connle helped Cassie onto the beach where the Boogan awaited their arrival.

"I didn't know you could fly a helicopter! What a brave girl you are!"

"I learned it from a computer game," said Cassie, "but I'm afraid I'm not brave enough." Cassie sobbed as she told him what had happened to Nancy. How she had shut her eyes at the last minute and in that second Balor had swallowed their poor little sister.

Connle tried hard not to cry. He wanted to be brave for Cassie's sake.

"I think that Jarlath might have been saved by the Merrows," he said when he could speak again. "This kind gentleman, the Boogan, saw someone wearing a red cap come to a drowning man's rescue."

Cassie finished off a nut and closed her eyes. She saw a vision of Jarlath being pulled through the water by someone wearing a red cap of feathers. Connle's eyes shone with hope when she told him. Granny Clíona instructed the Boogan to go to the top of the cliff to call out to the Merrows.

"But what of Thomas?" Connle asked Cassie.

Cassie told him that the last vision she saw was of Thomas as a stag about to do battle with Balor as a boar. "I fear the worst. And I can see nothing of Nancy, no matter how hard I try," she sobbed quietly. "Oh please, don't let Thomas be dead too!"

Just then the Boogan returned to them on the beach.

"I've been calling out to the Merrows," he said, "and all I can hear is laughing and giggling, like a pack of naughty schoolgirls. They're mad ones, they are, yerra. I pity the poor young fella who falls into their hands. They came here from Dublin Bay several hundred years ago and since then they've been nothing but trouble."

As the Boogan attended to the wounds on Cassie's face, Granny Clíona and Connle walked a little way off to the edge of the waves, deep in conversation. Then the Boogan went to fetch something from a fissure in a rock. He returned and handed Granny Clíona a broom. Her eyes lit up.

"You left this with me hundreds of years ago in case there was ever an emergency," he said, "and I think this is it."

"I didn't want to upset Cassie," said Granny Clíona, "but it will be no easy matter to get Jarlath back. The Merrows lay claim to any drowning man they rescue and I've never known one to come back."

Connle scratched his head and looked worried. "And, oh dear, what if they have already given him a fish's tail?" he said. "It's going to take another miracle to get him back in one piece!"

Leaving the Boogan to take care of Cassie, Granny Clíona and Connle climbed on board the broom. Soon they were sweeping over the waves trying to find the Merrows.

Connle pricked up his ears and he heard giggles and loud hoots of laughter coming from the north. At the bottom of the cliff, there was a small stony beach that could only be reached from the sea. As they drew closer they could hear someone talking in a sing-song voice.

"Jarlath, you make me scarlet!"

And then another voice, throaty and mocking. "Yer gorgeous! Can I be your mott, ye beut?"

"I think they are at the circle of rocks just off the shore," said Granny Clíona, "that we call Poolbeg Cove." She pointed the broom in that direction and they headed down from the cliff.

The fiery light from the burning yacht gave the beach a mysterious glow, matched by the comet lighting up the sky. They saw a group of young women sitting at a rock pool fussing over someone who was lying on a bed of dried seaweed. One of them had long blonde hair reaching down to her waist, another thick dark hair like tendrils of seaweed and a third deep brown curly hair with a little red cap of feathers perched on her head.

All of them had silvery tails like fishes. They wore belts of coral around their waists and pearls around their necks and very little else. In the middle of them, Jarlath was propped on his seaweedy bed. He looked dazed and blissful at the same time.

"Fand, see what your necklace looks like on him," said the blonde one to the dark one.

"Great idea, Mara," said the dark one. She took off her pearls and wound them around Jarlath's neck.

"Sionna," said Fand to the brown-haired one with the red cap, "give him your cap to try on."

Sionna laughed and perched her red cap on Jarlath's head at a rakish angle. Then she spoke to the blonde Merrow, "Go on, Mara, let's see the belt on him."

Mara took off her belt of coral. It shone like phosphorescence in the comet light. She was about to wrap it around his waist when Granny Clíona's voice rang out.

"Look at the state of him! I can stand it no longer. You are making an awful fool of the man!"

Granny Clíona brought the broom down to their eye level. Connle tried to hide behind her because he was afraid of the Merrows mocking him.

"Who's this, lover boy? Is it your oul' wan?" Fand asked Jarlath.

"And is that your oul' fella?" Mara said, tossing her blonde tresses and continuing to wrap the belt around Jarlath.

"Excuse me, I'm not his oul' fella," said Connle full of dignity, "and Mistress McColl is not my oul' wan. Jarlath is her many times great-grandson."

"I bet you'd prefer a kiss from our lovely lips than having to look at her wrinkled ould gob," jeered Sionna twirling her brown curls in her fingers.

Granny Clíona shook with fury, nearly causing Connle to fall off the broomstick.

"I'll have you know, Jarlath is spoken for," said Connle, "so put that in your pipe an' smoke it!"

"Well, you'd never have guessed from the way he was chasin' my tail!" scoffed Mara, the blonde.

"That's because he was drowning. He'd have to be that desperate to chase you!" Granny Clíona said, losing her temper.

"Ooh, get a load of yer one!" mocked Fand. "You spiteful oul' biddy! I bet you were burned at the stake."

Granny Clíona was getting angrier and angrier but she tried to hold her tongue.

"Now come along, Jarlath," she said, "there's a good lad. The children need you. Hop on board."

At the mention of the children, Jarlath tried to stir himself but the pearls around his neck weighed him down.

Connle was about to jump off the broom but Granny Clíona suddenly moved upwind and he was left hanging off the end. The Merrows tried to grab him by the leg but they couldn't reach.

"I'll-I'll be damned if I put another man in your clutches," Clíona shouted at them as Connle clambered back on the broom. She drove the broom off behind the rocks.

"Leave this to me," whispered Connle. "The Merrows are a bit like the fairy folk. They take a bit of humouring and fine talk. And with no disrespect, they don't like women."

Granny Clíona calmed down. "It is worth a try," she said.

The broom hovered back towards the rocks.

Connle smiled politely and blushed.

"I've sailed the seven seas," he said, "and met with the folk of the air, the earth and the next

world but the beautiful Merrows of Inish Álainn
are beyond compare."

The three heads tossed their hair. They seemed
interested in what he had to say. They preened
themselves and purred like cats, charmed by his
words.

He went on, "Neither diamonds, nor gold –"

But then all three of them exploded into
laughter.

"That's enough of your blarney," Sionna
jeered. "You can save that flowery rubbish for the
fairies!"

"I bet they'll give you short shrift when you go
and start moaning at them!" Mara scoffed.

"What do you mean?" asked Granny Clíona.

"You keep out of our business and we'll keep
out of yours," Sionna sniffed.

Connle was about to tell them to wash their
mouths out with soap when the earth shook with
a sudden tremor and even the brazen Merrows
jumped in fright.

They heard Cassie calling from the beach.

"Don't think you can get away with this, you

brazen hussies. We'll be back to sort you out later!" Connle shouted.

But the Merrows were too busy fussing over Jarlath to pay any heed.

As they gained the beach, there was a great whoosh of air and a wounded stag landed on a patch of sand between rock and sea. They gasped and knew in an instant that it was Thomas. The night was suddenly illuminated with a thousand bright colours as the comet entered their sky. Then they saw that the stag was badly wounded and was dripping blood on the white sand from his injured foot.

There was a terrible blood-curdling growl and a huge marauding boar landed heavily near the stag. His cruel tusks shone in the light of the comet.

"It's Balor!" shrieked Cassie.

The boar gave a snort through his pointy snout.

Without thinking of her safety, Cassie tried to run towards the stag, breaking away from Connle who tried to hold her back.

"I'm going to help my brother and if I can't I'll

die with him!" She pulled away with all her strength.

As she ran towards the stag, everything became a blur. The boar glared at her. She paused. She saw his thick grey skin, the tough hairs on his back, the snarling jaws. The boar pawed the ground and lowered its head, ready to charge through her. He ran at her, going faster and faster, gaining speed as he charged. She froze. In one second, she would be gored to death by his sharp yellow tusks. But just as the boar was getting closer and she could smell his evil breath, the stag leapt out of nowhere.

The boar followed her startled gaze and saw the stag land by her side. Thomas in his stag shape nudged his sister aside and stood to meet the charging boar. They locked antler and tusk, fighting to the death. As he pulled away, the stag managed to wound the boar on his back. The boar roared but didn't seem to be seriously hurt despite the big gash in his side and caught the stag on his hindquarters with his sharp yellow tusks. The stag fell to the ground near the water's edge and let out a cry of pain.

Thomas was slumped and wounded and couldn't go on.

"Death to the enemies of Balor!" the boar roared.

He grunted and snorted and charged towards the stag.

Cassie couldn't bear to watch and Connle and Granny Clíona cried in anguish. The boar charged, the stag didn't move. But, just as the boar was about to gouge the stag with his tusks, the stag disappeared and the boar ran straight into the sea.

Cassie ran to the place where the stag should have been. In the place of the noble animal was a small, squashed red hawthorn berry. Balor the boar arose from the waves as an angry wasp and flew over to the sand, ready to gobble up the red berry.

Cassie didn't hesitate. She picked up a piece of driftwood and whacked the wasp against a rock.

Connle and Granny Clíona ran toward Cassie.

"It's a hawthorn berry," Granny Clíona said.

"But can it be Thomas?" Cassie said. "Thomas and I never changed into non-animal things even if Nancy did."

"Magical things happen at the time of the comet. It must be him," Granny Clíona said. "It was well done turning into a berry because it made Balor think he had won the fight."

Then Cassie remembered their meeting with Cernunnos in the vales of the Otherworld and the promise of Uath in the Sacred Grove that her help would be revealed. "It's the berry of the hawthorn tree that was shown to us!" she cried.

The comet was now full centre in the sky and there was a ticking sound. Jarlath's watch was working again. And before their eyes, the berry transformed back into Thomas. Cassie ran to him and held him in her arms. He was covered in scars and badly wounded.

Connle picked up the piece of driftwood with the squashed wasp on it – all that was left of the mighty Balor in his latest incarnation, the evil Sir Dignum Drax.

The Boogan examined the piece of driftwood. "Quick, throw it out to sea," he said. It was in the shape of forked lightning and was harder than normal wood.

Connle handed it to Cassie. "The Mulally twins say you have the best throw on the island," Connle said to her. Cassie took the piece of driftwood and flung it with all her might towards the yacht. It sailed through the air and landed in the yacht like a stick of dynamite. The comet's tail sparked a rainbow of colours. Out at sea, *The Ocean Beast* exploded in a thousand shades to match.

The yacht erupted like a volcano. Then a huge black cloud of smoke belched up towards the sky. The smoke turned from violet to green, to sulphurous yellow, and billowed into many shapes, transforming one to the other. Hovering through it was a big yellow evil eye and through the smoke there was a giant foot, a boar, a wolf, a large satellite dish, a huge pylon, an otter, millions of television sets, billions of pounds, dollars, euros, yen, all the currencies of the world. And then, screaming in agony, the shape of Sir Dignum Drax. They all burned and screamed and withered away to be replaced by another smoking image under the intense heat of the comet's tail. They saw a Roman emperor, a terrible barbarian from Mongolia, a grasping fat monk, a giant Viking, a hideous obese English king, an explorer wearing an old-fashioned pith helmet.

"They must be some of the identities that Balor assumed when looking for the Star Splinter and waiting for the return of the comet," Granny Clíona said, but she looked worried. "I fear that's not the end of him. You have destroyed his earthly form. But Balor is a shapeshifter and he will find a new form to inhabit. The only one who can vanquish him forever is a god of his own kind."

But Connle was more concerned about Thomas who was badly wounded and could barely speak.

Cassie's poor little heart was broken. "Oh don't leave me too," she cried to Thomas. "You are so brave. You saved my life. I'll never call you chicken or scaredy cat again."

Thomas's face was white. "Nancy," he breathed, "did we save her?"

Cassie couldn't bear to answer and burst into tears.

"Balor ate her," she cried, "just before you turned into a fly. I closed my eyes because I was trying to see into the future. And in a second Balor swallowed her." She could hardly bear to say the words.

Tears ran down Thomas's cheeks.

"Now don't be fretting yourself," Connle soothed, taking some ointments from his pockets. And then from an inside pocket he pulled out Nancy's Dog, which he'd found on the lawn just after Nancy and Jarlath were abducted. The sight of it made him sob out loud but he disguised it as a cough and handed the teddy to Cassie.

The Boogan covered Thomas's wounds with strips of seaweed and Connle applied all kinds of potions. Cassie held on to the teddy as if for dear life, hugging it close to her chest.

Granny Clíona was lost in thought. "I wonder where the Star Splinter is? Cassie, are you saying you didn't actually see Balor swallow Nancy?"

Cassie shook her head.

"And Thomas, don't speak, just nod your head. Did you see Balor put Nancy in his mouth?"

Thomas shook his head.

"Nor did we hear the Banshee sing," said Connle. "I haven't seen sight nor light of her and she's a personal friend. She always wails when one of ours has died."

Granny Clíona nodded in agreement.

"Neither of you can say for definite that Balor swallowed Nancy," she continued. "So there might be a teeny, tiny hope that he didn't?"

"And surely if Drax had the Star Splinter we would not have been able to defeat him," added Connle, catching on to Granny Clíona's thought process.

"Was there anything strange that you can think of to do with the fairies?" Granny Clíona asked Cassie suddenly. "Those cheeky Merrows said something to Connle about saving his flowery rubbish for the fairies – that they'll give us short shrift when we go and start moaning at them. And when I asked them what they meant they clammed up."

Cassie rubbed her head. "Where do I begin? There was nothing normal about the Midnight Court!"

"Have you any long sight left?" said Granny Clíona.

Cassie found one of the last remaining nuts in her pocket. She nibbled it and closed her eyes.

"I can see only a cup," she said. "It is like a chalice, studded with diamonds and it contains a red juice. And I see a silver platter laden with berries."

Suddenly, Connle looked like a light had gone on in his head.

"You're thinking what I'm thinking!" he said to Granny Clíona.

"All aboard my trusty steed!" Granny Clíona said. "I'm a bit out of practice so it might be a bumpy ride."

"But where are we going?" asked Cassie. "I don't understand what has got you so excited."

"Wait and see, my Chingles," smiled Granny Clíona. "Wait and see!"

So they all squeezed onto the broomstick and flew off over the island, which was lit up by the bright light of the comet travelling across the sky. From high up in the clouds they saw lights switched on again in the houses. The fiendish fog that had shrouded the island was beginning to clear. They could see the angry gash in the ground where the Sacred Grove used to be and Mr Mulally's pub where things were beginning to stir. But it seemed their final destination was closer to home.

"The Fairy Fort!" Cassie exclaimed as Granny Clíona directed the broom to land in the field.

The ground with its flashing lights rose to meet them and the air parted as they dive-bombed down. As they came in to land, they saw some of the fairies they'd met at the Midnight Court, hovering near the haystack.

They heard their little sister before they saw her.

"I want my brudder and my sister and I want my Dog. *Woof, woof, woof!*" shouted Nancy.

Cassie and Thomas leapt from the broom and raced past all the fairies who had gathered to meet them. There, on a mossy bank, surrounded by attendants, Nancy sat large as life. She fidgeted with the catkin given to her by Fearn, the Alder, for protection in fairy realms that Áine had threaded on the bracelet. And when she saw her brother and sister, her face lit up to match the comet itself. She smiled and laughed and Granny Clíona and Connle sniffled and tried to hug each other to see her so happy, though to everyone else it looked like Granny Clíona was running through Connle.

Granny Clíona introduced herself to her youngest ancestor.

Nancy was delighted. "I'm a wish too," she cried, "but I'm not a ghost!"

But what of Cassie and Thomas? They smothered their baby sister in a huge hug. And

Nancy was even more delighted when Cassie produced Dog. Cassie felt so happy she thought she would burst. "I love you," Nancy said simply to everybody in turn, and finally asked, "Where's Uncle Jarlath?"

They explained to her that he had gone for a little swim and because she was only nearly three she just said oh, as if this was the most natural thing in the world. Then she grew a little frightened.

"And the nasty man?" she asked.

"Only you can help us now," said Connle gently. "Do you remember that Star Splinter that the Pike gave you?"

But some of the fairies were annoyed at the interruption to their court. Before Nancy could speak, her friend Dris butted in.

"Excuse us but we were in the middle of something," he said crossly, "Nancy was going to do her party trick!"

Cassie's face reddened with anger and Connle was about to shout an angry retort but one stern look from Granny Clíona made them all freeze.

"Control yourselves," she hissed at them. "Be careful with the fairies. We need their help!"

Remembering their last encounter over the porridge, Connle bit his tongue.

The fairies gathered round in excitement, waiting for Nancy to repeat the spectacular vomiting trick that had so impressed them the last time.

Gritting his teeth, Connle patted Nancy on the back and whispered in her ear. "Just pretend you're going to get sick."

Nancy was happy to oblige with a display of enthusiastic grunts and groans. The fairies watched in anticipation, following her every cough and splutter. But nothing happened and they began to flounce off in disappointment.

But then her stomach really did heave. She gave a sudden cough and out of her mouth shot the most spectacular multicoloured projectile vomit anyone had ever seen. Thomas and Cassie sniggered as the fairies were sprayed by vile globs. They were especially delighted that the cranky Dris was completely covered in a sticky-looking mess.

"Hope you got what you wanted," laughed Connle as the fairy wiped the vomit off his face in disgust.

Nancy gave one final heave and out of her mouth with the speed of a comet, shot the Star Splinter. It landed bang on a golden dish at the feet of King Finbhearra.

It was the first time any of them had had a proper look at it. It was a million different colours, shaped like a comet about the size of a walnut but when it was moved it had its own brightly coloured, flashing comet's tail. It was more beautiful than a diamond or a pearl or crystal or any precious stone they'd ever seen. They marvelled at it. They were glad Balor had never got his filthy hands on it.

"We are thrice blessed," exclaimed King Finbhearra, "to set eyes on the sacred Star Splinter that has been sung about in songs for thousands of years!"

"Yes, well, we must go now," said Granny Clíona. "We still have two more people to rescue. And Balor isn't done for yet." And she told them about the sickness of Áine and the disappearance of Jarlath.

"By your grace, we will look to Áine, Chingles," Queen Úna said. "Grant us the Star Splinter. It will restore her. And we will guard it from Balor."

The Star Splinter sat on the golden bowl, glowing gently, and it lit up at the mention of Áine's name. It looked beautiful and otherworldly and the children didn't hesitate.

"There is no time to waste," said Cassie. "Yes, take it. You are our friends and allies. We must go look for our uncle and see what Balor will do next."

The three Chingles and Connle climbed on to Granny Clíona's broomstick. With an extra person, Nancy, wedged between Cassie and Thomas, it was a tight squeeze, and they had to bunch up tightly together. Connle kept slipping and had to hang on at the broom end.

"How did you know she would be here?" Cassie asked Connle.

"You remember that first night we visited and Nancy swallowed a berry but then sicked up most of it? And it was agreed she would have to spend a little time with the fairy folk because she had eaten fairy food? When you saw the silver chalice and platter in your vision it sounded to me like a fairy feast," he explained, "and I thought maybe they might have come for her in her hour of need. Also Balor definitely didn't have the Star Splinter. Otherwise he would have activated it to take over the sun. Which meant she must be still alive." Cassie smiled but looked wan.

Granny Clíona looked back at the children with concern. They looked so young and vulnerable. They had stood up to the might of Balor but the battle had taken its toll. She hoped they still had some strength to face up to whatever terrible magic Balor would next unleash.

CHAPTER 16

G ranny Clíona directed the broom over the cliff.

"Something is rising from the boat!" Cassie shouted as they drew near and came in to land. "Look!"

They all scrambled off the broom and stared in horror.

Out at sea, a hideous spirit rose from the boat in a plume of smoke. The children clung to each other and shivered, frightened to the core. This was worse even than Balor as a boar, worse than smelling his evil breath up close. A smell of sulphur, like rotten eggs, invaded the beach. Nancy became hysterical.

"It's the bad man," she wailed, her little shoulders shaking with horror. Connle picked her up and held her tight. The hideous shape rose higher and higher from the boat until it loomed over the whole beach. Seabirds flew off in alarm.

"Ha, ha!" the shape laughed. "I am as old as the earth. You can destroy my body but my spirit lives on. And soon I will take a new form. All I need is someone whose burning desire outruns their strength." The hideous shape came closer and closer, rising from the blackened hull of the burning yacht. It seemed to suck all the life out of the Chingles.

It was hard to describe, a black vapour moving like a pestilent fog, but they knew it was the very essence of evil. They could outwit Sir Dignum Drax, the media baron and property developer, they could even do battle against Balor of the Evil eye with cunning and shapeshifting but how could they ever fight a vile black phantom that they could neither wound nor capture?

Granny Clíona rose on her broom and moved

towards the phantom. But his putrid breath blew her back.

"Foolish old woman! You thought you were so clever creating a vortex to keep the yacht afloat. I could swallow you whole in an instant!" It was the voice of Drax, of Balor, but even more harsh and unpleasant.

Granny Clíona was surrounded by a black vapour and suspended in the air. She was imprisoned in a cage of fog.

The phantom's cold, clammy breath shot out towards the Chingles. "You think you have cheated me of the Star Splinter," he whispered. "This is your last chance to surrender it. Then I might consider sparing your lives."

Connle, still holding Nancy in one arm, put his other around Thomas and Cassie.

"We don't have it," said Cassie in a shaking voice.

The vapour drew so close they could feel its breath on their faces. It was a horrible sensation, burning like ice.

"Tell me where it is," commanded the phantom.

But the Chingles didn't have to answer because a blinding light came into the sky, piercing the phantom's gloom.

"I have the Star Splinter," a clear voice rang out. "Or have you forgotten about me?"

In the East of the sky, surrounded by glorious golden light, a beautiful woman arose. She was dressed in gold, her hair blazed around her head and her eyes shone with the light of the sun. Her brow was radiant and she suffused the whole island with her golden light. Even her beautiful gown seemed woven from light shot through with the colours of the rainbow.

"It's Áine!" gasped Cassie.

And there indeed was their friend, restored to her full majesty, in her goddess state, as they'd never seen her before. In her left hand she carried the Star Splinter. Her radiant light shone through it and it refracted in thousands of beams in all the colours of the world – a prism of glowing light. Everyone watched in awe.

There was a high-pitched hiss like the sound

of air escaping from a million tires as the phantom retreated.

"Long have we battled, Balor of the Evil Eye, for supremacy of the Sky," Áine said in her strong clear voice. "Long have you tried to unthrone me as Goddess of the Sun. And you thought the Star Splinter would allow you to create a new sun in the old one's place under your evil will." She shone the Star Splinter towards the phantom and it hissed again. "But many small good things can unite and defeat one big evil thing. Before I destroy you forever, tell me of my sister Finnen. Where is she? Did you kill her?"

The vapour shuddered and Balor's voice came out, weaker but still terrifying.

"She was the only thing I ever loved. She could have been my queen. She left to go I know not where. Disappeared into thin air. At first I thought she took the Star Splinter with her. But in truth, I wanted her as much as the power of the skies. And then I realised. She had kept it hidden in the lake. All I had to do was come back for it when the comet once more roared near the earth."

Áine's bright rays burnt stronger and she flared once more at the vapour, which shuddered away.

Balor's voice came back smaller. "If you do not believe me, look into the Star Splinter – it records all that comes to pass around it."

Áine's blazing eyes looked at the stone. She saw reflected in it like a tape spooling backwards, first the recent events, the fairies coming to rescue her, Nancy vomiting the Star Splinter up, the children meeting the Pike, the capture in Ferdia's Cape, and many other previous happenings in the history of the Pike. And then it showed the battle of Glimmering Lake between Balor and her sister Finnen, the creation of the Worm from his snot and the Pike from his eyelash and Balor sinking in the lake himself. Then as he sank, Finnen rose from the lake as a swan. For one brief second, she looked out of the stone, straight into Áine's eyes and then disappeared into thin air.

Balor, for once in his life, had told the truth. Áine looked longingly at the stone as if she could reach her sister there. Her desire to find her sister burned strong.

Balor's voice came out of the vapour, all silky and persuasive. "I can help you find her."

Áine paused and her face went all dreamy and sad. For a moment, the vapour seemed to grow thicker and formed into Balor's former giant shape.

"Come towards me!" Balor commanded.

Áine took a step forward. The children, Connle and Granny Clíona cried out to her from the beach but she didn't seem to hear them and walked forward like a blind woman. With every step, the Balor shape seemed to grow more real and lifelike as if he was emerging from the vapour. And he was taking on Finnen's form, first as a swan, then as a woman. He seemed to be sucking the life out of Áine.

Cassie closed her eyes. She felt a panic in her breast as if her heart was a small bird trapped in her chest. She reached into her pocket and swallowed her last whole hazelnut, shaking with fear. She closed her eyes and saw a vision of a woman with red hair who looked like Áine calling out from beyond the stars. She was calling to her sister, saying, *"Do not trust Balor!"*

Cassie had to try to tell Áine!

"Stop!" she shouted. *"Do not believe Balor! He is tricking you! You will only find Finnen by searching beyond the stars!"*

The phantom shape that had been gaining life from the Star Splinter and Áine shuddered. But Áine heard Cassie's words and turned towards her. She saw in Cassie's face the pure light of truth. In a moment she saw through the deception of the phantom of Balor, who was trying to exploit her desperate need to find her sister. She turned her eyes back on the phantom and they blazed with anger.

Áine surged with golden light and the Star Splinter glowed in her hand. A ray of sharp light, silver like a blade, flashed from it. The vapour of Balor shrank back. It lost the shape of Finnen and became a filthy, dirty fog.

"Be gone, you evil presence! All you ever brought was pestilence and loss. You are nothing!"

Áine aimed the blade of light. There was a high-pitched scream and the vaporous phantom burned away into a plume of blue smoke. The smell was so acrid and horrible the children gagged. There was a long shuddering wail and the evil shape dissolved completely.

The children and Connle looked up. The vaporous ghost had vanished and the only trace left of him was the blackened stump of the yacht, which now listed to one side and began to sink into the sea.

Áine held up the Star Splinter.

"Splinter from space, older than the earth, go back to the heavens! And I name you Finnen, in honour of my sister!" She threw back her hand and flung the Star Splinter into the sky.

They watched as the Star Splinter spun into the heavens. The sky was now a rosy colour and for the first time in ages the island enjoyed the morning light again. The children held their faces up, welcoming the return of the sun. When they looked down again, Áine was before them, no longer the blazing goddess but a beautiful young woman with streaming golden hair, wearing a gorgeous dress of gold embroidery. She embraced them all.

"Thanks be that you are safe. And praise to you, Cassie, that you saw Finnen in your vision. You have given me hope of some day finding her." Granny Clíona, released from Balor's vaporous trap, fell down to earth with a bump.

"That was close," she said. "I would have nearly died of fright if I wasn't already dead."

"But where is Jarlath?" asked Áine, concerned.

"Well now," said Granny Clíona, getting angry, "I'm afraid he's fallen into the clutches of some right little baggages. Just over there by the cliffs." But Áine was already on her way, shapechanged into a seagull. Granny Clíona jumped back on her broom and Thomas and Cassie jumped on too, eager to see the cheeky Merrows.

They soon caught sight of their flicking silver tails resting in Poolbeg rock pool. They hovered over on the broom as Áine in her seagull shape circled nearby.

"Oh look, it's the oul' wan back!" said the

cheeky Fand with the dark hair, "and she has some chisellers to defend her."

"Hey, young fella," shouted Sionna with the curly hair, to Thomas, "would you like to join us? You're a bit young but I'm sure you'll grow up to be a dreamboat!"

"It's enough for you to have one of my great-grandchildren. There is no chance you are getting your hands on another one!" roared Granny Clíona, shaking her fist at them.

The Merrows merely laughed.

"We told you before, Granny Ghostface, that we are hanging on to this one," said Mara, the blonde, stroking Jarlath's hair.

"We think he's going to start growing fins any minute, now that all the fireworks have stopped. That Áine one is a terrible show-off," said Fand. "Just because her da is Manannan MacLir, King of the Sea, so-called, she thinks the sun shines out of her behind!"

"Little does she know!" whispered Cassie to Thomas.

"We ought to be getting back to our kingdom

under the sea," announced Mara, "not wasting time with these gas-bags!"

Jaralth was as dazed as before, with a stupid smile on his face, and merely said, "Goo, nan, gooo!" like a baby.

Then a strong clear voice rang out. "He's not going anywhere!"

The Merrows cocked their heads to see where the voice came from.

"Says who?" demanded Mara.

"Yeah, you and whose army?" asked Sionna, exchanging smirking glances with her friends.

The smirks died on their faces when blinding light came from the sky as Áine shapeshifted from a seagull to her full majesty.

"Says me, that's who," she said in firm voice. "We thank you for saving him, now hand him over to his family like good girls."

The Merrows watched her with their mouths open and then shrank back a little. Jarlath stirred from his daze for a moment.

"This is the best dream I've ever had," he said. "And since it is a dream, I can say what I like.

Áine, I think you are the best-looking woman on Inish Álainn, or maybe even the world. Though, of course, I haven't seen all the women in the world. And these ladies here are also fab –" Then he fell back into his daze.

Thomas and Cassie couldn't help giggling. They loved it when grown-ups behaved stupidly.

The cheeky Merrows blinked at Áine and shielded their eyes from her fiery gaze but held tightly on to Jarlath. But Áine reached down and plucked him from their grasp as if she was picking up a kitten.

"You can have your cheap tat back," she cried, tearing off his pearls and belt.

She set him down on the broom between Cassie and Thomas who gave him a big hug. They had to keep a firm grip because he was still in some kind of trance and kept sliding off. The broom really was very crowded now, so it was lucky that Áine could fly in her goddess state.

"Hey, young wan," Sionna shouted at Cassie, "give us me cap back!" Cassie took the cap off Jarlath's head and tossed it back towards the rock. Sionna caught it and set it back on her head at a cheeky angle.

"Thanks for nothing! And you, Áine, we'll get you back for breaking the law of the sea!"

Granny Clíona tutted but, cheeky to the core, the Merrows just stuck their tongues out at her. Granny Clíona held herself in a dignified manner.

"If you're quick, there a big fellow out there struggling to swim," she pointed towards the wreck of the boat.

Sure enough, out at sea, Stinchcombe was clinging to a lifebuoy and kept sinking under the waves. The Merrows saw him and with a flick of their tails they were gone.

"I know Stinchcombe has done many bad things but he tried to be nice to Nancy on the boat," Granny Clíona explained. And then she allowed herself the last laugh. "I think him and the Merrows were made for each other!"

Granny Clíona manoeuvred the broom back to Connle and Nancy on the beach. Áine was already there, once more a beautiful young woman. Everyone was overjoyed to see Jarlath, even if he could barely stand and was still in a dream world.

"We better get Jarlath home while he still thinks he is in a dream," Áine said.

"Oh this is the most wonderful dream I've ever had," Jarlath said in a slurred voice, embracing the children. "I feel so good I could almost ask Áine to marry me," he confided to Cassie in a loud whisper.

"I think somebody should have a chat with you about that first," she said, looking at Connle in alarm.

In the twinkling of an eye and two shakes of a lamb's tail, the children lay curled up in bed. In no time at all they were all warm and toasty and fast asleep. And this time they slept deeply and soundly and had pleasant dreams of . . . well, what would you dream of after an adventure like that?

They dreamed of brushing their teeth and tying their shoelaces, of playing in the garden and reading their books. They dreamed of lying in a bunch together on the sofa, watching cartoons.

All the ordinary, everyday things that can seem so boring but can be so sweet and comforting when things get too exciting and exotic.

And as they slept Granny Clíona and Connle spent an agreeable time catching up on the events over the last few hundred years. They pored over old photographs and paintings and shared memories of the olden days. And they swapped stories of Clíona's fourteen children including Jarlath and Mary and Cian and Sean and Clíona Óg and Hamish and Fiona. And there were stories of weddings and fights and feasts and births . . . well, five hundred years of stories to get through.

For the first time in centuries, Connle felt the old warmth return to the house and he no longer felt so alone. And, in the nicest possible way, the house had acquired a ghost.

CHAPTER 17

Next morning, it seemed the whole island was on the beach, watching the smoking remains of Sir Dignum Drax's boat. Róisín and Muiris rushed over to greet the children.

"Well, you'll never guess what's been going on!" Róisín's words tumbled out all breathless. "Sir Big Bum Drax has only gone and exploded!"

A helicopter buzzed overhead and landed on the beach. Out of it popped the television reporter Finbar Flash with the tired-looking assistant called Katy and a cameraman lurching behind him. Finbar Flash once more wore the widest fake smile the children had ever seen. He jumped right in front of a group of islanders and started bossing them around.

"Right, you two old folks," he pointed to Muiris and Róisín, "I'll interview you."

Katy, the assistant, whispered something in his ear.

"And where are the children that climbed the trees to protest against them being cut down?" he shouted.

Cassie and Thomas put their hands up shyly. Nancy clung to Jarlath and started crying.

"Well, leave the baby," said Finbar Flash irritably. He turned to his assistant and hissed, "This is the biggest story of my career. Now that Drax TV is going down the pan, I need to move to another network. So no screwing up, right?"

"I see his manners haven't improved," Cassie whispered to Thomas.

Finbar Flash looked daggers at them. "Quiet please, ten seconds to air . . ." He took out a mirror and added more hairspray to hair that already looked like a helmet. Then he coughed and made his face all serious.

Katy, listening down headphones, gave him a wave and muttered,

"Cue, Finbar."

Finbar Flash glared down the lens and barked his piece to camera.

"One month ago, Sir Dignum Drax, international media magnate, came to this god-forsaken island to drag it into the twenty-first century. But now out at sea his yacht is a burning wreck. And he himself has gone missing, feared dead or drowned. His international media and property empire is on the brink of collapse. With me are the island's postmistress and master, Róisín and Muiris."

Finbar Flash turned to them and thrust a microphone in their faces.

"Early reports suggest that the boat might have been hit by a fireball or a comet. I understand that you may have an eye-witness account?"

They looked at him as if he had two heads.

"Excuse me," said Róisín, "but less of your 'god-forsaken island'. We never wanted that Drax and we say good riddance to him. And to you too."

Róisín gave a signal and Macdara and Conán, the Mulally twins, rushed over, grabbed Finbar Flash by a leg each and threw him in the sea.

"That'll teach you!" Róisín wagged her finger.

The whole island burst into applause. Even the camera crew smiled and Katy, the assistant, laughed. The camera crew continued to film. And the studio told Katy to take the microphone. She spoke to camera.

"Obviously feelings here run very high about Sir Dignum Drax. But now his plans to turn Inish Álainn into a celebrities' paradise are up in smoke, along with his media empire and this very television station you are watching. We ourselves might not even get paid, so what the hell." She turned to Róisín. "Tell us what happened."

"Well," said Róisín, "last night there was this almighty explosion. At first I thought Muiris had farted in the bed."

"Shut up, woman," said Muiris. "Nobody wants to know about that."

"We then realised it was coming from the beach," Róisín continued. "There was this comet going overhead and it was like a big fireworks display. And when we got here, lo and behold, it was what you can see before your eyes."

Katy turned back to camera and spoke to the presenter in the studio.

"An extraordinary end to one of the most colourful careers in recent history. Sir Dignum Drax came like a buccaneer into our lives and now he is gone. But here on Inish Álainn, he will not be mourned. One of the most extraordinary stories is how three small children tried to stop him destroying a forest by staging their own tree protest but his guards forcibly removed them. Some photographs survive thanks to the secret photography of the local publican, Ignatius Mulally, who managed to save some film before his camera was destroyed." She held up some blurry black and white photographs to the camera showing the children pinging acorns on the head of Drax's workmen from the branches of the oak tree. Katy then turned to Cassie and Thomas. Nancy now ran over to join them of her own free will and spoke into the microphone.

"He was a monster," she said, "and I spit at him! We are the Chingles from the East and we beat him!"

Everybody laughed.

"Bedad, she's right, you know," Muiris said. "That's the prophecy I was trying to think of – how the one-eyed one would return and the island would have to be saved by the Chingles from the East."

"What is that old fool blathering on about now?" Róisín interrupted.

Katy smiled politely but Muiris gave the children a big wink.

As they spoke, the blackened remains of the yacht sank a little further into the sea. Then it sank out of sight, swallowed up by the waves.

"Tomorrow divers will search the wreckage for any clues. But this is Katy Burke from Inish Álainn for what is left of Drax TV."

Everybody cheered. All around the beach, the islanders spoke about all that had happened in the last few weeks. The disappearance of Sir Drax was a complete mystery. Everyone had lots of theories that he had been struck by the comet, that he had killed himself and staged it to look like an accident. One person thought it might even be the fulfilment of an ancient prophecy. People smiled politely at Nancy when she talked about his evil eye and said children had such vivid imaginations. But Cassie and Thomas said nothing and each smiled a secret smile.

Jarlath stood on a rock and clapped his hands. "Ladies and gentlemen," he said, "there has been much turmoil and destruction on this island in the last few weeks. I propose we replant the Sacred Grove and begin to heal the island."

Everyone murmured their agreement and gave him a round of applause. Jarlath was so overcome he had to mop his brow with his handkerchief and was amazed to find a pearl in his pocket. He blinked at it and looked out to sea. "Weirdest dream," he said to himself, rubbing his eyes.

Down by the water's edge, a wet and angry Finbar Flash hauled himself out of the sea, spluttering and crying.

"My moment of glory gone!" he sobbed. "And

I'm ruined, ruined! All my money was in Drax stocks and shares. And that little vixen, Katy, stole my limelight."

Katy, the assistant, went around thanking the islanders for allowing them to film. "I'd like to come back and report on the restoration of the island," she said. She looked at their faces, which showed no enthusiasm. "Well, maybe it is best to leave you all in peace for a while," she smiled. And with that the film crew got back in the helicopter, dragging a wet Finbar Flash behind them. Everybody booed him and this time there was no chance that he could pretend it was some strange Inish Álainn cheer. In a few moments they took to the sky and were gone.

Jarlath wanted to go and have a look at his workshop that he hadn't been able to visit in days. So he rounded up Connle and the children. He had a bit of trouble getting Nancy to leave the beach because she said she was looking for the Boogan. Jarlath humoured her and said they'd come back and look for him later.

The workshop was in a right state. The barn

doors had been blown open and papers lay scrunched up all over the place. Clearly Sir Drax and his evil henchmen had paid a visit. Worse still, Jarlath's big equation on the blackboard was completely wiped out by the long fog. Jarlath peered sadly at where it used to be.

"Well, I'll definitely get thrown out of the university now."

"You can always rebuild the fog-machine," Connle said brightly. "We can all help you."

"But I'll never remember all that equation," Jarlath said, with tears in his eyes.

Then Cassie had an idea. In the depths of her pocket she found the remains of a half-eaten hazelnut. Jarlath was a McColl and it was their family tree, so it might just work.

"Eat this," she said, handing it to her uncle.

Jarlath looked puzzled but did as he was asked.

They watched him munch the nut without enthusiasm. But when he swallowed it, his face lit up with wonder. He hugged Cassie and jumped two feet in the air.

"I know the significance of the number 9!" he exclaimed. He put Cassie down and immediately grabbed a piece of chalk.

Then Thomas had a brainwave.

"Why don't you use one of your own indelible pens?" he suggested. Jarlath looked at him in awe and gave him a bear-hug too.

"You are a genius," he said.

Luckily Connle had one of the pens in his pocket. Jarlath grabbed it but just as he was about to use it, he stopped.

"But it is black, I won't see it on the blackboard.

"It changes ink depending on what the surface is," Thomas said, "or don't you remember your own inventions?"

Jarlath tried it and it wrote white. "Sometimes I'm just too clever for my own good." He was so deep in concentration they all decided to leave him to it and he didn't notice them slipping out the door.

Later that afternoon, at four o'clock, they set off

for the Sacred Grove. Cassie carried in her basket all the seeds for replanting. She had the last nut from the Hazel, an acorn from the Oak, a catkin from the Birch, a winged nutlet from the Alder, a berry from the Hawthorn, a pip from the Apple Tree, a silky plumed seed from the Willow. Alongside them were the ashes from the fire still wrapped in Áine's scarf.

As they turned towards the castle, Jarlath came bounding up the road.

"Children," he said, "I've got some news. The ferry came back today and Tadgh was on it and he had a telephone call from your mammy. You are going to have a new baby brother and sister or brother and brother or sister and sister."

They looked at him, amazed.

"Your mammy is going to have twins!" he exclaimed.

They all opened their mouths and shouted hurrah.

"That's just like Granny Clíona. She had twins," Cassie said.

Jarlath gave her a puzzled look. Little did he

...ow that at that moment his ancestor was in Connle's pocket.

People streamed into the castle grounds from all over the island. Mr Mulally and his twin sons, Macdara and Conán, rolled up barrels of beer. Muiris and Róisín came bearing trays of fairy cakes and amazing sweets including new ones called the *Exploder* and the *Comet Cake*. Tadgh, the librarian, brought streamers and banners decorated with magical Ogham symbols. He had spent the whole afternoon tidying up his tower and the children offered to help him later, for which he was very grateful.

"There's only one thing missing," he said, "my silver 'witch in a bottle'. Perhaps Drax stole her. I wonder if she has escaped? Though I'm sure she's very nice."

"She is," Nancy said. "She lives in our house."

Tadgh smiled and Jarlath nodded at him.

"Kids eh," their uncle said. "Such imaginations."

Everyone was delighted that Tadgh's petition had been a success and the government was thinking of granting the castle grounds to the whole island.

"It would be great if we could find that will where Clanswoman Clíona McColl promised the castle grounds to everyone," said Tadgh to Connle.

"I'll see what I can do," Connle replied fingering the silver bottle in his pocket.

Eamonn, the fiddler, had his fiddle and Donnacha, the bodhrán-maker, had several bodhráns for anyone who wanted to make a big noise. The farmer, Stephen Guilfoyle, brought along a whole lot of food for a barbeque. Mrs Moriarty, the Knitting Champion, had donated her finest blankets for the picnic and Emer Cassidy, the cheesemaker, had made some special cheeses. It really was a tremendous occasion. Then Áine arrived looking lovely in a white dress and with white blossoms in her hair.

Everyone gathered in the place where the trees of the Sacred Grove used to grow. Cassie held the basket and the islander took turns digging the holes and preparing the ground. Then Áine took the birch catkin and held it up for all to see.

"First, we plant silver mother, Beith, nurse to other trees." Then she planted the Alder saying, "Here is Fearn from the hearth of the earth." By the brook she put down the seeds of the Willow, hailing it as the tree of enchantment and mysteries. Then the Hawthorn, tree of shapeshifters, for love and the Apple, Quert, for its sacred fruit. In the middle of all the trees, she placed the acorn in the ground for protection and knowledge and called on Dair, Spirit of the Oak, to once more dwell amongst them. Then she planted the hazelnut beside the well. "This is your special tree," she said to the children. "McColls, sons of the hazel. Its fruit is the food of the gods."

Everybody cheered.

Finally, Áine scattered the ashes from her scarf around the whole area.

"And, now, I would like to suggest that this sacred place be now called Chingle Grove in honour of our three young friends. Without them, we wouldn't have saved even these seeds."

Everyone clapped their hands in approval and Muiris proposed a toast to them.

"Three cheers for Cassie!"

"Three cheers for Nancy!"

"Three cheers for Thomas!"

Jarlath and Connle beamed at them, thrilled and as proud as punch. Music started up and lots of people danced in a big circle. Jarlath looked shyly at Áine. She gave him a dazzling smile.

"Isn't Áine the most beautiful thing you ever saw?" he said to Connle.

"She's a fine girl all right," Connle replied.

"I'm thinking of asking her to marry me," Jarlath said, blushing all the way to the roots of his hair.

Connle looked at him in alarm.

"There's one thing you should know," he said.

"Oh she's not spoken for, is she, or already married?" Jarlath said, going deathly white.

"No, no," Connle said. "It's just that, well, she's a goddess . . ."

Jarlath looked relieved and his face went all dreamy.

"Oh, I know she's a goddess," he said. "I'm glad you see her that way too. I bet everybody does."

Connle scratched his head. "I don't think you and I mean the same thing!"

But Jarlath wasn't listening. He had gone off to ask Áine to show him how to do a jig.

Connle fingered the little silver bottle in his pocket.

"Did you hear that?" he said to Granny Clíona who was curled up inside. It was the only way she was able to go to the party without giving loads of people heart attacks.

"That's all we need," he said, "a goddess in the family. And soon there will be twins!"

Hoots of laughter came from his pocket.

"I hope she's good enough for a McColl." Granny Clíona's voice continued. "Never a dull moment in the McColl family! Now where did I put that will about the castle?"

Connle joined in the laughter and went off to join the children in the dance. It was fast and furious and, for years afterwards, some islanders claimed they'd even seen the fairy folk taking part!

Thomas, Cassie and Nancy were swinging each other round with such fury that they all got dizzy and fell down laughing. Somehow, they had spun a little way off behind a gorse bush and they stopped to catch their breath there.

They were surprised to be approached by three strangers, two men and a woman with raven feathers in her hair, who asked what the celebration was about.

They looked like warriors. They wore cloaks clasped with beautifully crafted designs like Áine's tattoo and waistcoats of leather. The woman's hair was plaited and she had a weather-beaten face with fierce blue eyes. She carried a club. One man with a grey beard, who was somewhat older than the others, carried a staff and the third who was blond and younger was clad in golden armour and held a spear.

The strangers radiated a force so powerful that without hesitation the children told them that the reason for this celebration was their victory over Balor of the Evil Eye.

They recounted everything from the discovery

of the Star Splinter at Glimmering Lake to the waning of Áine and the shapeshifting battle with Balor.

The warriors listened intently and when the tale was finished bowed low to the children.

"Well," said the older man to the warrior woman and blond young man, "they will not be needing us here."

"True," the fierce-eyed woman replied. "We feared we were too late but fate has sent others in our place."

"It is said that each age brings forth its own heroes," said the young blond warrior, his golden armour glinting in the sun, "and so it has come to pass. We salute you."

"What are your names?" asked Cassie.

"I am Lugh," said the blond warrior, "and my companions are Scáthach and Sennan." He indicated the woman and the grey-haired old man.

"And where have you come from?" Thomas asked.

"We are of the Sean Gaels, the old Irish,"

Scáthach, the warrior woman replied. "We have come from the East." She pronounced it "shan gales".

Cassie looked in amazement at Thomas. The 'Shan Gales' sounded awfully like 'Chingles' if you said it quickly. They turned round to call Connle and Áine. But when they looked back, there were no ancient warriors to be seen. In their place, perched on a gorse bush, were three ravens that took wing and flew off into the sky.

The End

Acknowledgements

I owe an enormous debt to the good people at Poolbeg who set up the competition to write a bestseller for children and to the judges who have made my dream come true. A special thanks to publisher Paula Campbell for her enthusiasm, vision and support and to Claire McVeigh and Lynda Laffan who have steered the book to publication. My editor, Gaye Shortland, has been a guiding light and is so in touch with myth and fairy lore, I have my suspicions!

Winning the competition brought me to the attention of the Literary Agency Curtis Brown and I would like to thank Euan Thorneycroft and Nick Marston for their guidance. Also thanks to Geraldine East for her kindness and support.

I am truly grateful to my first readers. As well as all the Murphys and O'Learys, I thank Julia Kennedy, Genevieve Deffarges, Rafael, Ivan and Louis Ramirez and the Smith family, Claudia, Mikey, Amelia and Lorelei.

I owe a debt to the Irish countryside whose secrets, buried in a name or a feature in the landscape, inspired me to find out about our mythology.

I am indebted to a number of books that have instructed me and fired my imagination including *Mythic Ireland* by Michael Dames, *A Guide to Irish Mythology* by Daragh Smyth, *The Celtic Wisdom of Trees* by Jane Gifford and *The Celtic Shaman* by John Matthews whose accounts of shamanic journeys inspired the Chingles' visits to the Otherworld. Many thanks to Dr Siobhán Ní Laoire of the Dublin Institute for Advanced Studies for her great help with the pronunciation guide.

Much love to my husband Marc for putting up with a wife who is literally away with the fairies!

And, of course, to Chingles everywhere. You know who you are.

Also published by poolbeg.com

THE CHÌNGLES GO WEST

PATRICIA MURPHY

ON HOLIDAY IN THE WEST OF IRELAND ON REMOTE
INISH ÁLAINN, THE CHINGLES – CASSIE, THOMAS
AND NANCY – JOIN THE SUN GODDESS ÁINE IN HER
DANGEROUS QUEST TO FIND HER SISTER FINNEN
THE SWAN MAIDEN WHO IS "HIDDEN AMONG
THE STARS".

Their search for the Swan Maiden takes them into
perilous other worlds in Europe and America and even
the glamorous world of Hollywood movies. But their
special powers seem useless against the wicked
sorceress, Caitlín of the Crooked Teeth, who has
vowed vengeance on the Chingles for their defeat of
her husband, Balor of the Evil Eye.

Will they manage to crack the mysterious Ogham
code and master Celtic battle craft to find Finnen and
defeat their most deadly enemy yet?

ISBN 978 18422 32167
ISBN 1 84223 218 5